VIEUX CARRÉ
VOODOO

Visit us at www.boldstrokesbooks.com

Praise for the Scotty Bradley Series

"Fast-moving and entertaining, evoking the Quarter and its gay scene in a sweet, funny, action-packed way."—*New Orleans Times-Picayune*

"Herren does a fine job of moving the story along, deftly juggling the murder investigation and the intricate relationships while maintaining several running subjects."—*Echo Magazine*

"An entertaining read."—*OutSmart Magazine*

"A pleasant addition to your beach bag."—*Bay Windows*

"Greg Herren gives readers a tantalizing glimpse of New Orleans." —*Midwest Book Review*

"Herren's characters, dialogue and setting make the book seem absolutely real."—*The Houston Voice*

"So much fun it should be thrown from Mardi Gras floats!"—*New Orleans Times-Picayune*

"Greg Herren just keeps getting better."—*Lambda Book Report*

By The Author

The Scotty Bradley Adventures

Bourbon Street Blues

Jackson Square Jazz

Mardi Gras Mambo

The Chanse MacLeod Mysteries

Murder in the Rue Dauphine

Murder in the Rue St. Ann

Murder in the Rue Chartres

Murder in the Rue Ursulines

Murder in the Garden District

AS EDITOR:

Full Body Contact

Shadows of the Night

Upon a Midnight Clear

FRATSEX

Love, Bourbon Street (with Paul J. Willis)

VIEUX CARRÉ VOODOO

by

by

Greg Herren

A Division of Bold Strokes Books

2010

CREDITS
EDITOR: STACIA SEAMAN
PRODUCTION DESIGN: STACIA SEAMAN
COVER DESIGN BY SHERI (GRAPHICARTIST2020@HOTMAIL.COM)

Acknowledgments

As hard as it is for me to believe, this is my twelfth novel.

There are a number of people to thank, as always with one of these—so I appreciate your patience.

First of all, I need to thank everyone who works with me at the NO/AIDS Task Force, and most especially Jean Redmann, Allison Vertovec, Diane Murray, and Larry Stillings (who never forgets the jalapenos). I work at a satellite office, the Community Awareness Network in the Marigny—and I need to thank my co-workers for putting up with me: Josh Fegley, Mark Drake, Ked Dixon, Tanner Menard, Martin Strickland, Kyle Morse, Jon Pennycuff, and Michael Robinson. Pity poor Tanner and Martin—they have to share an office with me.

My three graces and their spouses are certainly angels in human guise: Julie Smith and Lee Pryor, Patricia Brady and Michael Ledet, and Bev and Butch Marshall.

I want to especially thank Radclyffe, Stacia Seaman, and everyone at Bold Strokes Books for welcoming me, and my wacky Scotty, with open arms. I just hope you won't be sorry.

The Compound is a wonderful home away from home, filled with warm loving people and lots of laughter: Becky Cochrane, Tom Wocken, Timothy J. Lambert, and of course the original Ninja Lesbians: Rhonda Rubin and Lindsay Smolensky.

Also worthy of mention are such gracious people as Richard Labonte, Anthony Bidulka, Michael Thomas Ford, William J. Mann, Philip Rafshoon, everyone at Murder by the Book in Houston, Mark Richards, John Messenger, Michael Carruth, John Angelico, Al and Harriet Campbell-Young, Thea Mars, Ellen Hart, Nevada Barr, Stephen Driscoll, Stuart Wamsley, Todd Perley, Famous Author Rob Byrnes, 'nathan Burgoine, Dan Smith, Jeffrey Ricker, Michael Wallenstein, David Puterbaugh, Steve Soucy, and so many others I don't have enough room to name. But you know who you are.

And of course, my dear, wonderful Paul Willis, who makes every day an adventure and my life worth getting out of bed for.

Dedication

This is for
POPPY Z. BRITE
Thanks for always believing I could write about Scotty again,
even when I didn't.

"Don't you just love these long rainy afternoons in New Orleans when an hour just isn't an hour—but a little piece of eternity placed into your hands—and who knows what to do with it?"

—Tennessee Williams, *A Streetcar Named Desire*

"New Orleans can break your heart and wreck your liver."

—Julie Smith, *The Axeman's Jazz*

PREAMBLE

No live organism can continue for long to exist sanely under conditions of absolute reality; even pigeons and palmetto bugs are supposed, by some, to dream. New Orleans, not sane, stood by itself inside its levees, holding darkness within; it had stood there for almost three hundred years and might stand for three hundred more. Within, walls continued to tilt, bricks crumbled sloppily, floors were termite-chewed and doors sometimes shut; silence lay steadily against the wood and stone of New Orleans, and whoever drank there, drank alone.

Yeah, right. People only drink alone in New Orleans by choice.

My name is Scotty Bradley, and I'm a private dick who works the mean streets of New Orleans. I right wrongs. I help the downtrodden find justice. I punish the guilty. I ferret out crime, and protect the innocent while punishing the guilty. Criminals tremble when they hear my name, and get out of town if they know what's good for them. Dame Justice may be blind, but I see all too clearly. The helpless come to me when everyone else has failed, when hope is gone, and the night seems darkest. I've got a mean right hook and never back down from a fight. I drink my martinis shaken, not stirred—because I like my gin like miscreants who cross my path, bruised and a little battered. I am on a never-ending quest for truth, justice, and preserving the American way of life. I rescue dreams and bring nightmares to an end. Don't call me a hero, because any one of you would do the same if given the chance. There is no case too small for me to handle, and there is no case so large that it is intimidating. I've taken down a corrupt political machine, and would gladly do it again tomorrow. I've found lost treasures and stared down the Russian mob. I've stared evil in the face until evil blinked and backed away in mortal terror. I have—

Yeah, right. And I have a bridge across the Mississippi for sale, if you're interested.

My name is really *Milton* Bradley, like the board game company— my parents have a slightly twisted sense of humor. Scotty is my middle name, but it's what everyone calls me. I really *am* a private eye— bonded, and licensed by the state of Louisiana. I was born and raised in New Orleans and have lived here my entire life except for two misspent years at Vanderbilt University up in Nashville. I live on Decatur Street with my partner, Frank Sobieski. We're business partners, and life partners. We met on a case a couple of years back, and it was pretty much love at first sight. Frank is one of the most gorgeous men I've ever seen outside of a porn movie. He's in his early forties, about six foot two, and when he had hair, it was blond. Now that he's balding, he shaves it down to a little buzz. He has the most hypnotic blue eyes, a strong chin, and a scar on the right side of his face. He also started lifting weights in his twenties—and there's not an ounce of fat on his hugely muscled, amazingly defined body.

He also has one of the most amazing butts I've ever laid eyes on. Woof!

Well, okay—it was lust at first sight. Love came later.

Back in the day, I was just a personal trainer who moonlighted as a go-go dancer. That's what I was doing when I first met Frank—but after I foiled an evil right-wing conspiracy to commit mass murder, Frank convinced me I had the makings of a first-class private eye. I was a good personal trainer, but I was getting bored with it—and I liked the sound of Scotty Bradley, dick for hire. Frank took early retirement from the Feds, moved to New Orleans, and we hung out our shingle. My older brother Storm (I told you my parents have a twisted sense of humor—my sister's name is Rain) is a lawyer, and he threw us some work every now and then.

That one-eyed bitch Katrina swamped our business like she did ninety percent of the city. After the city dried out and people slowly started trickling back home, private detectives weren't in much demand. Oh, sure, there was some insurance work—fraud by policyholders, fraud by the soulless suits in the corporate office—but frankly, insurance work sucks. But it pays the bills and keeps the lights on, so we took the cases even though the work left us feeling slimed.

I think that was part of the reason Frank decided to chase a lifelong dream and go to pro wrestling training school.

"Seriously?" I said, staring at him in shock when he brought it up.

He blushed. He's awful cute when he blushes. "Seriously, Scotty. I know it might sound silly, but it's something I've always wanted to do." He shrugged his big shoulders. "And you know, if we learned anything from Katrina…"

"Grab every brass ring that comes along because there might not be another." I finished the thought for him. We'd talked about that a lot since the water receded. "You really want to do this?" I pondered it for a moment.

"Yes," he replied, turning an even deeper shade of red. Before he'd gone bald, his hair had been blond. He was one of those lucky blonds who turn that gorgeous shade of golden brown when tanned—and he was always tanned. But when embarrassed, that skin tone also turns a deep red that's almost purple. Frank doesn't blush often, but it's really cute when he does. Even his neck turns red.

It makes me want to kiss him.

"When I was a kid, pro wrestling was my porn," he went on with a sheepish smile. "I used to love watching them wrestling around in those little trunks, sweating, rolling around." He winked at me. "So, yeah, that's part of it. But it's also pretty amazing, you know, the things those guys can do."

"So, it was pro wrestling or the FBI?" I teased him. We were sitting on the couch in our apartment in our underwear, watching some stupid reality TV show about a bunch of incredibly spoiled and selfish women who'd been to the plastic surgeon a few times too many—one of those awful so-called "real housewives" shows, or as we liked to call them, *Trailer Trash with Cash*—and I couldn't resist adding, "It was the WWE's loss. You're going to look amazing in one of those outfits."

And so one chilly morning in mid-March, I put Frank on a plane to Ohio. The training school that had accepted him was one of the best in the country. I kissed him good-bye and watched him go through security. He turned and looked back just before he went through the metal detector—and I forced a smile on my face and waved.

The drive back home sucked. I don't think you ever realize how much space someone takes up in your life until they aren't around anymore. The apartment seemed so vast and empty with Frank gone. I spent the first few days finishing up paperwork on cases we'd finished, doing billing and other busywork that I had a bad habit of putting off.

Then the days until Frank would be back stretched before me like an endless boring nightmare.

"When did I get to be so boring?" I asked my best friend David at the gym one afternoon. We'd been working out together for almost eight years. He is about my height, but has one of those metabolisms that make it hard for him to gain weight of any kind. He has fair skin and a massive tattoo of a dragon curling around his left shoulder. He's a great guy, and you couldn't ask for a better friend.

"You need to come out," he replied as he put another twenty-five-pound plate on each side of the bar we were using for shoulder presses. "Your fans miss you in the bars."

I laughed and started my next set. But as I lifted the weights and my shoulder muscles screamed in protest, I began to think he might be right. It was dumb to just mope around the apartment feeling lonely and sorry for myself.

I finished my set and put the bar down. I stood up, and David took my place. I stepped behind the apparatus to spot him. As the bar moved up and down, I starting thinking about everything that had happened the year I turned thirty. That was the year everything had changed.

Frank and I had met just after I'd turned twenty-nine. It was during Southern Decadence—one of the great gay party weekends here in town, every Labor Day weekend—and he was here on a case that I wound up accidentally getting involved in. I wanted him the first time I laid eyes on him—but we didn't have the usual courtship. Instead of dating, our "getting to know you" period was spent stumbling over bodies and racing against the clock to foil a madman's destructive schemes. I also got kidnapped.

Nothing like a wild adventure for bonding, right?

After Decadence, he put in for early retirement and decided to move to New Orleans.

Unfortunately, I also met someone else during that same Southern Decadence. He told me his name was Colin Cioni, and he worked for an international detective corporation known as the Blackledge Agency. Frank and Colin fell for each other as well, so the three of us worked it all out. We had a nice three-way relationship (the sex was mind-blowing), and all three of us went to work for the Blackledge Agency. We even opened up our own little office on Frenchmen Street in the Faubourg Marigny neighborhood, just a short walk from where we lived on Decatur Street between Barracks and Esplanade in the French Quarter.

Alas, our happily ever after was rather short-lived. Over Mardi Gras, another case dropped into our lives involving the Russian mob, Chechnyan terrorists with ties to al-Qaeda, and my family. I discovered that my maternal grandfather had had an affair with a Russian ballerina who'd given birth to triplets. As my half-uncles were being murdered, one after the other, it turned out that Colin wasn't who he said he was—he was actually an international assassin who'd been after my uncles all along. He didn't get all three of them—we managed to keep Uncle Misha alive, and he was now an integral part of my family.

In the wake of finding out someone we'd welcomed into the family was a sociopathic murderer, probably wanted in most civilized countries for crimes too numerous to even begin to list, it would have been easy for all of us to be bitter, hurt, and angry. But even though it was hard, we all stayed positive. We may have lost two of our Russian uncles, but the one who was left was truly a gift from the Universe. I know that whenever I started going down that dark path to anger and bitterness, all I have to do is pick up the phone and call Uncle Misha—once I hear "Hello?" in that thick accent I am cheered immeasurably.

And even if everything Colin had ever said to us was a lie, we *did* have good times together.

The only thing he took with him when he fled the country was a photograph of the three of us in our Halloween costumes. That had to mean something, right? He wouldn't have taken it if he hadn't cared on some level.

Every once in a while, I'd miss him—and wonder where he was, if he was even still alive. I never really doubted he was alive—the man had more lives than a herd of cats—but I couldn't help but wonder if sometimes when he was lonely, if that picture of the three of us in our harem boy costumes made him feel better.

What can I say? I'm sentimental by nature.

So we survived, and got through it all with our spirits intact. Our little detective agency wasn't doing so great—turned out the Blackledge

Agency was another one of Colin's little lies, and I didn't want to know where the funding he provided came from—but we picked up little jobs here and there, and there was Frank's pension from the FBI.

But I kind of missed the old excitement of murder investigations. At the time, I didn't think they were all that fun or exciting—you never get used to stumbling over a dead body, having a gun pointed at you, or being kidnapped—but now that those times seemed to be past, I was getting a little, well, *bored.*

I also used to have a bit of a psychic gift. I could usually channel it through a deck of tarot cards—and sometimes the Goddess Herself actually spoke to me. I'd go into a trance (which usually scared the shit out of people who saw it happen) and go to a place between dimensions where She would give me hints and clues as to what was going to happen in the immediate future. There was even a time, during a murder investigation, when I communicated with a dead man.

But after Colin's betrayal, I wasn't interested in communing with Her anymore. How could She have let me—and everyone I loved—be completely deceived by a sociopathic killer? She never even gave me one of Her "figure this out for yourself" vague clues.

She was dead to me, and good riddance to you, bitch.

Okay, maybe I was a *little* bitter about the Colin thing.

So the summer of 2005 dragged on, and about mid-July my family and friends suddenly woke up to the fact that my thirtieth birthday was approaching.

And the teasing started.

My birthday is in August, which means I was born under the sign of Leo. (And every single time someone asks me for my astrological sign, I always get the same reaction when I tell them I'm a Leo. They smile, nod knowingly, and say, "Of course you are." *I* choose to take it as a compliment.) All the weeks leading up to my birthday, there seemed to be a concerted effort by every single person I know—relatives, friends, etc—to convince me that I was going to wake up on my thirtieth birthday to discover that my life was over. I personally didn't think it was a big deal—age is just a number, and I believe you can enjoy life at any age—my grandparents and parents are prime examples of this. When they started giving me shit about it, at first I just laughed it all off. But after a while, the constant teasing and warnings started to get inside my head a little—which, of course, was their evil plan all along. My best friend and workout partner, David—who I might add is almost *forty* and was one of the worst teasers—finally let me off the hook the day before my birthday at the gym, when I was freaking out a little bit.

"Get a grip, girl." He laughed and rolled his eyes as I struggled with the leg press machine. "You're not going to wake up tomorrow and have no sex drive, no hair, and no teeth. My thirties were way better than my twenties. You look great; you have a hot as hell boyfriend, a great family, and lots of friends—so you're going to be thirty. Forget about the number and just enjoy yourself." He winked at me, shaking his head. "Such a drama queen."

I absolutely love David. He's a great friend—and through all the murders and things he was always right there by my side. Considering the fact being my friend has directly resulted in his car being totaled, his nose broken, and his house shot up, I really am lucky he still talks to me.

And he was right. In fact, my thirtieth birthday rocked pretty hard, to be honest. It fell on a Saturday, and Frank woke me up with breakfast in bed wearing just a black jock. "Now this is something I could get used to every morning," I said as I sat up in bed, giving his amazing body a longing once-over with my eyes. He'd made my absolute favorite breakfast—blueberry pancakes with strawberry syrup, with some bacon crisped up in the microwave—with a mimosa and a cup of coffee spiked with Baileys. Frank climbed back into the bed with me, and when I finished everything on the tray he gave me a pretty nice dessert.

Ah, if only every day could start that way!

And that was just the start of an absolutely amazing day. I got lots of nice presents (an iPod I'd been coveting, a new laptop, tons of clothes, and an ounce of killer pot from Chico, California, from my parents)—and maybe the best present of all came from my two grandfathers.

They released my trust funds. They'd frozen them when I'd dropped out of Vanderbilt, and to be honest, I kind of figured the money was gone for good. Instead, with a couple of signatures and notary stamps, I went from having eight dollars in my checking account and about fifteen in my savings to having a net worth (on paper) of about eight figures. I had no idea there was that much money in my trusts. I couldn't touch the principal—all of our family's trusts are set up that way, to protect us from fortune hunters and our own stupidity, as my mom says—but I could access the interest income. That was enough so that I never had to work another day in my life if I so chose.

Timing is everything. As I said before, our little private eye agency wasn't exactly a smashing success. We'd even been considering closing the office and just working out of the apartment to save money. It had even gotten to the point where I was seriously considering breaking out my thongs and shaking my ass on bars for dollars again.

The other thing I hadn't known about the trusts was that all the money was invested in oil and health insurance stock, so it was just going to continue to increase in value.

I felt a little guilty about that. In my mind, those two industries are the modern-day epitome of evil. So I asked my mother about it—I mean, this is a woman who has chained herself to the front gates of nuclear power plants. She just shook her head. "Scotty, blood money spends just like any other kind," she said, "and when a charity is cashing your check, they don't care where the money originally came from." She sighed. "I know that might seem like a justification, but real life isn't black and white—there's an awful lot of gray." She winked at me. "It helps me feel better about the money. I mean, if the oil companies knew what I did with my share of their profits, a lot of high-powered executives in board rooms would need to change their underpants."

So I wrote a nice check to the NO/AIDS Task Force, and Frank and I decided that every quarter when I got the interest checks, we'd donate half of it to charity.

And there would still be more than enough money left over for us to live on, quite well.

That night, my best friend David provided us all with some of the best Ecstasy I've ever had and we went dancing at the gay bars in the Quarter, going back and forth from Oz to the Parade and back again. The deejays played the best music ever, and I danced and danced and danced like there was no tomorrow. I felt beautiful, and happy, and loved.

All in all, it was one of the best birthdays I ever had.

And the next afternoon when I woke up in Frank's arms, I remember thinking how blessed I was. I lived in the greatest city in the world with the man I loved, I had the best friends and family any gay man could ask for, I had more money than I knew what to do with, I had my health, and I just couldn't imagine life getting any better than it was at that very instant.

How was I supposed to know that just around the corner was the biggest bitch-slap reality could come up with?

Just eight days after that wonderful lazy afternoon in bed with Frank, a Category 5 one-eyed bitch named Katrina came roaring ashore just to the east of New Orleans. For those of you who don't have televisions or computers, the storm surge came into Lake Pontchartrain, and the federally built, funded, and maintained levee system that was supposed to protect the city from just such a thing was a little, shall we say, *inadequate.*

I'm not going to talk about Katrina and the aftermath. I lived it, and I don't want to relive it, thank you very much. If you didn't see me on CNN being interviewed by Anderson Cooper, I'm sure it's on the Internet somewhere.

Okay, maybe I'm still a *little* bitter about the Katrina thing. You would be, too.

But when Katrina was out in the gulf, and the entire city was engulfed in panic, I decided to try to talk to the Goddess for the first time since Mardi Gras. I got out my cards and gave it a try. But apparently She wasn't happy that I'd turned my back on Her, because no matter what I did, the gift was gone.

In a way, it was also kind of a relief. Being able to see the possibilities the future holds might seem like a really cool thing, but it actually isn't. It's a lot of responsibility, and people look at you funny when you try to convince them you've spoken to the Goddess.

It's funny how fast time goes by when you get older. Granted, it wasn't like I had a foot in the grave or anything, but time just seemed to start slipping through my hands. After the floodwaters receded, we just took life one day at a time and did what needed to be done. We didn't sit around and mope. We didn't mourn for what was lost. Instead, we girded our loins and did what was needed to bring the city back to life. Rome wasn't built in a day, and New Orleans wouldn't be rebuilt in one, either. My parents, Frank, and I did a lot of volunteer work after they finally managed to pump all the water out of the city—gutting and rebuilding houses, driving around the devastated parts of the city handing out supplies to people working on houses in areas without water and power. And slowly but surely the grand old lady known as New Orleans began coming back to life again.

She's not what she once was, but she's still one hell of a great city.

It's going to take a hell of a lot more than a flood and federal incompetence to wipe us off the map.

And by the way, all you haters who thought the city should be abandoned? Fuck you, and don't think you are ever welcome to come here and enjoy our special magic.

And remember that Mardi Gras you didn't think we should have that next year? It was the best one *ever*. Ninety percent of our city might have been in ruins, but New Orleans could still throw a better party than any other city in North America.

No flood could ever kill our spirit.

Like I said, I guess I'm still a little bitter. You would be, too.

But even as I was gutting houses and pulling up linoleum in wrecked houses, my mind would sometimes go back to Colin. It seemed like he was *always* in the back of my mind. Despite everything I knew to be true about him, I still had feelings for him. You don't just stop loving someone, no matter how much they've hurt you. There were just so *many* unanswered questions. We hadn't gotten *closure*, and I didn't think we ever would. Whenever I was out dancing, or in a crowd, I'd find myself looking through the crowd, scanning their faces, and then would realize what I was doing was looking for him. I just couldn't believe we were never going to see him again.

I missed him.

I couldn't help feeling, even though my gift was gone, that there was unfinished business there, and that he'd turn up again one day when we least expected it.

"Earth to Scotty, come in, Scotty," David said, bringing me back out of my mental time travel. "Are you there?"

I just laughed and helped him put the weights away.

"Easter's this weekend," David said as we moved over to the preacher curl machine. "Come on out for Tea Dance. It'll be fun—you'll see. It'll get you out of this funk you've been in ever since Frank left."

"Yeah," I replied as he started his set. He was right, I knew. Frank wouldn't want me to sit around the house and mope. Besides, Mom and Dad were making me ride in their float in the Gay Easter Parade. Mom and Dad own a tobacco shop at the corner of Royal and Dumaine called the Devil's Weed. Mom and Dad were far left liberals, and probably the best, most accepting parents a gay man could wish for. "Maybe. I have to ride in the Easter Parade, so maybe…"

"You're turning into a hermit," David said when he finished his set. "You *need* to get out of the house."

"But what if Frank calls? I'd hate to miss him," I replied stubbornly.

"You are *whipped*, Scotty," he teased me. "Meet me out this weekend. What's it going to hurt? Have a few beers, smoke a joint, dance a little—you owe it to everyone in New Orleans to show off that body again." He winked. "It's been a long time since your adoring public has seen you shirtless."

"Fat Tuesday wasn't that long ago," I replied.

"A month and a half is an eternity in gay years."

I laughed. "Well—"

"You need to go out and get in trouble, is what you need."

I made a face. "No, I've had enough of trouble, thank you very much." I shook my head. "I've had enough trouble to last me a lifetime."

"True dat." David rolled his eyes. "I don't miss having my car totaled, or my house shot up, or my nose broken, or—"

I couldn't help but laugh.

After we finished our workout, I went home and looked at the calendar. Another two more weeks before Frank came home.

He wouldn't want you to sit around the house and mope.

I lit a joint and decided that I would go out and have some fun on Easter. David was right—what would it hurt? Frank was having a good time up in Ohio, doing something he wanted to do.

But I'm quite sure if Frank had known the kind of trouble I was going to get into while he was gone—he'd have never bought that damned plane ticket.

Chapter One

EIGHT OF SWORDS
New beginnings are possible.

O ne of the rules of walking in the French Quarter when the weather's warm is always look up when you walk underneath a balcony, or you'll be sorry.

You'd think having lived in the Quarter all of my life, looking up would be second nature for me by now. But I was lost in thought as I hurried up Governor Nicholls Street. I was really missing Frank and wishing he were here instead of in Ohio. I was on my way to ride on my parents' float in the Gay Easter Parade, and it felt really strange to be doing it without Frank. I was debating myself as to whether my relationship had descended into an unhealthy level of codependency. I was paying absolutely no attention to my surroundings, other than making sure I wasn't about to walk into a support post for a balcony. I had just decided there was nothing neurotic in missing your boyfriend, and that I should just relax and enjoy myself. It was a beautiful spring day, after all, and riding in a parade was always fun. I took a deep breath, cleared my head of all negativity, and started walking faster so I wouldn't be late.

And that was when I was completely drenched by a cascade of cold water from above.

My reaction was reflexive and instinctive. *"Fuck!"* I screamed at the top of my lungs, which got me a really nasty look from the couple pushing a stroller across the street. I sighed, gave them an apologetic shrug, and their disapproving frowns turned into slight smiles at my expense.

I was soaked. Water was running down my back and chest, dripping out of my hair, and to my horror, I realized the white bikini my mother had so thoughtfully provided for me to wear in the parade apparently became see-through when wet. I immediately dropped my hands to cover my crotch as my eyes darted back and forth, looking for other pedestrians. The couple with the stroller shook their heads, gave each other a look, and started pushing the stroller a lot faster.

Obviously, they were tourists.

I shivered. The cool damp breeze coming from the river was much colder on wet skin. I *knew* I should've worn sweats over the costume.

"Scotty? Is that you? Oh, dear, I'm so sorry!" a familiar voice said from above me. There was apologetic concern tempered by a slight bit of amusement in the tone.

I looked up and my initial irritation faded away to embarrassment. "Oh, it's okay, Doc," I called up to the bald older man peering down at me through gold-rimmed spectacles. "I wasn't looking, like an idiot." I sluiced water off my arms and shook my head from side to side. Droplets of water flew away from my hair.

"Well, come in and let me give you a towel." He shook his head. "I'll buzz you in." His head vanished for a moment before reappearing almost instantly. "And you can explain to me what you're *doing* in that *ridiculous* get-up." His face broke into a wide grin, and I couldn't help but laugh as I dashed over to the metal gate at the side of the building in time to open it when the buzzer sounded.

Dr. Benjamin Garrett was a friend of my parents. He'd taught them both when they'd attended the University of New Orleans. He had been a full professor in both history and political science, and my mother frequently credited him for "opening her eyes to all the injustice in the world." We all called him Doc—well, when we were young we'd called him "Uncle Doc" until he asked us to drop the "uncle" because he said it made him sound like a relative of the former dictators of Haiti. He loved to debate politics with my parents into the wee hours of the morning over bourbon, his eyes twinkling as he deliberately took an opposing viewpoint to wind my mother up. I'd always liked Doc. He was fiercely intelligent, a bit of a curmudgeon, and one of the funniest people I knew.

No matter the situation, he always managed to have the absolutely perfect, droll thing to say on his lips. He was the epitome of the old-style Southern gentleman, and he was always dressed stylishly and appropriately. In the summer, he wore seersucker suits, bow ties, and Panama hats. After Labor Day he switched to navy blue suits and dark red ties. He liked his bourbon and cigars, and he always seemed to have a mischievous twinkle in his blue eyes. He walked with a cane now that he was older, and had been completely bald for as long as I could remember.

I paused long enough to take a look at myself in the plate glass window of the candle shop on the first floor of Doc's building. I'd been working hard at the gym since Frank left. Now that I was in my thirties, my body seemed determined to develop love handles. Frank said he didn't mind them, but I did. My goal was to be as lean as I'd been when we first met by the time he came home, and I was making progress. The wet white bikini was unforgiving, but I didn't see any pesky fat hanging over the sides. I winked at myself and dashed down the dark passageway alongside the building until I reached the back stairs. Another blast of wind brought up goose bumps on my skin as I climbed the stairs. Doc was standing in the door to his apartment holding a huge fluffy white towel, which he handed to me. One of his gray eyebrows went up as he peered at me over his round gold spectacles.

"It's for the Gay Easter Parade," I explained as I toweled my hair and wrapped the towel around my waist. "I'm riding on thc Devil's Weed float."

"And your mother decided you should dress up as a gay Easter Bunny." He nodded as he stepped aside to let me in. "And to her, that means a white bikini with a cottontail and rabbit ears." His eyes twinkled. "Now slip off that bikini—I'll throw it in my dryer for a few minutes."

Frank had laughed out loud when my mother first broached the idea to us a few weeks ago. It didn't bother me—when you've danced on bars for years in a thong you don't really have many inhibitions left about public displays of skin—but Frank had resisted. No matter how many times I tell him resistance is futile with Mom, he never listens. Mom suspected his decision to train as a pro wrestler was rather conveniently timed to get him out of bunny duty on the float.

She might not be far wrong, at that.

I slid the bikini off and handed it over. The towel was warm and felt good against my skin. "Frank was going to do it, too, but then, you know, the training school thing came up," I added as I took a seat in the room just beyond the back door.

"I have to say, I admire your Frank for taking the chance." Doc took the bikini and walked through the door on the other side of the room. I heard the sound of the dryer being started. "That took some courage," he said as he came back into the room. "Would you like a drink?" he asked as he walked over to the bar. Despite the fact that he was home alone, he was impeccably dressed in a white shirt and a pair of blue slacks that matched the vest straining to stay buttoned over his stomach. He poured himself two fingers of bourbon. After I declined his offer, he sat down in a wingback chair and propped his feet up on a hassock. "One should always reach for the brass rings in life, you know."

Doc was always encouraging people to grab for brass rings. He gave me a lascivious look and winked. "And I should think your Frank would look marvelous in those little tights they wear."

"He does," I admitted. A few days earlier, Frank had e-mailed me a photo of him in his ring attire—white leather boots to the knee that laced up the front, white knee and elbow pads, and the trunks were electric blue with a silver lightning bolt across the crotch. He'd been standing in a corner of the ring, his left foot up on the bottom rope, every muscle in his body flexed and tightened, glistening in the light.

I'd really missed him at that moment.

Doc gestured at me with his glass. "You miss him, don't you?" He gave me a little smile. "I can see that you do…don't worry, Scotty, he'll be home sooner than you realize."

I opened my mouth to reply but his phone started ringing. "Tut, tut." He hoisted himself out of his chair. "I should get that. Though I can't imagine who'd been calling me on Easter Sunday." I knew he had a sister who lived up in Vicksburg, but they weren't particularly close. Doc was a confirmed bachelor, a polite Southern euphemism usually substituted for "gay" among the older, more genteel generations. I'd never seen any evidence he was actually gay. Sure, every once in a great while he'd say something that *could* be interpreted that way—his remark about Frank looking good in the tights, for example—but as far as I knew, he'd never had a lover, male or female.

He had a lot of artistic nudes, paintings and photographs, hanging throughout the apartment, but the models were both men and women—

and the artists were all famous. His art collection was worth a small fortune. The room I was in—which he called the "back parlor"—had several works by George Dureau, among others, on display.

Doc was a bit of a pack rat—his entire apartment was crammed full of books and art. Every available surface seemed to be stacked high with books. When I was a little boy and we'd come over, I'd spend hours reading the names on the spines of the books. Doc always encouraged me to read—"Reading makes you smarter, even if you read trashy books," he always said—and while the adults talked, I'd curl up on a sofa and read one of his books. He had just as many "trashy novels" as he did classics.

I doubted many other people had Jacqueline Susann next to John Steinbeck on their shelves.

But his absolute favorite books were mysteries. He had probably the most extensive collection of mysteries outside of a library. In fact, the latest S. J. Rozan novel was sitting on the table next to his chair, with a bookmark stuck close to the middle.

The dryer made a buzzing sound. I got up and walked into the little alcove where his washer and dryer sat next to a very deep sink. Even the shelves in the little laundry space were crammed full of books. I couldn't help but grin when I noticed dried drops of laundry detergent on the spines of the books piled next to the orange plastic bottle. I opened the dryer and grabbed my bikini. The white ball on the back had fluffed larger, but it was dry. I slid it on and looked at myself in the full-length mirror hanging on the wall.

The bikini material had dried enough so it no longer was like wearing cellophane. I ran my fingers through my curly hair to fluff the curls out some more. I'm only five-nine, but I weigh about a hundred and eighty pounds. I examined myself in the mirror thoroughly. I looked pretty good for thirty-three. I turned sideways and looked for the love handles. Damn, they were still there—but they were smaller than they had been. They'd be gone before Frank got back, I vowed. I turned to face the mirror, and grinned at myself. I still looked good. Maybe not quite as good as I did when I danced for tips in a thong, but my body still had definition.

I placed the towel in the washer and grabbed a book called *The History of Time Inc 1941–1960* from one of the shelves. I walked back into the back parlor, flipping through the pages, and sat back down.

Doc limped through the doorway. His face was reddened, and he was breathing heavily. "Are you okay, Doc?" I asked, concerned. He'd had an incident with his heart around Christmas, and I knew Mom worried about him. Her lectures about his cigars and bourbon fell on deaf ears.

"I'm—fine." He picked up his glass of bourbon and took a drink. "Just an upsetting call, nothing to worry about." He waved his hand.

"Well, thanks for the towel and drying my costume," I replied, giving him a wink. "But I'd better get going or I'll be late—and you know what Mom is like when someone is late."

"Oh." He looked disappointed. "I was hoping to have a nice visit."

I looked at my watch. "I really am going to be late," I apologized. "Maybe I could stop by tomorrow?"

He struggled up out of his chair. His face was still red, and his breathing hadn't calmed either. "I have something for you—I've been meaning to give it to you for years, and that outfit"—he suppressed a laugh—"reminded me. Give me a moment." He walked out of the room, leaning heavily on his cane.

I was a little worried about him, actually. He wasn't in the best health—maybe I shouldn't leave him alone unless I was sure he was all right. I hadn't brought my cell phone with me—all I had room for in the boots I was wearing was my house key and my wallet—but I could call Mom on his phone and let her know...the thought died in my brain when he walked back into the room with a ratty-looking stuffed animal in his free arm. "That's for me?" I asked, wondering why on earth he would think I'd want it.

Doc's skin was back to its usual color, and he was breathing normally as he walked back into the room. "Do you remember him?" He smiled as he held the thing out to me.

I took it from him and looked at it. It was a rabbit, missing an eye, one of the ears was hanging on by a thread, and it was a dirty yellowish-brown color that might have been white at one time. I held it at arm's length. "No, I'm afraid I don't." It slightly stank of dust.

"You don't remember him," he said a little sadly. "Of course, you were just a little boy...you never went anywhere without that rabbit. You left him here when you were about four, I think, and I always meant to give him back, but he got buried in a closet I had my maid clean out a few days ago." He peered at me over his glasses. "You really don't remember him?"

Obviously, it meant a lot to him. I smiled. "A little bit." I tucked it under my arm.

"Seeing you in that outfit reminded me I'd found him. You used to call him Mr. Bunny." He shook his head. "He makes a nice accessory for your parade ride."

"Are you sure you don't want to keep him? I can drop him off after the parade." The thing was filthy, and the mottled plush fabric felt scratchy against my skin.

"He's a piece of your childhood." He sounded a little hurt. "You should always hold on to pieces of your childhood. But if you don't want him…"

I've never understood why older people set such a store on things like that. My old room at my parents' was exactly the way it looked the day I moved out, like a creepy Scotty shrine. Of course, I'd pretty much lost everything I owned when my apartment burned down, so I'd lost whatever sentimentality I'd had toward possessions. But Doc was a sweet old man, and for whatever reason, giving me the dirty old rabbit meant something to him. I didn't want to hurt his feelings. "I'll keep him," I said. "Thanks, Doc." Impulsively I kissed his cheek. "It's really sweet of you."

"You can sleep with him until Frank comes back so you won't be lonely." He patted me on the shoulder. "Now, run along—I know how your mother is about being tardy—although she wasn't that way when she was in my classes, God knows."

"I'll come by tomorrow afternoon," I promised as I started down the back stairs. "You're sure you're okay?"

"Fine. I look forward to a nice long visit tomorrow." He smiled and shut the door behind me.

I shook my head as I opened the gate to the sidewalk. As if a filthy old stuffed rabbit could replace Frank. I rolled my eyes and resisted the urge to toss the thing into a garbage can as I hurried up Governor Nicholls.

I was late, and Mom would be pissed.

I broke into a run, vaguely aware of the funny looks I was getting from other people on the sidewalks. Well, from tourists—locals didn't give me a second glance. It *was* Easter, so *not* seeing a man in a white bikini wearing bunny ears would seem odd to the locals. The weather had changed while I'd been at Doc's. The wind felt wetter and the sky was now full of gray clouds. It was going to rain, and I hoped it would hold off until after the parade ended. The temperature had also dropped some.

I should have brought my sweats, I thought as I finally reached the corner of Rampart and Governor Nicholls. The buggies and carriages making up the Gay Easter Parade were lined up in front of Armstrong Park.

The Gay Easter Parade was the brainchild of Rip and Marsha Naquin-Delain, and was a fund-raiser for the Food for Friends program of the NO/AIDS Task Force. I hadn't ridden in it for years—well, since before the flood. Frank and I had gone to Palm Springs for the White Party every Easter till this year. Mom and Dad swore it was one of their favorite times of the year. Everyone wore Easter bonnets and dressy clothes—and you haven't seen an Easter bonnet until you've seen the ones drag queens come up with. The parade wound its way through the Quarter, the riders tossing beads and whatever else they could come up with. I spotted the carriage for the Devil's Weed and headed over there.

"You're late," Mom said as soon as I walked up. She was wearing a lovely yellow spring dress with a matching bonnet, and holding a bouquet of daisies. "Is that Mr. Bunny you've got?" She smiled. Mom is beautiful. She has amazing skin, wears very little makeup, and always wears her long black hair in a braid that reaches her waist. Frank thinks I look just like her, which I consider a major compliment.

I climbed up into the carriage. "Yeah. Doc stopped me on my way here. That's why I'm late," I explained, "and he wanted to give me this."

"It *is* Mr. Bunny." Her eyes widened as she took him from me and smiled at him. "Oh, how you loved this rabbit when you were a little boy." Mom looked over at me, and her smile was sad. I knew she was remembering when I was little, and was touched. "I'm amazed he kept it all this time. But then Doc has always a bit of a pack rat." She handed me the bunny.

I handed it back to her. "I don't want it. I thought you might."

She gave me that sad smile again. "Yes, I do think I want him. All he needs is a run through the washer and he'll be just fine." She kissed my cheek. "Your beads are all up in the front of the carriage. You know what to do."

I did. She wanted me to stand up front, next to the mule driver, and throw beads from there. She figured I'd get everyone's attention and then they'd notice the Devil's Weed sign behind me, which would be good for business. Dad handed me a go cup filled with mimosa—it was their drink of choice for the parade. I climbed up front, hugging my brother and sister.

"Nice outfit." Storm smirked. He's a lawyer, and loves nothing more than giving me shit. He's put on a lot of weight since the flood, and his face is starting to take on a permanent reddish hue.

My sister Rain punched him in the arm, making him yelp. Rain is beautiful, married to a doctor, and loves nothing more than giving Storm shit. "You're just jealous because there's not enough Lycra in the world to fit your fat ass."

I laughed as Storm spluttered a bit. I left them to their bickering and climbed to the front. I said hello to the other riders. Most of them worked for my parents at the shop. They were an eclectic mix of Goth kids, adorable young lesbians, and a couple of cute gay fraternity boys from Tulane, proudly wearing their Beta Kappa letters. Mom and Dad treated them like members of the family, and they all worshipped Mom and Dad. Then again, there weren't many employers in the world who kept their workers supplied with the best pot to be found in southeastern Louisiana. They were all nice kids, but my favorite was Emily, a cute lesbian who shaved her head and performed with a street band. She had an amazing voice, better than most with lucrative recording contracts and hit records. She'd come down for Mardi Gras from Chicago one year and decided to stay. I gave her a kiss on the cheek and she put a strand of gold beads around my neck. "Was afraid you weren't going to make it," she said as she gave me a big hug.

"And risk the wrath of Mom? Perish the thought." I grinned at her, stepping over the rise at the front to the driver's bench.

"Hey, Scotty." Tanner Strickland was driving our carriage. He used to work for Mom and Dad in the shop for a few years while he was getting his master's at Tulane. He was working on his PhD now, and worked driving tourists around on buggy tours of the Quarter. He was a nice guy, his handsome face concealed by a heavy beard. His fiancée, Anna, was a living statue in Jackson Square—a brass bride. "Hope the rain holds off until we're done." He whistled and grinned. "Nice outfit."

"Thanks, Tanner." I stood on the bench next to him. Bags and bags of beads lined the floorboards. I reached down and grabbed a couple of handfuls, draping them over my arms. Just as I did, the carriages in front of us started moving.

I really had cut it close.

Another gust of cold, damp wind made me shiver as the carriage started rolling and I struggled to keep my balance. It's not easy balancing in a moving vehicle, and the last thing I wanted to do was take a header off the stupid thing. Eventually I found my center of gravity and looked off into the distance. The clouds in the distance over the West Bank were dark and ominous looking, and the way the temperature kept dropping by the minute was not a good sign.

"Let's get this party started!" I yelled back to everyone in the back, and they cheered.

There's nothing like riding in a parade in New Orleans, even a small one like this. Everyone in my family—excluding me and my parents—belonged to one or more Mardi Gras krewes. Rain had let me ride with her in Iris one year, and that had been one of the best experiences of my life. The ladies of Iris know how to party—I was hungover the rest of the day and almost missed the parades the next day because I was afraid to be too far away from a toilet. The parade turned into the Quarter, and the sidewalks were lined with grinning people holding drinks and cheering, waving for beads with their free hands. I started waving and tossing beads at people, a stupid grin plastered on my face. "Happy Easter!" I shouted, and people cheered and yelled back at me. Cameras pointed at me, and I grinned happily, sometimes flexing for the photographers.

What can I say? I like being the center of attention. It's *fun.*

The carriages rolled up St. Ann, and soon we were in front of a crowd of people in front of Good Friends Bar. The parade paused for a moment, and the crowds pressed closer to the carriage. I started tossing beads with both hands, waving at people I knew and making sure they got the best throws I had. The carriage started rolling with a sudden jerk, and I had to catch my balance again. The next corner on the route was Gay Central—the corner of St. Ann and Bourbon. The crowd was even thicker there, spilling out of the open doors of both bars and filling the sidewalks. They cheered and started jumping and waving. The parade came to another stop right when our carriage was directly in between the Pub and Oz. I started looking for David—he'd said he'd be out in front of the Pub, but couldn't see him anywhere. I was throwing beads with both hands to hot guys on both sides of the street when I felt a strange chill go down my back.

It was a feeling I hadn't had since—well, since before the flood.

I felt a little dizzy, like I was about to…

Have a vision.

I reached down and grabbed on to both sides of the front of the carriage. I closed my eyes and took some deep breaths.

Something—something is wrong, something is terribly wrong. Just look, and you will see. Look, you have to see!

And then, as quickly as it had started, the feeling was gone.

My body was covered with goose bumps.

I turned and looked at the front door of Oz. I scanned the smiling faces of all the guys with drinks in their hands, looking for I didn't know what.

And then, out of the corner of my eye I saw someone in the crowd who looked terribly familiar. My heart started pounding loudly in my ears.

No, it couldn't be him…

I turned my head quickly. All I saw was the crowd, the same faces that had been there before. I scanned their faces again, searching. But he wasn't there.

It had just been my imagination, obviously, but the feeling had been so strong…

I've always been a bit psychic. I read tarot cards to help me focus, and sometimes they gave me answers. In the year before the flood, it seemed to be getting stronger and more intense. I'd communicated directly with the Goddess, going into trances and seeing Her in visions. There had even been a time when I'd been psychically linked to a man who'd been dead for almost twenty years. But after the levees failed, it hadn't seemed to work anymore. The cards had just been cards, there had been no more visions, and I figured it was gone for good. Maybe it had become so much stronger that it had burned itself out. Maybe it was the negativity that followed in the wake of that last pre-flood Mardi Gras. I didn't know, and probably never would know for sure.

It wasn't like it was a science, or anything.

The only thing I'd known for sure was it was gone, and to be honest, I didn't really mind all that much.

Was it coming back? Why? And why now?

Of course, it could have just been the mimosas.

I sat down, grabbed my go cup, and downed what was left in a few gulps. I passed it back to my dad, who refilled it.

"You okay, Scotty?" he asked as he handed me back my drink. Dad is tall and skinny, with a full beard and a graying ponytail. He was wearing faded jeans ripped at the knees and his *I love my gay son* T-shirt. His eyes were concerned. "You look a little pale."

"I'm fine," I said, taking another drink and standing back up.

"You're sure? Maybe you should sit for a while."

"Seriously, I'm okay, Dad." I patted his shoulder and grabbed another handful of beads, which I tossed up to some guys on the balcony of Oz. I turned and tossed some more into the crowd in front of the Pub.

I still felt a little woozy. Was it possible that the gift was coming back?

Did that mean I was in *danger*?

Most of my life it hadn't been much; a twinge here and there, knowing who was calling before the phone even started ringing, and getting answers sometimes from the cards.

It had become more powerful only when I was in danger of some sort.

Hardly a reassuring thought.

It wasn't him. It wasn't anything. You just got a little dizzy from the mimosas and not having lunch. Get a grip on yourself.

"Idiot," I said to myself as as I grabbed another handful of beads and tossed them to the waving hands. "The gift is gone, and it's not coming back again."

The parade started moving again, but I wasn't into it anymore. Oh,

I smiled and posed for pictures, tossed beads to friends and strangers with a big grin on my face, but I just wanted the whole thing to be over so I could go home. I'd promised David I'd meet him at the Pub later for Sunday Tea Dance, but that didn't sound like much fun anymore.

All I wanted to do was go home and smoke pot until I passed out.

CHAPTER TWO
PAGE OF CUPS
A young man with brown hair and hazel eyes

The parade came to an end at the corner of Bourbon and Esplanade. All the floats and carriages were turning left to head back to Rampart Street. There was an after-party for the riders at a bar called Starlight by the Park I hadn't planned on attending even before whatever it was I'd felt in front of Oz. As our carriage got to the corner, a drop of rain hit me in the forehead. The wind was picking up as well, and was getting colder. Lightning forked over the river, and a loud clap of thunder followed almost immediately on its heels.

I just wanted to head home, and I needed to get going before the rain started.

"Scotty, are you okay?" Mom asked as I climbed into the back of the carriage. "You look like you've seen a ghost." She grimaced a little as she examined my face. She can always tell when something's wrong with me—it's a little spooky. "Here." She dug into the huge carpetbag she carried with her everywhere and pulled out a T-shirt with *Devil's Weed* on the front and a pair of ratty sweatpants. "Put these on before you catch your death." She gave me a faint smile. "I figured you wouldn't bring anything to put on over your costume."

"Thanks, Mom." I pulled the sweatpants on over my shoes. Another drop of rain hit me in the head as I was putting the T-shirt on. "No, I'm fine, Mom." I forced a huge grin, hoping it would fool her. "I'm just missing Frank, I guess."

"My poor baby." She kissed my cheek and mussed the curls on the top of my head with her free hand. "Well, next year he's not getting out of riding, even if he's hospitalized. We'll just tie his hospital bed to the back of the wagon." She grinned, taking a small one-hit pipe out of her purse, and took a long drag in full view of a mounted cop. He pointedly turned his head away. Mom was well-known to the French Quarter cops, and they never bothered her. She offered it to me.

I just shook my head and smiled back at her.

"He'll be home before you know it." She took another hit. "You want to come by for dinner later? Everyone's coming." She waved her hand, taking in all the riders. "Even Storm and Rain."

"Really?" That was a surprise. Mom and Dad were strict vegetarians, and we all avoided meals at their place as much as possible. I'd vowed when I was a kid that once I was grown up I'd never eat tofu again if I could possibly help it. "No, thanks. I have some leftovers I need to get rid of," I lied. "I don't want to have to waste it." It was the right tack. Nothing infuriated Mom and Dad more than wasting food.

I hugged everyone good-bye and jumped down from the carriage. I stood there waving as they turned the corner and headed back up Esplanade.

I made it around the corner on Decatur Street just as the skies opened. Fortunately, every building on my block has a balcony that covers the sidewalk. The wind picked up, too, and I shivered as I ran the last few yards to the iron door on the left side of my building. The narrow passage that ran alongside the building to the big courtyard behind wasn't covered, and as I unlocked the gate I prepared to get soaked. The rain was coming down hard, and the gutters were starting to fill with water.

I was sopping wet by the time I got to the back, where the stairs to the upper floors were. I dashed up the stairs, stopping on the second-floor landing to strip out of the wet clothes. My landladies, Millie and Velma, lived on the second floor, and their washer and dryer were on the landing. I stuffed the clothes into the dryer and turned it on.

I lived on the third floor. It was an old town-house style building just across the street from the Old U.S. Mint building. The first floor was a coffee shop. Neighborhood rumor had it the woman who ran it was a Mafia princess—but I didn't believe it for a minute. I liked Donatella. She was sweet, and always comped my coffee whenever I stepped in. The fourth-floor apartment had been vacant for years until recently. A college student in his early twenties named Levi Gretsch was currently renting the apartment up there. He'd moved in the week after Frank left for wrestling school. I hadn't seen him since the day he'd moved in, although I'd heard him moving around up there a couple of times. He was good looking in that young straight boy kind of way. He hadn't set off my gaydar, but that didn't mean anything anymore. He seemed nice enough, if a little on the shy side. All I really knew about him was that he was from Ohio and had moved down here to go to college. That was all Millie and Velma had told me about him when I'd asked, and I'd let it drop. Either they didn't know anything more about him, or weren't willing to say.

I'd find out his life story eventually—in New Orleans, you always do.

I fit my key into my lock and heard the door upstairs shut, followed by footsteps on the staircase. I'd just opened my door when I heard Levi say, "Hey, Scotty, do you have a minute?"

I paused, and turned to look at him. Levi was over six feet tall, with a mop of wavy dark hair and startling green eyes. His face was square. His forehead was square and high beneath the thick shock of hair, his jaw was square, and his chin was a small triangle pointing down from the straight line of his jawbone. His nose looked like it had been broken a couple of times. His neck was thick and strong. He was built like a football player, stocky and powerful. My guess was he'd either been a linebacker or a tight end. His shoulders were broad, his hips and waist narrow, and he was still in the full flush of youthful beauty that seems to fade so quickly in straight men. He was wearing a pair of hideous multicolored shorts that didn't fit right, didn't flatter his body at all, and hung down just past his knees. His red T-shirt with the Nike swoosh across the front fit tightly in the chest and shoulders, dropping from there loosely almost to his thighs. He was barefoot, and his weight shifted awkwardly from one foot to the other in that loose-hipped way straight boys affect as he stood there. His thickly muscled calves and forearms were covered with curly black hair. He had razor stubble on his face and neck. A couple of pimples dotted his forehead.

"Sure, come on in. You want a beer?" I offered, wondering for a brief moment if he was of age.

"Um, sure. Okay." He bit his lower lip, still shifting his weight from one foot to the other. David thought he was gay, "just didn't know it yet." I was pretty sure it was just wishful thinking on David's part. David was convinced every good-looking man was gay, or leaned that way.

I got the sense Levi wasn't totally comfortable going into a gay man's apartment.

Like once I got him inside I was going to rape him or something.

Please. He was at least four inches taller and had at least forty pounds on me. If anyone was going to be overpowered, it wasn't going to be him.

Besides, if I wanted that, the bars weren't that far away. I might be a little older and have love handles trying to take root at my waist, but I'm still capable of finding a hot guy.

I walked into my empty, lonely apartment and turned on the hall light. "The beer's in the fridge—grab one and have a seat in the living room while I put some clothes on." As soon as I said it, I had to suppress a smile. *Maybe he isn't homophobic, but what I'm wearing would make most straight boys nervous. It would make most gay men nervous, for that matter.* My bedroom was the first door on the left, and I shut the door behind me. I slipped off the bikini and pulled on a pair of boxer briefs, a pair of khaki shorts, and an AIDS Walk T-shirt. I slid my feet into my house shoes. I grabbed a beer from the refrigerator for myself and walked into the living room.

Levi was sitting on the couch, clutching a sweating bottle of Abita Light in both hands. He was bouncing his legs. Outside, the rain was beating a steady tattoo on my balcony. A flash of lightning lit up the room. The thunder that followed was so loud and close the house shook a bit.

"You don't have to be so nervous," I said, keeping my tone light. "I won't bite you or anything."

He gave me a weak smile. "I'm not worried about that," he replied, and took a long pull off the beer. "Storms make me a little nervous."

"Ah, this is nothing to worry about. Storms here generally don't last long." I opened a drawer in my coffee table and pulled out the box I keep my pot in. I'd rolled a couple of joints the day before, and retrieved one. "You don't mind if I smoke?" I asked as I put it in my mouth and flicked a lighter on.

He swallowed, his eyes fixated on the joint. "No. I don't smoke pot." His face reddened.

"You want to try?" I asked before taking a long drag. I blew out a stream of smoke. I offered it to him, but he waved it away, distaste written plainly on his face. *You need to lighten up a bit, straight boy.*

"What's up, Levi?" I gave him my friendliest smile. "You didn't come down here to watch me get stoned. Or did you?"

He shook his head. "Well, I've been meaning to ask you something for a while now." Levi took another nervous drink. "Millie and Velma told me you're a private eye." He took a deep breath. "I need to hire you."

Okay, then, this is going to be interesting. "You need a private eye?" I gave him a smile. "Are you sure? I mean, I don't charge a lot, but depending on what the case might entail, it could be expensive." I shrugged. "And any expenses I'd incur wouldn't be included in the daily rate, of course. I could give you the neighbor's discount, but it can still add up in a hurry. And I require a retainer, some of the money up front."

I've found that most people who think they want to hire a private eye really just want someone to talk to. They think their significant other is cheating on them, they think this or that or the other. Usually, talking about how much it's going to cost makes them rethink their options. When I bring up the cost, their faces usually fall. That's when I ask a few questions, and then it all comes pouring out of them. Nine times out of ten, they just need a friendly ear to listen to them. Once they've given voice to their suspicions, they feel better and find they don't need a private eye anymore. It annoys Frank no end, but I don't mind.

"I have money." He took a deep breath. "The reason I came to New Orleans—" He hesitated. "My grandfather—he was all I had, you know? He raised me after my parents were killed in a car accident when I was a kid." He paused again, gathering his thoughts. He emptied the beer and put the bottle down on the coffee table, covering his mouth to mask a burp. "Excuse me."

I took another hit. I was starting to feel a lot more mellow—it was very good pot. "I'm sorry about your parents," I said, waiting for him to go on. "That must have been very rough on you."

"Thanks. My grandmother—his wife—died before I was born, so I never knew her. He was all I had." He hesitated again. "A couple of months ago, my grandfather was—was—well, he was *murdered*." His eyes swam with tears. "I was supposed to go home that weekend, but I was behind on a paper. I should have been there!" Angrily he drove one fist into the palm of his other hand.

"You might not have been able to save him," I said gently. "You might be dead, too."

"That's what the police said. I still should have been there." He closed his eyes. "They called me on Sunday night to tell me. The police said—" He closed his eyes, and a tear came out of his right eye. He wiped at his eyes. "The police said he'd been *tortured.* I had to—I had to identify the body." He shuddered again. "I could barely recognize him."

I take a great deal of pride in my ability to find the right thing to say in any situation, but in that moment I couldn't think of anything. I just sat there and stared at him. I couldn't begin to imagine how awful that must have been. I've stumbled over any number of dead bodies in my life, and it's not something you ever get used to. I couldn't imagine how awful it would be to have to identify the body of a relative—especially if it was your *only* relative—and one that had been tortured. Gruesome images filled my mind, and I forced them back out.

He swallowed, and visibly pulled himself together. "Anyway." He reached into his shorts pocket. "He'd written me a letter—I got it when I went back to school to clean out my dorm room." He wiped at his eyes. "I should have gone home. I mean, I'd called him earlier that week to tell him I wasn't going to be able to come home, and there was—I could tell there was something wrong. He said everything was fine"—he swallowed—"and I had that paper due, so I…" He closed his eyes and shuddered.

"You poor, poor kid," I replied, finally finding my voice, and wincing at how lame my words sounded. "You can't beat yourself up about it, Levi. I'm sure your grandfather is glad you weren't there. He wouldn't want anything bad to happen to you. Do the police have any leads?"

He shook his head. "No."

"Do you want me to find your grandfather's killer…" I left my voice trail off. He was a nice kid, but I wasn't about to go looking for criminals that tortured people before killing them. "That's best left for the police. They have a lot more resources than I do."

He shook his head as he unfolded the letter and passed it over to me. "No, that's not what I need you to do." He wiped at his eyes. "Just read this. This is the last letter he wrote me."

I took it from him. It was a piece of notebook paper, with three holes on the left side. It was wide-ruled, and the folds were deep. The handwriting was a barely legible scrawl. I started reading.

Dearest Levi:

I fear that when you read this letter, I will most likely be dead. The past has come back to haunt me—a past that would be better off left in the past. The thing I have always feared the most—the actions of three foolish young men in a time of war are now coming home to roost. I always believed that somehow we'd escaped, and that the past would never come back to affect us in the present. But pretending something didn't happen doesn't mean that it didn't, and actions always have consequences.

I won't tell you any more than that—because the less you know, the better off you will be. But I have to warn you. You have always been a son to me, and I couldn't be prouder of you than if you were my son. Of the three young men in the picture, you are the only descendant. The first died over there. The other now lives in New Orleans, and has no children. The consequences of what we did—well, I don't believe that you will come to any harm if you don't know anything. But if I am indeed dead when you read this letter, you need to go to New Orleans and find Moonie. Moonie has what they are looking for, and he is the only one who can save you from their wrath by returning it.

It has to be returned before more blood is spilled.

I love you, my grandson.

Marty Gretsch

"Moonie? He couldn't tell you his name?" I shook my head as I put the letter down on the coffee table. "That's no help at all." My mind was racing. "But your grandfather seemed to know what was going to happen to him. Do you have any idea what it is that Moonie supposedly has? Or what it is they did over there?" I got up and walked over to the big windows that opened out onto my balcony. Had they committed war crimes, like what's his name, which'd massacred those people—what

was the name of the place? I wracked my brain. It was My something…
I shook my head and turned back to face him, figuring I could just
Google it later. "And after you got the letter, you came down here?"

"Scotty, I'm *scared*." His lower lip started quivering again. "I
mean—I don't know what these people *want*—and what they did to my
grandfather—" He started choking up again.

"Have you gotten any weird phone calls or letters?" I watched his
face. "Noticed people following you?"

He took a deep breath. "No, nothing like that. But that doesn't
mean—" his voice trailed off. After a moment, his body shook as he
tried to keep control of himself.

What else could I do? I walked over, sat on the arm of his chair,
and put my arm around him. "We'll figure it out, and I'd be happy to
help you find Moonie," I said, hoping I wouldn't regret the words later,
and suspecting it was likely. "Was there anything else?"

"I also have this."

He pulled an old photograph out of his pocket and handed it over
to me. It was of three young GIs standing in front of what looked like
a jungle base camp. It looked like Vietnam, but all I knew of that war
was from movies and television shows. It could have been any jungle,
anywhere in the world.

The three young men were all smiling, holding cigarettes in one
hand and rifles in the other. Jungle camouflage helmets were low on
their foreheads. They were wearing jungle camouflage shirts, open to
reveal white T-shirts underneath and dog tags hanging from their necks.
Their camouflage pants were tucked into black boots. The picture had
faded and yellowed with age. The one on the left looked older than the
other two, but not by much. A white margin framed the picture, and
across the bottom was printed the date it was developed: 06/07/66.

Over forty years ago.

I turned the picture over. On the back were written three names:
Marty, Moonie, Mattie. It was in the same scrawled handwriting as the
letter.

I turned it back over and looked at their faces more closely. "Your
grandfather is the one on the left?" There was a slight resemblance to
Levi in the shape of the face and the square jawline. The one on the
right rang no bells in my memory.

The one in the middle, however, looked slightly familiar.

Well, according to the letter, he lived in New Orleans. Maybe I'd seen him around somewhere. It was possible. New Orleans was really nothing more than a big small town—everyone was one degree of separation from everyone else. But I couldn't recall ever meeting or hearing about someone who went by Moonie.

He nodded. "I don't know what to do," Levi went on. "I have no idea how to find this Moonie guy. I don't even know what I'm supposed to do when I *find* him. I mean, the only people I know in New Orleans are Millie and Velma. And you." He finished the beer and put it down. "Do you think you could help me find him?"

I stared at the picture. That middle face—I was sure I recognized it. *Shouldn't have smoked the damned pot,* I cursed at myself. "How do you know them, anyway?"

"I really don't know them. When I decided to come down here, to try to find Moonie, I went on craigslist and found this apartment listed. When I called, it turned out that Millie went to school with my grandmother. She was from New Orleans." He hesitated again. "Millie doesn't know about any of this, by the way. I didn't know if I should tell her—about the letter. I mean, she knows Grandpa was murdered, and then she mentioned one day you were a private eye"—he swallowed—"so I thought I would come to you. I have some money—"

I cut him off. "We'll worry about that later." My curiosity was aroused. Turning the picture over in my hands again, I looked at the names written on the back. I flipped it back and stared at the faces again.

I *knew* I'd seen Moonie before, but I couldn't quite put my finger on where.

And as I stared at the picture, it started to swim out of focus.

Everything started going dark around the edges of my vision, and my mind started slipping down into darkness.

I had time to think *crap* before everything went dark.

It was hot. The air hung thick and damp, making my skin damp. I could feel sweat running down my back into my already soaked underwear. My armpits were dripping, and I wiped my hand across my face to keep the sweat from running into my eyes. I was in a jungle, in the middle of the afternoon, but everything was still and quiet. No insects were humming, no birds were singing, and nothing was moving anywhere. I could hear the sound of a river off to my right as I crept along the path. I was carrying a machine gun, and the ground was a little muddy underneath my feet.

The silence was strange, oppressive, and not right. It shouldn't be so quiet. The jungle was always alive with sound. Usually, such silence meant they were out there. Moving silently through the underbrush. Maybe even now I was being sighted, a gun aimed into the center of my back.

I could feel dread rising inside me, but I fought it back down. They were out there somewhere. I had to find them before they found me. I felt like I was being watched, but even though I kept scanning my eyes back and forth across the thick foliage, I saw—and heard—nothing. It might just be my imagination, but the silence—that wasn't, and that meant they were out there somewhere. Maybe they were afraid, like I was. Maybe they were afraid I would spot them before they spotted me. I stopped moving and wiped my hand across my eyes again.

That was the worst part of it, really—how silent the enemy was. They slipped through the jungles like wraiths, soundlessly, and you never knew where they were until they opened fire.

I couldn't shake the feeling I was being watched.

"Mattie?" someone whispered from my right. It was Marty. I heard a branch snap underneath my feet. It sounded like a gunshot in the silence.

We just had to get through this mission, and then we could go on leave. Two glorious weeks away from the jungle...and then we would be set. For life.

I heard a rustling in the bushes ahead of me.

"Scotty! Are you all right?"

I opened my eyes. I was lying on the couch, and Levi was hovering over me, his face pale. "I'm fine," I said, struggling to sit up. My mind was still foggy. He started to say something else, but I held up my hand to silence him. The vision was fading, and I needed to remember as much of it as I could.

It was gone.

I cursed to myself and reached for my beer. I took a long pull on the bottle and glanced back over at Levi. He was still standing, his face white, shifting his weight from one foot to the other as he watched me. His Adam's apple bobbed in his neck as he dry swallowed. I put my beer back down and gave him a weak smile. "Levi, I don't know if Millie or Velma said anything, but I'm a little psychic."

His eyes widened and he licked his lower lip. "No, they didn't say anything about it."

"Please. Sit down. You're making me nervous." I waved him into one of the wingback chairs. "It's nothing to worry about, and really, it's been such a long time since I've had anything, I'd really thought it had gone away." I hesitated. "Sometimes I have visions—and when that happens, I guess the best way to describe what happens is I kind of pass out, in a way." I shrugged. "I'm sorry—I would have warned you, but when it happens it's very sudden. And like I said, it hasn't happened in a long time." I crossed my arms.

As a rule, I didn't like to tell people about the gift. But I didn't have much choice in this instance. I waited for him to say something, bracing myself to be asked for the Powerball numbers, or something equally stupid.

Instead, he leaned forward, his face curious. The color was coming back into his face. "What did you see?"

I shook my head. "Sometimes I remember, sometimes I don't. This time I don't. That's why I shushed you—I wanted to try to remember what I saw, in case it was important." I noticed the picture had fallen out of my hands and was lying on the floor. I reached down and picked it up. "All I really remember was being in a jungle." I looked at the picture again. "This is Vietnam, right?"

He nodded. "My grandpa didn't really like to talk about it, but I knew he served." He shook his head. "He got a Purple Heart, there were pictures of him in uniform in his den—but whenever I asked him about it he didn't want to talk about it. I guess that's normal with war veterans."

"And you said the police don't have any leads on his killer?"

"No." His eyes got wet again, but he seemed to shrug it off. "The sheriff said it was more than one person…I mean, the house was trashed. And they tortured him before they killed him." His voice broke, and my heart went out to him, the poor kid. "I don't know what they did to him—I don't want to know."

"And nothing was missing?"

"Not as far as I could see. I mean, I didn't know what all he had in the house." He shrugged. "But it didn't make any sense, you know? I mean, what could he have had that someone would want so bad…" He paused and swallowed again.

So bad they would torture him to find it.

I got up and walked over to my desk. I handed him one of my business cards. "All of my numbers are on there," I said, "so if you think of anything else, let me know."

"So you'll find Moonie?" His face lit up. He really was a gorgeous young man.

"I'll do my best." I led him to the door. "I'll get started in the morning." I shut the door behind him, cutting off his thanks.

I walked back into the living room and plopped down on the couch. A case! I felt positively rejuvenated. Besides, looking for Moonie would help me pass the time until Frank got back.

I picked up the joint and sparked it up again. I grabbed a notepad and started making notes.

The easiest way to find Moonie would be to contact the Veterans Administration. They would have records—they might not be willing to open their files to me, but I was sure after I told them the story, they could find out the names of the other guys who served with Marty Gretsch. But if I couldn't convince them, maybe Storm could do something. My older brother was a dreadful tease who loved to pick on me, but he was also one of the best lawyers in New Orleans. And wasn't there some law that allowed people to request records? What was it called?

Damn, it was good pot.

Oh, yeah, the Freedom of Information Act. I made a note to look it up online and find out what information could be requested.

My cell phone started ringing. I answered. "Yo."

"You coming to tea?" It was my best friend, David. "I'm down at the Pub already. You're late."

I glanced over at the clock on my mantelpiece. "Oh, man, sorry about that. I was meeting with a client."

"Well, get your ass down here—there are hot guys everywhere."

I sighed, and debated with myself. There wasn't really anything I could do until the morning, anyway. "All right. I'll be there in a few minutes."

"Well, hurry your ass up." David hung up.

I wandered down the hall to get dressed.

CHAPTER THREE
NINE OF SWORDS
Death of a loved one

I had a slight buzz going as I headed home from the bars about nine.

David had been right—the bars had been packed. They usually were on holiday evenings. After spending the day with family, most guys couldn't wait to get to the clubs and get their gay on. It was a lot more festive out than a usual Sunday, and everyone seemed to be drinking quite a bit more. Usually, I love to meet people and flirt, but I hadn't been into it tonight. Frank and I had an open relationship in theory, but so far neither one of us had strayed—and anyone I would have met would have been a poor substitute for him. Instead, I avoided making eye contact with anyone and just stood in a corner, nursing beers while David kept a running commentary on the fuckability of every guy who walked past us. Every guy I saw I compared to Frank— and they came up on the short end of the comparison. Finally, David zeroed in on a hot young Hispanic, and as they went through the gay mating ritual, I tossed my beer bottle into the trash and beat it out of there. I said good-bye, but David was so caught up with the Hispanic I don't think he even noticed.

The evening was cold, and I shivered a little bit. The rain had passed, but the sidewalk and streets were still slick and wet. I walked down Bourbon Street, stopping into the Nelly Deli to get a Coke. A cute guy was in there, waiting for his food, and he started cruising me. I just smiled and took my Coke to the cash register.

When did you turn into such a dull boy? I scolded myself as I walked home. *You're in an open relationship, and even if you don't want to hook up with someone, there's no harm in flirting with people.*

It wasn't just about missing Frank, though. As I took a swig of my Coke, my mind went back to Levi.

I felt really sorry for him. I couldn't imagine how rough it would be to be all alone in the world at that young an age. I was glad I'd taken his case. Was it likely his grandfather's killers were after him? Probably not, unless they thought he had whatever it was they'd been looking for in his grandfather's house. I made a mental note to do an Internet search for information about his grandfather's murder when I got home. All I needed was the name of the investigating officer. I doubted he'd give me any information about an open case, but he could let me know if he thought Levi was in any danger. The most important thing was to find Moonie. He had whatever it was they wanted.

I wondered again what the three young GIs had done over there.

I turned the corner onto Governor Nicholls and stopped dead in my tracks.

A block ahead, past Royal Street, several police cars were pulled up on the sidewalks, their lights flashing. An ambulance was parked in the middle of the street, its lights also flashing. I recognized the van from the police crime lab. Several cops had cordoned off the block and were keeping a crowd of people back.

I sighed. The crime rate had been going back up in the city as more people returned. There had been several shootings in the Quarter in recent months, and the residents were starting to get restive. I debated just turning down Royal and walking home down Barracks Street, but curiosity got the better of me.

"What happened?" I asked a tall, beautiful woman with red hair when I got to the crowd behind the barricade. She was holding a gorgeous King Charles spaniel on a leash. I leaned down to pet the dog. It started jumping on my legs excitedly.

"Down, Rambla," the woman commanded. The dog ignored her and placed her front two paws on my thighs. "Some poor man fell from a balcony, from what I gather." She shook her head. "It's a wonder there aren't more balcony accidents. He was probably drunk."

I scratched the spaniel's silky ears and cooed at her. "That's a good girl, yes."

I straightened up. The dog started sniffing around my feet. "Which balcony?"

"The one above the candle shop."

My heart sank into my shoes. I left her and pushed my way through the crowd of spectators to the barricades, all the while telling myself, *No, it's not Doc, it can't be Doc, I was just there this afternoon, it's not...*

I took a deep breath.

There was a body lying in the middle of the street, covered with a tarp from the coroner's office. The feet were uncovered, and I saw a pair of navy blue loafers and navy blue pant legs.

I grabbed hold of the barricade as my body started to sag.

Out of the corner of my eye I saw a door open, and two police detectives I recognized walk through it out to the sidewalk.

It was Doc's door.

I turned my eyes back to the corpse.

I looked up at Doc's balcony. There were several cops up there, and someone was dusting the railing for fingerprints. A camera's flash went off. I felt the beer in my stomach trying to come back up. I took a deep breath and fought the nausea down. Tears started to well up in my eyes.

Memories started flashing through my mind. I saw Doc lighting a cigar and enjoying a glass of bourbon as he explained the sociopolitical situation in the Middle East to my parents. I remembered Doc explaining to me the significance of the Stonewall Riots and the birth of the gay rights movement. I remembered Doc, who always hung a black wreath on his door on the anniversary of Lee's surrender at Appomattox, arguing with my mother that it wasn't racist to take pride in ancestors who fought on the wrong side of the Civil War. I could hear Doc saying that the only good Republican was a dead one. And I remembered how kind he had always been to me. I remembered how, after the flood, he had told Frank and me that how we chose to move forward with our lives was more important than anything awful that had happened to us that year. I remembered him telling us we had to grab for every brass ring life offered to us, and that the worst thing would be to look back on our lives and regret not doing things, not taking chances, not living our lives.

I choked back a sob.

No, no, no! There must be some mistake, it can't be Doc there under that tarp, it must be someone else, there must be some mistake, yes, that's it, Doc can't be dead.

"Venus!" I shouted at the two detectives. "Blaine!" I started waving at them.

Venus Casanova is a tall, striking black woman of indeterminate age. She wears her hair cropped short, and years of exercise have kept her body fit and strong. Her partner, Blaine Tujague, is a sexy guy in his early thirties with dark black hair and bright blue eyes. I'd dealt with them before on several murders I'd gotten involved in, and while I know I got on their nerves, they were thorough professionals.

Venus made a face when she saw me, and started walking toward me. Her heels clicked on the pavement. She was wearing a navy blue pantsuit over a yellow silk blouse. Her eyes narrowed, and she sighed. "Scotty Bradley. What are you doing here?'

"Is that"—I swallowed—"Benjamin Garrett?"

"Let him through," she said to the cop standing in front of me. The cop stood aside and let me pass. She turned her back to me and started walking over to the corpse. I followed her. "We're not sure who this is, there was no ID on him. But he came from that balcony up there, and the name on the box is Benjamin Garrett," she said, squatting down next to the tarp. "Can you handle taking a look?"

I nodded, and took a deep breath. She pulled the tarp back.

I felt gorge rising up in my throat. "It's him."

His face was down against the pavement. Blood was pooled under his face, and his nose was flattened. There was no sign of his glasses.

She replaced the tarp and waved for me to follow her. Somehow, I managed to get back to my feet and start walking. My mind was numb, but that was better than hysteria. *Doc is dead, Doc is dead, Doc is dead* kept running through my head like some kind of twisted refrain.

I followed her until we were standing underneath Doc's balcony. "At least this time you didn't find the body," she said, her face impassive. She folded her arms. "No offense, but I was hoping I'd never see you again."

"None taken. I was kind of hoping the same thing, to be honest." I turned and looked back at the corpse. "What happened, Venus? Did he jump?"

Venus's face didn't move. "We're trying to figure that out, Scotty. When did you last speak with him?"

"I—I just talked to him this afternoon." I leaned against one of the balcony support posts and took some deep breaths. "Oh, no, no."

The numbness was starting to spread through my body. I made an effort to pull myself together. I wasn't going to allow myself to melt down in front of Venus Casanova, no matter how justified it was.

"This afternoon? How did he seem?"

"The same as always." I shook my head. "Fine. He was perfectly fine. I was heading up the street to ride in the Easter Parade. I walked under his balcony—" *Was it just six or so hours ago?* I swallowed again. "And when I came out he dumped water on me. He invited me up, gave me a towel, and I hung out with him for a little while. I was afraid I was going to be late, so I left and he invited me to stop by again tomorrow afternoon." I looked at her. "He wouldn't have done that if he was planning to—you know." I couldn't bring myself to say it. "And I can't believe in six hours he would have gotten depressed enough to—you know."

Venus watched me, and when I had myself back under control, said, "How did you know him?"

"He's an old family friend. He taught my parents in college." I turned my back on the street. I didn't want to keep looking at his body. "I've known him my entire life. He is—*was*—a really great guy—a little cranky sometimes, but he was old, you know?" I thought of something. "He walked with a cane, Venus. He had hip problems, I think it was— and he also had heart problems. I think he had a mild heart attack last December. I don't think he could have climbed over the railing. No way." As the words came out, I knew what they meant.

The only way he could have gone over the railing was if he'd had help.

That made it murder.

But why would someone want to murder Doc?

"You're sure he gave you no hint of any trouble this afternoon?"

I thought for a moment. "You know, he got a phone call while I was there. I don't know who it was—he took it in another room. But when he came back his face was flushed and he was having trouble breathing. At the time, I just thought he might be having another one of his attacks, you know? I wasn't sure, though, because I wasn't completely sure what was wrong with his heart. I think it was a heart attack." I was babbling, so I clamped my mouth shut and stopped talking. I wrapped my arms around myself. I was shivering.

"You think it may have been the call that upset him so much?"

I nodded. "It had to be. I was worried about leaving him. But after a few minutes, he was back to normal, so I thought he was okay."

Venus looked out into the street for a moment before turning back to me and shrugging. "At first, it seemed pretty clear that he jumped. But when we saw the inside of his apartment…" She let her voice trail off. "You're positive he couldn't have jumped?"

"He couldn't have jumped." I kept my voice steady. "There was no way he could have climbed over the railing. He wasn't that agile."

She nodded, her face impassive. "His apartment was ransacked," Venus went on. "Would you know if anything was missing? Can you come up and take a look?"

"I could try." I thought for a moment. "Although my mother"—I swallowed. Mom. Someone was going to have to tell my parents— "would probably be better, or his maid. He was kind of a pack rat." I shrugged. "He kept everything, and the place was really cluttered. You think it was a robbery?"

"You mind taking a look around?" she asked, ignoring my own question. "We're going to need to take your prints, too—if you were there this afternoon, we need to rule your prints out."

I took a deep breath. "Okay, let's go."

I followed her down the passage to the back stairs. The numbness and shock were starting to wear off. I still was having some trouble wrapping my mind around the idea that Doc was dead. I was also dreading having to call my parents and tell them. When we reached the staircase, Venus turned and asked, "Did he have any relatives?"

"He has a sister up in Vicksburg, I think." I shook my head. "He never really talked about her much. But my parents—they'd know."

Venus nodded and started up the stairs with me right behind her.

I don't know what I was expecting to see when we got up to the apartment, but it was a shock.

Ransacked wasn't a strong enough word for what had happened to Doc's apartment. It looked like a bomb had gone off inside. The back parlor, where I'd toweled dry earlier, was completely destroyed. The couch and the chairs had been slashed. Their stuffing spilled out of the rips and was scattered all over the floor. Tables were overturned. Books had been pulled down from the shelves and scattered all over the carpet. Some of them had been torn apart, their pages scattered here and there.

The big mirror on one wall in its gilt frame had been smashed. His bric-a-brac, once carefully arranged on tabletops and on the shelves, lay everywhere. Some of it was in pieces. Art had been removed from the walls. Some of it had been ripped from the frames and tossed aside like so much junk. Other frames still held the art, but the glass had been smashed, the prints scarred and slashed. The floor was covered with shards of glass that glittered in the light. My jaw dropped. "Oh, wow," I whispered. "This is *awful*."

Venus just nodded. "You said Garrett was an old family friend?"

"Uh-huh."

"Did he have any enemies?"

"Doc?" I turned back to her in disbelief. "No. Well, yeah. He used to feud with other historians, but it was all academic stuff. He used to talk about it some, but I really didn't pay a whole lot of attention. But to kill him? And do all this?" I shook my head. "I can't believe someone would be angry enough over an academic dispute to do this."

"You'd be surprised what people will do," she deadpanned.

"I guess," I replied dubiously, trying to remember what the last feud had been about. We'd been at Mom and Dad's for dinner in January. Doc was telling us about some scathing critique he'd done for some historical magazine about some book about—what had it been? I hadn't paid much attention; it all seemed kind of silly to me. "Someone had written a book about the occupation of New Orleans during the Civil War—I don't remember who or what the name of the book was, but—" I closed my eyes. I could see us all sitting around Mom and Dad's table. Frank was next to me, and had been rubbing my calf with his foot under the table. Mom, Dad, and Doc had been at the other end of the table. "The book was a defense of Spoons Butler, and Doc was furious about it." He had been. His face had reddened and he had pounded his fist down on the table a few times to accentuate his points. Benjamin "Spoons" Butler, or Butler the Butcher, had been the military dictator of New Orleans after the city fell to the Yankees. He'd been called "Spoons" because he used his authority to steal everything he could get his hands on—even the silverware. A hundred and fifty years later, Butler was still reviled in a city that never forgot. "Apparently, he'd shredded the book and its conclusions. He really enjoyed that kind of thing, frankly."

She made a note on her pad, and asked, "I know it's a mess in here, but can you tell if anything is missing?" When I shook my head, she walked into the hallway.

I followed her. The mess was just as bad in the hallway. I didn't see how anyone could tell if anything was missing—not even his maid would be able to tell. Room after room was more of the same. Not a single book was left standing on a bookshelf. The art had all been yanked down from the walls. Not a single chair or couch had escaped being slashed to pieces. Drawers were open, their contents dumped on the floor. I tried not to step on anything, but glass crunched under my feet with every step.

"Some of this art is really valuable," I said, pointing at a ruined canvas tossed into a corner, scarred from the broken glass. "That's an original Dureau, it's worth a lot of money. He lent it for a show at the Museum of Modern Art last summer." I shook my head. "This couldn't have been a simple robbery. The art is worth a lot of money, Venus. Why would they damage it rather than steal it? It doesn't make sense. Whoever did this was looking for something." A thought tried to form in my mind, but slipped away.

"You have no idea what they could have been looking for? Was there something really valuable he had hidden somewhere in the apartment?"

I shook my head. "No, Venus, I'm sorry. I just don't know."

I heard a voice in my head. *The entire place was torn apart.*

Levi's grandfather's place had been trashed, too.

I put that thought aside. It didn't make sense.

I walked into his bedroom. The mattress and box springs had also been slashed and tossed off the bed. The bed covers were piled in a corner. It was more of the same. The floor was covered in debris from shattered bric-a-brac, destroyed books, and framed art. The carpeting had even been slashed methodically.

"They had to have done this before they killed him," I said aloud.

Venus nodded. "That's what we think. This kind of destruction took time. Once he went off the balcony, they only had a few moments to get away before someone called the police—they certainly didn't have the time to trash the place and get away."

I winced at the thought of Doc having to witness all of his belongings being destroyed. "Unless he was already dead when they tossed him." But that didn't make sense, either. In fact, tossing him off the balcony seemed kind of dumb. While the balcony was certainly high enough for the fall to be deadly, there was also no guarantee the fall would kill him. He could have landed in any number of ways that would have caused serious injuries that might not have been fatal. And if he was already dead, why throw him off the balcony in the first place? They could have just left the body in his apartment, and there was no telling how long it would take before he was found. It could have been days before anyone noticed he was missing. He wouldn't have been found until his maid showed up.

"Was Garrett in the habit of hiring hustlers?"

"What?" I spun around and stared at her. "I can't imagine..." My voice trailed off. As long as I'd known Doc, he'd never had any romantic entanglements of any kind. I'd never even been sure he was gay. And while I could hardly picture Doc sitting in a bar hitting on someone, it was equally impossible to imagine him hiring a hustler. He was so fastidious I couldn't picture him letting a hustler into his home. "I'm not even sure he was gay, Venus. But on the other hand, I can't imagine him at the Catbox Club tipping the women there." But surely, he had to have some kind of sexual outlet. Everyone did—whether they liked to admit or not. But I couldn't picture Doc hiring hustlers, or even letting one into his apartment. He was so fastidious...but maybe he associated sex with being dirty... I put that thought out of my head with a shudder. I didn't want to go there. "Maybe my mother would know, but I don't."

She shrugged and gave me a little half-smile. "Just making sure. All the nudes here in the bedroom are male." She leaned down and picked up one. "But these are more artistic than pornographic."

I leaned against the wall. *If Doc weren't already dead, hearing this conversation would give him a stroke.* I started to laugh, knowing it was completely inappropriate, but I couldn't stop myself. The laugh sounded strange to me, and before I knew it I was crying.

Venus just stood there watching me until I got hold of myself.

"Sorry." I wiped at my face.

"Are you okay?" she asked, not unkindly.

"It's just a bit much." I sighed. "I mean, not five hours ago, I was sitting with him in the back parlor, just talking, you know? And now he's dead. Maybe if I hadn't left—"

She shook her head. "Then you'd most likely be lying next to him in the street." She shrugged. "This wasn't the work of just one person. And there were no signs of forced entry—Garrett let his killers in."

"Oh God." I started to retch, but took some deep breaths until it passed.

"And whatever it was they were looking for, they didn't find it." She went on, kicking a picture frame out of her way as she headed back to the bedroom door.

The frame skittered across the floor, smacked a book, and flipped over face-up just a few feet away from me.

A young male face in military dress blues stared up at me.

I caught my breath as I recognized the face.

I'd just looked at it earlier that afternoon in a different picture.

Three young GIs in a jungle base camp, mugging for the camera.

I knew he'd looked familiar.

Doc was Moonie.

"Venus!" I called, kneeling down next to the picture. I picked it up, staring at it.

There was no question about it. Doc was Moonie, the friend Levi's grandfather had sent him to New Orleans to find.

Marty Gretsch had been tortured to death, his house ransacked in much the same manner as Doc's apartment.

My instinct had been right.

"Yes, Scotty?" Venus said from the doorway.

I stood back up and took a deep breath. "You're going to need to talk to my upstairs neighbor, Venus. His name is Levi Gretsch, and his grandfather was murdered a few months ago...and his house was trashed the same way."

Venus raised an eyebrow. "And the connection is?"

"His grandfather wrote him a letter before he was killed, telling him to come to New Orleans and find an old army buddy of his." I swallowed, pointing down at the picture. "He hired me this afternoon to help him find his grandfather's friend. All he had was a nickname and an old picture of three Army buddies. Doc was one of the three soldiers—the only one who was still alive." I sighed. "I thought the guy in the picture looked familiar, but I couldn't place him. The picture was forty years old. And I never saw this one before."

"All right, let's get moving." She gave Blaine some directions I didn't hear, and we walked down the back stairs.

We walked the two blocks to my apartment in silence. My mind was racing. Surely it couldn't have been a coincidence that Levi had rented the apartment upstairs from me, and was looking for a man who just turned out to be an old friend of my family? But it had to be coincidence. If he'd known Doc was Moonie, he didn't need to hire me to find him.

I hate coincidences, but they do happen. In a city like New Orleans, they happen a lot. Levi had said his grandmother was from New Orleans, had gone to school with Millie. Doc was from Vicksburg, had lived in New Orleans for forty years. Maybe that was the connection. Maybe Doc had introduced Marty to his bride. But why didn't Marty just tell Levi in the letter who Doc was? Maybe he was afraid whoever was after them would find the letter…which meant Levi might be in danger. If the same people had killed his grandfather and now Doc…

I tried to remember every little bit of our conversation, tried to get a sense of whether Levi had been lying to me. I tried to remember his tone of voice, his body language, everything he'd said and how he said it. He'd seemed a confused young man, torn with grief and confusion. Unless he was an incredibly gifted actor, I was pretty sure my impressions were correct.

What the hell was going on? What had the three GIs done over there?

I got my keys out to unlock the iron door at my house, but it wasn't latched.

I turned to Venus as I reached out and pushed the gate. It swung open, hit the wall, and swung back. I put my hand out to stop it from shutting.

Millie and Velma were sticklers about making sure the gate was locked. If the gate was left open, anyone could just walk down the passage and would have easy access to the back stairs—and everyone's apartments. Millie had even put a spring lock on it so it would slam shut. The only way the gate could be left ajar was if someone had deliberately tried to keep it from shutting.

Millie and Velma would kill for far less than that. Velma had lectured me more than once about the importance of keeping the door closed. "Leaving it open, for any reason, at any time, is grounds for immediate eviction." Her tone made it clear she was not joking. "Anyone could walk in here. Anyone. And I don't really want to be robbed, raped, or killed simply because you got careless." I'd gotten the message, and had passed it along to Frank when he'd moved in. I was certain Levi had gotten the same lecture.

No one who lived in the building would leave that door open.

I looked at Venus. "This isn't good. I know I shut the door when I left. I heard it slam." I explained how security conscious my landladies were.

Her eyes narrowed as she flipped open her phone and called for backup. She pulled her gun and slipped the safety off. "He's on the top floor?"

I nodded.

"Stay here." Her heels made no noise as she moved down the passageway. "When the squad car gets here, let them know I went in."

I stood there in the doorway, my armpits clammy with cold sweat. A couple of cars drove past heading uptown. I could hear music from a live band playing at Checkpoint Charlie's on the other side of Esplanade. Some people were hanging out in front of Charlie's, drinks in hands, talking and laughing loudly. Further up Decatur Street, I could see street kids camped out in front of some of the closed shops, spare changing people going from bar to bar. The night sky was clear of clouds, stars twinkling in a sea of deep blue velvet. The wind still felt cold and damp. I shivered and rubbed my arms.

I hoped Levi was okay. I said a quick prayer for him.

It seemed like I waited forever, but only a few minutes passed before she finally came back. She was talking into her cell phone as she waved me to come down the passage and join her in the dark courtyard. She was standing inside a yellow cone of light being cast from one of the fixtures on the back staircase—but it was much darker back there than usual. Millie and Velma liked to keep all the courtyard lights on all night.

My legs were wobbly. I let the gate slam shut behind me. I put my hands against the walls on either side of the passageway to help me keep my balance. When I reached Venus, she was putting her gun back into its holster.

"Is he—" I asked, afraid to hear her answer.

"He's not there," she said, giving me a look I didn't like. "His door is wide open, but there's no sign of him." She folded her arms, her face carved from stone. "Why don't you start at the beginning? And don't leave anything out."

Chapter Four
THE MOON
Unforeseen perils

Venus finally left just before midnight.

Frankly, I was beginning to think she would never leave. She's a good cop, which means she is very thorough. She'd made me go over my encounter with Levi so many times I'd begun to feel like I was reciting from a script. She'd taken lots of notes, her face impassive. Any time I started speculating, she'd cut me off with a curt "Stick to the facts, Scotty." Properly humbled, I'd shut up and wait for her next question. Finally, she closed her notepad and put it into her jacket pocket.

"So, what do we do now?" I asked.

She gave me a look that made me squirm a bit. "We?" she replied, a faint smile playing at the corner of her mouth. "*We* aren't going to do anything. You, on the other hand, are going to play nice with the police for once."

"I've always played nice with the police," I objected. "Name one time I didn't cooperate."

Her smile broadened. "I don't have all night." She stood up and stretched. "All right. This is what I'm going to do. I'll get in touch with the police up in Ohio and see what I can find out about this Marty Gretsch's murder, okay? There may be a connection, there may not be." I started to protest but she held her hand up for silence. "It's a starting place, at any rate. But from all indications, Garrett *wasn't* tortured before he went off the balcony. And you only have this Levi's word about this murder in Ohio." Her forehead wrinkled. "I would like to talk to him."

"Are you going to put out an APB?"

Her smile faded a bit. "Don't use police lingo, Scotty." She sighed. "I really can't do a whole lot until he's been missing for twenty-four hours. For all we know, he might be out on Bourbon Street and just left his door unlocked."

"But—"

She held up her hand again. "If he shows up, call me. I don't care what time it is, you call me. Got it?"

I nodded.

She glanced at her watch. "All right, I'm heading back to the station."

I walked her out and shut the gate behind her.

I took a deep breath and started climbing the back stairs. I thought about knocking on Millie and Velma's door, but it was late. They hadn't responded earlier when we'd knocked, but they might have come back home while Venus was grilling me. They wouldn't be happy to be awakened—they never were—and I was too tired to deal with a pair of angry lesbians.

All I wanted to do was take a long, hot shower and go to bed. *You need to call your mother and tell her about Doc,* I lectured myself.

I didn't want to make the call.

But when I got to my own door, I hesitated. I looked up the stairs. Venus was a good cop, which meant she never bent the rules. She had probably just gone up there, made sure he wasn't there, and that was it. Bound by rules of admissible evidence, she wouldn't have searched the place. My word was not enough probable cause for her to search the place, and if there was no "in plain sight" evidence that Levi had been taken against his will, her hands were tied.

That didn't mean it wasn't there for someone with a little less scruples to find.

I went into my apartment and scrounged around in my kitchen junk drawer. Millie and Velma had given me keys to every door in the building, in case of an "emergency." They'd never told me exactly what qualified as an emergency, but I had never once abused their trust by using my keys to go anywhere I wasn't supposed to—like their apartment or the carriage house on the back side of the courtyard where they stored things. They might not like the idea of me going into Levi's apartment without his permission, but I felt I could make a pretty strong argument to justify my quasi-legal entry. But where were the damned keys? The junk drawer was a mess. Frank and I both just threw things in there that didn't have a specific home elsewhere. Whenever I had to try to find something in there, I always swore I would clean it out and organize it—and promptly forgot the vow once I found what I was looking for. I started digging through the mess—cigarette lighters, key rings, stamps, blank envelopes, old clogged pipes, paper clips—and began to fume with irritation. *Tomorrow I am cleaning out this stupid thing,* I swore just as I spotted the Saints key ring. With a smile of triumph, I grabbed it and slammed the drawer shut.

Millie was a little anal, so each key had a label taped to it.

Feeling enormously proud of myself, I made sure the key marked APT 4 was on the ring before heading out the door.

It was raining again, and it had gotten even colder. I shivered and started up the stairs to the fourth floor.

I hadn't been up there since I helped Frank move down into my apartment. Back in the days when there'd been the three of us, he and the Liar had shared the fourth-floor apartment. We spent most of our time down in my apartment, but once the Liar was gone, it just didn't make sense to keep both apartments. We converted my spare bedroom into a room for Frank to keep his clothes and things in, and left the guest bed there. I'd never liked going up to the fourth floor much, frankly. Even though my apartment was pretty high up, going up to the fourth always gave me a touch of vertigo. The first three floors all had sixteen-foot ceilings, so the top floor was at least fifty feet up in the air. The wind always seemed more blustery and stronger the closer you got up there, and it didn't take a lot of imagination to see the wind blowing me right off the stairs and falling to my death in the courtyard.

An overactive imagination can be a curse sometimes.

Finally, I got to the top landing. The bright yellow light outside the door lit up the landing pretty well. It was also the smallest landing, and even though the building had been rebuilt after the fire four years ago, it had a slight downward tilt from the building settling. Right by the railing overlooking the courtyard was a small metal ladder attached to the wall by screws that led up to the trap door that opened onto the roof. Other than roofers, no one ever went up there.

There wasn't enough money in the world to make me climb that ladder. For one thing, you had to hold on with one hand while opening the trap door, and the ladder was too close to the edge for me. One slip and next stop—the courtyard.

I tried the doorknob but it didn't open. Venus must have locked the door behind her when she'd left. I slipped the key into the lock and smiled when I heard the deadbolt slide back. I opened the door and flipped the light switch.

All three apartments had the exact same floor plan. The front door opened into a hallway. The two bedrooms were to the left, with a bathroom located in between them. On the right wall, just inside the outside door, was a door to a massive closet. The kitchen was the next door on the right, and the hallway ended in a one huge room sectioned off into a living room and a dining area. On the far wall of the lower-floor apartments were three sets of French doors that opened out into the balconies. The fourth-floor apartment didn't have a balcony, so there were only windows on that wall.

Levi's hallway was bare. No tables, nothing on the walls, and no rugs. I opened the closet door and flicked on the switch. It was empty, not even empty boxes from when he'd moved in. The floor was dusty, and cobwebs hung in the corners near the ceiling. I turned the light off and crossed the hall to the first bedroom.

It, too, was empty. No furniture, nothing. I closed the door and headed into the bathroom.

The bathroom was spotless—which I wasn't expecting. Given Levi's age and sexual preference, I was expecting a bathroom that bordered on being a public health hazard. But the sink and the counter gleamed in the light. The toilet was scrubbed clean. There were no telltale spots of toothpaste on the mirror like there were on mine. The only thing on the counter was a small, clean glass. I opened the medicine cabinet. On the bottom shelf were his razor and shaving cream. The second shelf held his toothbrush and a rolled-up tube of toothpaste. The top shelf held a bottle of face wash designed to fight acne. I smiled a little—I'd used that brand when I was in high school.

I closed the door and looked at the shower. The bathtub was completely clean. There were no hairs or soap build-up in the drain. A huge purple bath towel was drying on the rack for the shower curtain. The floor mat next to the tub matched the towel. Underneath the sink I found more rolled-up purple towels, and a stash of toilet paper, along with a toilet brush and other cleaning supplies inside a blue plastic bucket.

I walked into the kitchen. The refrigerator was empty other than a half-empty gallon jug of milk, a six-pack of Diet Dr Pepper, and some sandwich meat in plastic containers. There was nothing in the freezer. A quick glance through the kitchen cabinets revealed some inexpensive dishes and glasses, a box of Honey Nut Cheerios, and an unopened loaf of bread. The rest of the cabinets were empty, as were the drawers, except for one filled with local take-out menus and some cheap flatware.

The bedroom he used, on the other hand, was a little sloppier. The shorts and T-shirt he'd been wearing when he'd come down to my apartment were thrown into a corner on top of some other dirty clothing. The single bed was unmade. A can of Diet Dr Pepper sat on the nightstand, along with an ashtray overflowing with cigarette butts and ashes. A straight porn magazine was open to a quite nauseating picture of a large-breasted bleached blonde servicing two well-endowed, tattooed men who looked a little malnourished. All that was in the nightstand drawer was an opened box of condoms.

Definitely straight, I thought as I tore my eyes away from the lurid magazine.

The walk-in closet was next. As I opened the door and reached for the light switch, it crossed my mind that if Levi had just gone bar-hopping I was seriously invading his privacy, and it would probably be best if I got out of there—

The closet flooded with light, and I whistled to myself.

The closet was a walk-in, just like the ones in my bedrooms. At eye level was a shelf that ran along one wall, across the back, and back up the other side. To my left hung the shirts I was accustomed to seeing Levi in: sweatshirts and sports team jerseys. Dirty, worn-out running shoes were placed neatly on the shelf above. There was a pile of cheap-looking cotton boxer shorts neatly folded next to the shoes, and beyond that were the unflattering shorts he usually wore. On that side of the closet, everything was as it should have been.

But the right side was a completely different story. I pulled down a pair of expensive-looking black leather shoes and checked the inside sole for the brand name. I whistled. Storm wore that brand, and they cost a minimum of $200 a pair. There was a black wool suit with a

Versace label, Dolce and Gabbana slacks, shirts from Hilfiger. Next to the designer shoes on the upper shelf were two stacks of brief-style underwear, all with designer labels.

I remembered him saying to me, *I've got money.*

I put the underwear back on the shelf. Apparently, he hadn't been kidding.

I closed the closet door and walked out into the living room, thinking.

He'd said his grandfather had a farm, and he was a college student. That had, to me, implied poverty.

I heard my mother sneer in my head, *Classist. Just because his grandfather was a farmer didn't mean they were poor.*

But it wasn't just the farming thing, I answered her back in my head. The way he dressed—and from the closet, it looked like he deliberately chose to dress that way to create the impression of a poor college student. Why, for example, would a college student need all those expensive dress clothes, or shoes that cost over two hundred dollars a pair?

He wouldn't.

There was nothing of interest in the living room. His laptop sat on a computer desk in the dining area, but it was password locked. The computer desk drawers were empty, other than a bankbook from the Whitney Bank, an old-time New Orleans bank. I opened it.

The balance showed $523,000. The account had been opened the day Levi had moved in here. There had been two withdrawals since then, both for twenty thousand dollars, two weeks apart.

What on earth did he spend forty thousand dollars on in the last month?

The clothes? Maybe, but it didn't seem like there were forty thousand dollars' worth of clothes in there. They were expensive, but still.

What the hell is going on?

I put the bankbook back and turned off the lights, locking the door behind me. A cold blast of wind almost knocked me back against the door. Shivering, I started down the stairs when I thought I heard something.

I stopped, and listened.

It sounded like it came from the roof.

I went back up to the landing and waited for a few moments. *It was your imagination,* I scolded myself, and headed downstairs.

Once inside my apartment, I headed for the couch and plopped down. I reached for the half-joint I'd left before going to Tea Dance in the ashtray and froze with the lighter halfway to my mouth.

Great. I'd left it sitting right there in plain sight with a New Orleans police detective in my apartment.

"Who are you, Levi Gretsch, and where are you?" I asked out loud as I blew a plume of smoke toward the ceiling. The money and the clothes—they didn't fit in with the image Levi projected. But to be fair, maybe he wasn't trying to project an image. I'd made assumptions, based on his age and what he wore whenever I saw him.

And if you hadn't invaded his privacy, you wouldn't know any different.

As I sat there on the couch, I started feeling overwhelmed. Okay, some of it was probably the pot intensifying things, but still. A little over eight hours ago I was riding in the Easter Parade, not a care in the world. Now my client might be missing, and—

Doc is dead.

I fought the feeling off. There was nothing I could do for Doc, but Levi was still alive—so what I should be doing was focusing on finding him. At least, I *hoped* Levi was still alive. It was possible Venus was right—this was the French Quarter, after all. He could have just wandered off, maybe gone barhopping, or hooked up with some girl on craigslist. It was also possible he hadn't pulled his door completely shut, which was why the latch hadn't caught. But that explanation didn't cover why the gate hadn't been closed, and it was the gate that concerned me more than anything else.

Or maybe I was just making too much out of everything. Maybe Doc's murder—*oh, sweet Goddess, Doc is dead*—and the similarities between that murder and the story Levi had told me were playing havoc with my imagination.

But I couldn't shake the feeling there was more to Levi's disappearance than the simpler explanations.

I reached under the couch and pulled out the box with my ancient deck of tarot cards. I hardly used them anymore—since the levees failed, the few times I tried to read them had been utter failures. But I always kept them under the couch, where I always had, and figured it was worth a shot. I'd already had two episodes; maybe the Gift was coming back. Nothing ventured, nothing gained.

I lit the white candles I always kept on the coffee table, and sat down on the floor and cleared my mind. When I felt peace, I opened the box and slipped out the deck of cards, wrapped in a white silk scarf for purity. The deck felt warm and alive in my hands. I clasped them with both hands, closed my eyes, and offered a prayer to the Goddess. I unwrapped the deck and shuffled.

They felt good in my hands.

I sent my question out into the universe, and laid the cards out.

An untrustworthy figure from your past will return and possibly cause problems.

There is danger from the past that must be faced.

A handsome young man is not who he seems.

Pray for a brave heart.

I frowned. Well, that was much clearer than many of the other readings I'd done, but it still didn't tell me a whole lot. *An untrustworthy figure from your past...*

My mind went back to that moment on the float as we passed Oz. Surely—

No, I dismissed that thought immediately. That had been my imagination, surely. Colin could never come back to New Orleans. He was wanted for murder.

When we'd first met, Colin had told me he was a cat burglar. That was just the first of the many lies he'd told me. Frank and I thought he worked for an international detective agency, the Blackledge Agency, and we had even thought we worked for them as well. It wasn't until after Colin had murdered two people that we found out his real name was Abram Golden, and he not only didn't work for the Blackledge Agency, he was actually a paid assassin. He'd fled the country before getting caught, leaving everything he had behind him.

It had been hard getting over that, but Frank and I had managed. There was bitterness and anger, hurt and fury to get past. Time actually does heal—that isn't just an annoying platitude. When Hurricane Katrina slammed into New Orleans and the levees failed, we all got a little perspective over what's important and what wasn't. I'd always had the feeling, though, that we weren't done with Colin.

I picked up the cards and put them away, taking another hit off the joint. *You need to call your mother,* an annoying little voice reminded me. I emptied my beer and went into the kitchen to get another one. As I opened the refrigerator door, I noticed the light on my answering machine was blinking, and the digital 1 was lit up. Wondering if Frank had called back for some reason, I reached over and hit the Play Message button as I took a swig from the beer.

"*BEEP. Frank, Scott, this is Angela Blackledge. I have a business proposition for the two of you. Could you please return my call at 030-234-9876? Thank you.*"

I almost dropped the beer.

Angela Blackledge. I played the message again, writing the phone number down on the pad we kept by the phone. It was a foreign number, that much I knew, but I didn't know the country code. I picked up the phone, and put it down.

I swallowed. *How weird that I was just thinking about Colin, and here's a message from Angela Blackledge.*

When Colin's true identity had been revealed, Angela Blackledge had claimed she had no idea who he was—that he didn't work for her, never had, and our little agency here in New Orleans was not affiliated with hers in any way. We'd had no choice but to believe her—neither Frank nor I had ever spoken to her on the telephone, and Colin had handled all of the business arrangements. At first, I'd been certain she was lying—but in fairness, I was still trying to clear Colin in my head at the time. What she'd said had not been what I'd wanted to hear at the time. What I'd hoped for was an explanation, some magical *deus ex machina* to come down from the heavens and explain why Colin had killed two men and kidnapped Frank.

It was very hard to accept that you were in love with a paid killer.

But still, I hesitated. Maybe, just maybe, I'd sensed she was going to call—and since she and Colin were so completely linked in my mind, that put thoughts of him into my head?

And just because the cards were warning me about someone untrustworthy from my past didn't mean it was Colin. There were a lot of untrustworthy people in my past.

But, I reasoned, it had been a long day, and there was no need to call her back right away. I didn't owe her anything. I didn't have to call her back at all.

I did want to know what she wanted, though.

I sat down in front of my computer and opened the Internet browser. I pulled up a search engine and typed in *country code 30*. The little wheel spun for a few seconds, and a directory popped up. I stared at the screen for a moment. *Greece. She was calling from Greece.* The city code was Athens, apparently; there was a list of the different city area codes on the page. I pulled up a time zone site. Greece was six hours ahead of New Orleans. I glanced at the clock in the bottom right corner of my computer screen. 12:27 a.m., which meant it was 6:27 a.m. in Athens.

What the hell, I thought, *if it's too early for her she doesn't have to pick up.*

I dialed and waited as the phone rang on a scratchy connection. On the fifth ring, voicemail picked up. It was one of those toneless voices that come with the service that gives no information other than the number and to leave a message at the tone. When it beeped, I said, "Ms. Blackledge, this is Scott Bradley returning your call. Please call me back—bearing in mind there is a six-hour time difference. It is currently 12:27 a.m. in New Orleans. I will wait up for another hour and a half. If you do not call within that period, please wait a minimum of eight hours before calling. Thank you."

I hung up the phone and took another drink from my beer. *If I'm going to wait up to see if she calls, I should make use of this time a little better.* I pulled up a search engine and typed in *Benjamin Garrett*.

There wasn't much there, mostly links to conference speaking engagements and articles he'd published in academic journals.

I thought back. I couldn't remember ever, not once, hearing him refer to his service days in Vietnam. That wasn't surprising, I supposed. Vietnam had been one of those horrible times in history where public opinion was horribly divided—between those who thought we should be there and those who thought we shouldn't. Mom and Dad certainly had strong opinions about our "imperialistic intervention in Vietnamese affairs."

I picked up Levi's grandfather's letter again and reread it.

"...the actions of three foolish young men in a time of war are coming home to roost..."

I typed *Vietnam War Atrocities* into the search engine, and clicked on the first link that came up.

It was an article for a history Web site by a woman doing her dissertation on the Vietnam War. I started reading. I didn't really know a whole lot about the war, other than the brief week we spent on it in U.S. history in high school, and movies I'd seen. As I read, I grew more and more horrified.

> In 1971, the Army began a four-and-a-half-year investigation of the alleged torture of prisoners, rape and murder of civilian Vietnamese women, the mutilation of bodies, murder of civilians, assault, and dereliction of duty. No one was ever court-martialed; on the contrary, soldiers under investigation "resigned" from the military during the investigation. The vast unpopularity of the war at home made it necessary for the Department of Defense to sweep any alleged American war crimes under the rug. Several American newspapers did remarkable investigative pieces on these crimes, notably the Toledo Blade in 2003.

Had Doc been a war criminal?

But that didn't make sense to me. If he and his friends had committed war crimes, someone seeking revenge would certainly want to kill them—but the ransacking of their homes didn't fit into the equation. Levi's grandfather had been tortured, but Doc hadn't. The only common denominators between the two murders were the ransacking and the old photograph.

Unless—

I swallowed. *Unless they tortured Levi's grandfather to find out where Doc was hiding.*

But they had to be looking for *something* as well.

The question was, what? And the way they'd left Doc's apartment, I doubted they'd found whatever it was. The whole place had been ripped apart, which would have only been necessary if whatever it was they were looking for had been in the last place they'd looked. What were the odds of that?

Of course, whenever I was looking for something it was *always* in the last place I looked.

The phone started ringing, startling me out of my thought processes. "Hello?" I said, picking it up.

"Scotty." It was my mother, and she seemed short of breath. My heart sank. *I should have called her and told her about Doc.*

"Hey, Mom," I croaked out, taking another swallow of beer to bolster my courage. "I was meaning to call you…"

She cut me off. "Scotty, I need you to come over to the apartment, right now. I am serious. Now."

"Mom? Are you okay?" There was something in her tone that seemed off.

"I can't discuss this on the telephone, Scotty. You need to come over. Now."

I started to protest but she'd hung up. That, too, was unlike Mom.

I sighed, glancing at the clock. It wasn't likely Angela Blackledge was going to call me back anyway, and what else did I have to do? And it would be better to tell Mom about Doc in person, anyway. She always said she hated getting bad news over the phone.

But what was wrong? I wondered. The way this night was going, it could be anything.

I pulled on a pair of shoes and grabbed my keys. I locked the door behind me and went down the stairs. Millie and Velma's apartment was still dark. I made my way down the passage and out the front gate, making sure it slammed shut behind me. I started walking quickly, turning the corner at Barracks and heading up the street. It was deserted, which was normal for this hour on a Sunday night.

I had almost reached the corner at Royal Street when I was grabbed from behind and slammed against a brick fence, knocking all the breath out of me. My head hit the bricks, and stars swam in front of my tearing eyes.

I didn't have time to yell or do anything before a very sharp knife was pressed to my throat.

Adrenaline coursed through my body.

The man who was holding the knife to my throat was wearing a black hooded sweatshirt with the hood pulled low over his forehead. I couldn't make out his features above his nose, which was long and crooked. His lips were thin over yellowed teeth, and he smelled bad, of a mixture of tobacco and body odor that made me slightly sick. "Where is the eye?" he said in thickly accented English.

"I don't know what you're talking about." I tried to keep my voice calm, which wasn't easy. My heart was pounding loud enough to be heard blocks away.

The blade pressed harder against the base of my throat. "You lie! Where is the eye?"

He pressed closer against me, and I scanned the street in both directions. No one was around. No police cruiser conveniently patrolling the lower Quarter, no group of drunken tourists staggering back to their hotel, no gutter punks walking their dog and spare changing people.

It was then I realized he'd made a huge mistake. My right leg was in between his, giving me a clear shot.

"I don't know what you're talking about," I said again, then raised my knee as fast and as hard as I possibly could.

He let out a strangled moan, the knife dropped away from my throat, and he collapsed to the sidewalk.

I took off running. I ran around the corner at Royal Street and just kept going. I didn't slow down until I got to the corner at Dumaine, fumbling for my keys to the gate to the stairs behind the Devil's Weed that led up to my parents' house. I slammed the gate shut and took the stairs two at a time, and paused to try to catch my breath before opening the back door.

Finally, I put my key into the lock and pushed the door open.

"Mom? Dad?" I called as I walked through the kitchen into the big living room.

What I saw stopped me dead in my tracks.

"Hi, Scotty." Colin smiled at me from the couch.

Chapter Five
SIX OF CUPS, REVERSED
Living in the past rather than the present

For just over three years, I had imagined what this moment would be like. I'd imagined all kinds of witty bon mots I would toss off nonchalantly, wounding him the way he'd scarred Frank and me. I'd wondered if it would be better to be cold and distant, and not give him the satisfaction on knowing the damage he'd left in his wake. I'd wondered if I would get angry, lose my cool and start yelling at him. I'd wondered if it would be better to simply be indifferent. There was a part of me that wanted to somehow get even with him. Those kinds of thoughts bothered me. That wasn't the kind of person I wanted to be, that I tried to be, that I was raised to be.

So I'd tried to cleanse my soul of negativity and bitterness. I tried to put aside my pain, and prayed for him and his safety. I'd wondered if he were alive, or if his line of work had finally proved fatal for him. I'd wondered if he had really cared about us, or if we'd simply been a convenient cover for him in New Orleans. Had he loved us or been using us? There hadn't been a single word from him in all that time. There were times when I'd tried to understand him, tried to get inside his head and figure it all out. Maybe he was afraid to get in touch, maybe he was afraid we hated him, maybe he knew there was no way he could repair the damage he'd caused.

Maybe, maybe, maybe.

But in all my fantasizing about this moment, I'd never imagined it would be like having someone reach inside my rib cage and squeeze my heart with both hands.

I just stood there, gaping at him like a fool incapable of speech. My mind was racing through thoughts and emotions I'd thought I'd be finished with years earlier. My body felt numb from head to toe.

My breathing was too fast, and if I wasn't careful I was going to hyperventilate.

I closed my eyes and tried to clear my mind. *Focus on getting your breathing under control,* I thought as blackness started to crowd into the edges of my consciousness. I leaned against the door frame, and as I took deep controlled breaths the blackness started to fade away.

My mouth opened and closed several times, but no sound came out.

The truth was I didn't know what to say or how to react.

It was really annoying.

He was still one of the most gorgeous men I had ever seen. He had an extraordinary masculine beauty that was mesmerizing, almost impossible to look away from. His thick curly blue-black hair was longer than I remembered, and his olive skin contrasted nicely with his almond-shaped bright green eyes that always looked dewy beneath his long black lashes. There was a bluish shadow on his cheeks and chin that usually showed up within hours of him shaving. He had dimples, even white teeth, and thick sensual lips. When he smiled, his entire face lit up, and he was smiling at me now. He was a little shorter than me, maybe about five-seven, and his body was thickly muscled from years of working with weights and strenuous exercise. His shoulders were broad, his waist narrow, and his stomach completely flat. He had gotten bigger since I'd last seen him, and he looked as powerful as a tank. He was wearing a pair of baggy black jeans and a black T-shirt stretched tightly across his hard chest.

I closed my eyes and remembered the first time I'd ever seen him—wearing a yellow thong in the manager's office at the Pub before we went out to dance on the bar. And like then, I just stared at him without speaking.

I opened my eyes and noticed he had gauze wound around his upper right arm—and there was a slowly expanding dark red dot in the center of it. *He's injured,* I thought, sympathy welling up inside me. I resisted the urge to go to him, put my arms around him, and kiss him.

I gritted my teeth. *Oh, but hell no,* I thought, pushing all the sympathy I was feeling behind a door in my mind and slamming it shut.

"Give me one good reason why I shouldn't call the police right now," I said. My teeth still clenched together. I realized my hands were trembling, so I shoved them into the pockets of my jeans.

His smile never faltered. "Go ahead and call them," he said in an even voice and shrugged. "If that's what you want. We can finally get everything cleared up."

I wasn't expecting that. There was an outstanding warrant for his arrest, for committing two murders over that crazy Mardi Gras weekend so long ago. Maybe he was just calling my bluff. I stepped out of the dark kitchen and into the living room, pulling my phone out. "Yeah, maybe it would be best if I just went ahead and called them."

His smile faded, and his eyes widened. "My God, Scotty, your neck is bleeding! What happened to you? Are you okay?" He started to get up out of the chair.

"Stay where you are!" I commanded in a shaky voice as my hand flew up to my neck and felt wet stickiness. When I pulled it away, it was covered in blood. "I—*oh.*"

The adrenaline high I'd been riding chose that moment to crash, and my legs got wobbly in the knees. I felt myself starting to get dizzy, and I managed to stagger over to a wingback chair before collapsing completely. That bastard *cut* me, I thought, staring at the blood on my hand. My heart was pounding in my ears, and I was vaguely aware Colin was calling for my mother. She came into the room, but I couldn't really hear what was being said. I saw my mother kneel down in front of me and her face go pale. I blinked and she was gone, and Colin was there, with a paper towel, daubing at my neck. I tried to push his hands away but my arms had no strength in them. The numbness was spreading through my body. *Breathe, Scotty, focus on your breathing, you're going into shock.* Colin covered my legs with a blanket. I was shaking, the adrenaline rush long gone, and I ached with exhaustion. I closed my eyes, and when I opened them again my mother was kneeling in front of me, gently patting my neck with a warm, wet cloth. "Honey, what happened to you?" she asked, placing a piece of gauze at the base of my throat before anchoring it in place with a bandage. "It's a small cut, but you're bleeding like a stuck pig. What on earth happened?"

Has the entire world gone crazy? I wondered as I watched her get up. Colin had sat back down on the couch, and she sat down next to him, patting him on the leg. She smiled at him, like having a murderer sitting on her couch was not a big deal, just the most normal thing in the world.

"What is he doing here?" I blurted the words out at last. I'd stopped shaking, but was still exhausted. "Mom, why haven't you called the cops?"

Mom looked at me like I'd lost my mind. "The cops?" Her voice was puzzled, and then her expression broadened into a smile. "Oh, of course, you mean because he's been *shot*. No, we agreed there's no need for us to call the cops." She patted Colin's shoulder gently, and he smiled up at her. "He doesn't want us to, and since it's just a small flesh wound I could fix up—"

I said, very carefully enunciating each word, "No, Mom, I thought maybe you might have called the police because he's wanted. You know, like his picture is on a poster in the post office?"

"Don't be silly." She dismissed that with a wave of her hand. "It most certainly is not. I was just there yesterday, and I can assure you—"

"Mom, he killed two people?" *And who knows how many others?* "They were your brothers? Hello? How could you forget that?" Okay, granted, they'd had connections to the Russian mob and terrorists, and she'd never met them, but *still*. And I remembered we'd never told her he'd been trained by the Mossad, and worked as a paid assassin. Frank thought we should tell everyone the truth—but what Colin had done was bad enough, I'd thought. Frank finally came around to my way of thinking.

At least Frank wasn't here to say *I told you so.*

"Hey, I'm sitting right here," Colin said, looking from Mom to me and back again.

Mom ignored him, a stern look on her face. "Colin did *not* kill them." Her eyes narrowed as she continued speaking. "He said he didn't do it, and that's good enough for me." She gave him a huge smile. "He's not a killer. I would know if he was." She folded her arms in front of her. Her tone clearly implied *and that's the end of that unpleasant subject.*

"Maybe we should leave that to a jury?" I wanted to shake her. "And there's a little thing called aiding a fugitive from justice? Accessory after the fact? You could go to jail!"

"Hello? I'm right here," Colin said, his eyebrows coming together over his nose.

"You're starting to sound like your brother." Mom frowned. "And I don't mean that in a good way, Scotty."

"Well, he's not always wrong, Mom," I said, thinking *I cannot believe I just said that.* "Storm would go through the roof if he knew…" I let my voice trail off and buried my face in my hands. There was no point in arguing with my mother. She was probably the most loyal person I knew. I usually thought that was one of her better qualities, but it apparently also came with a severe downside. I knew my mother. If the police showed up to arrest Colin, she would fight them with everything she had. She would hide him, she would help him escape, she would give him money and—my head was starting to seriously hurt. Yes, she would most certainly risk jail to protect him.

Okay, yelling would only make her more obstinate, so I decided to try another tack. I knew it was a hopeless fight, but I had to try at least one more time so that when Storm eventually met us at the police station, I could say I tried everything. I took a deep breath and said in my most even, reasonable tone, "Mom, please. I just don't want you— or me—to be in trouble with the law, Mom. We could be arrested. We could go to jail."

"I wish you would stop talking about me like I'm not even here," Colin said.

She didn't even look at him. She waved her hand dismissively. "Please. We wouldn't go to jail. If it came to that—and I'm not saying it will, mind you—you know we can afford the best lawyers in the country. And you know as well as I do how heavily weighted our justice system is in favor of people with money."

I stared at her in disbelief. "And the reason I know that is because you've spent your entire life protesting against it and fighting to correct it—and now you're saying you're willing to compromise your principles and beliefs to take advantage of that inequity? Isn't that kind of hypocritical, Mom?"

"What, you think I should stand on principle?" She rolled her eyes and shook her head. "No, Scotty, I don't think our system is fair. I don't think the poor—or even the middle class—can afford the same justice the privileged can. But if it were my child—or someone I love—you bet your ass I'm getting them the best lawyer—or lawyers—money can buy. Does it make me a hypocrite? Maybe it does, maybe it doesn't. That's not for us to decide. But I would rather be a bad person than a bad mother." And with that, she folded her arms. The subject was officially closed. We would not be turning Colin over to the police. Not now, not in the future, and probably not ever. For better or worse, we were now accessories after the crime, harboring a fugitive from justice, and whatever else the district attorney decided to throw at us after we were caught.

And we would be caught.

"Now, what happened to your neck?" She had switched from her don't-argue-with-me tone to concerned mother.

"Why is he here?" I asked, and hated that my voice sounded whinier than I'd intended.

"For God's sake, I'm sitting right here!" Colin exploded. "Quit talking about me like I'm not here!"

I ignored him. "Is this why you wanted me to come over here? And where's Dad?"

"Oh, dear." Mom rubbed her eyes. "That's right, you don't know. Oh, Scotty—"

"If you must know, I called your mother because I didn't know where else to go," Colin interrupted her. "I'm here on a case—didn't Angela call you? She was supposed to call you—"

I interrupted him. "She called me." I still couldn't bring myself to look at him. "She left a message on my machine. I called her back, but she didn't answer. I left her a message. She didn't say what she was calling about." I smiled at him, but it wasn't a pleasant smile. I certainly wasn't there yet—and didn't know if I ever would be. "How do I know she wasn't calling to warn me that you were in New Orleans?"

"Obviously, since I knew she was going to call you, it stands to reason she was calling to ask you to help me." Colin sighed. "You have to believe me, Scotty."

"I don't *have* to do anything." I snapped. "So, you're saying you do, in fact, *work* for Angela Blackledge? That isn't what she said three years ago, as I recall. So which is it, Colin? Or Abram or whatever your name really is? Do you work for her, or do you not?"

"Scotty, you're being rude. You could listen to what he has to say." She gave me her *I raised you better than this* look.

I sighed. "I'm getting a headache." I rubbed my forehead.

Without saying a word, she walked into the kitchen. I heard the sink come on, and a moment later she was handing me two capsules and a glass of water. I took them and drained the glass. She sat back down on the couch next to him and took one of his hands in hers. He smiled at her before turning back to face me.

"I *do* work for Angela Blackledge," Colin said. "I know, I know, after the Mardi Gras case, she denied that I work for her, but she had to. She didn't have a choice. We couldn't let the local police get involved. It was just easier to let everyone think I was the killer." He took a deep breath. "I didn't kill your uncles, Scotty, you have to believe me. I was undercover, yes, deep undercover, and the case was a lot more complicated than you know. Once my cover was blown, I had to get out of here as quickly as possible. There wasn't time for explanations." He swallowed. "If I'd stayed, you and everyone I love would have been in danger." Mom smiled and kissed him on the cheek. "And if anything like that happened—" He choked off a sob.

I rolled my eyes. Mom, of course, was eating this up with a spoon.

He cleared his throat and went on. "And even now, I can't tell you everything. I wish I could, you know I wish I could." He looked at me pleadingly. I recognized that expression, all right. It used to melt my heart, make me want to do anything he asked.

Well, it wasn't going to work on me now.

"Yes." I smiled thinly. "I suppose if you told me, you'd have to kill me. Like Sasha and Pasha. Remember them? The uncles I never got a chance to know?"

"Scotty!" Mom said warningly, but I ignored her.

"You killed them both." I went on, worked up into a high state of righteous indignation. "Your thugs kidnapped Frank, and beat him. He could have been *killed.*" In spite of myself, I felt tears coming to my eyes. I took a deep breath and got hold of myself. I'd be damned if I was going to let him see me cry.

"Scotty." Mom walked back over and sat on one of the arms of my chair. She put her arm around me. "Trust me, son. I know it's hard. But do you really think you were wrong about him? Do you really believe he could have done such a thing, lied to us all, kept up a charade like that twenty-four/seven?" She kissed me on the cheek, and squeezed me hard. "I'm sure Colin is good at his job, but no one is that gifted an actor, Scotty. He would have slipped up at some point, or contradicted himself—no one can keep that many lies straight. And none of us are stupid people, Scotty. At least one of us would have caught on at some point, don't you think?" She started stroking my hair. "At the very least, Frank was in the FBI for twenty years. Do you really think anyone could fool Frank for that long? I mean, it was his job—and he was good at it, remember?"

I hated to admit it, but it was a good point.

On the other hand, she hadn't held Frank every night until he fell asleep for about three weeks after that fateful Mardi Gras, either.

Let it go, Scotty, just let it go.

So, hoping I wouldn't regret it later—and suspecting I would—I made a decision. I took a deep breath, and said, "All right. You have until tomorrow morning to convince me to help you." I looked at my watch. "And then I'm calling the police."

Colin started to say something, but Mom cut him off. "You never said what happened to your neck, dear."

"Someone tried to mug me." I leaned back in my chair. I was so tired. "It was very weird, though, he didn't want my wallet or anything. He just shoved me up against a wall and put a very sharp knife to my throat. All he said was, 'Where is the eye?'" I shuddered at the memory. "I kneed him in the groin and ran the rest of the way here."

Colin and Mom exchanged glances.

"What?" I asked crossly. "What the hell is going on around here? And you never told me where Dad is."

"Oh, honey. I started to tell you before, but—" She bit her lip. "But you just wanted to argue." She glanced at Colin and got up off the couch. Mom walked back over to me and sat back down on the arm of my chair. "Scotty, I'm afraid I have some terrible news. Your father is at the morgue, making arrangements."

"The morgue?" My eyes widened. "Papa Bradley? Maman? Not Storm. Please, Mom, tell me it's not Storm."

"No, honey, it isn't a member of the family. Well, sort of." She patted me on the head. "Honey, I'm afraid Doc is dead."

My body, which had gone completely tense at the word *morgue,* relaxed and I blew out a sigh of relief. "Oh, *that.*" The absurdity of the entire situation hit me at the moment as funny, and I started laughing nervously.

"He must be in shock," Mom said over her shoulder to Colin. "Scotty, are you okay?"

"I'm not in shock." I wiped at my eyes. "It's been a pretty crazy night, I'm sorry. It's just that—I already knew about Doc, Mom. I kept meaning to call you and Dad and tell you, but the night's been kind of crazy." I rubbed my eyes and ran my hands through my hair. "I went out tonight to Tea Dance, met David there, in fact. On my way home from the bars, I walked up Governor Nicholls Street, and right into the crime scene. Venus Casanova and Blaine Tujague were in charge. They had me go look around the apartment, to see if I could tell if anything was missing." I darted a look back at Colin. "I couldn't tell, of course. The place was trashed. I told them you'd have a better idea, or his maid."

"That Blaine Tujague called here, asked your father to come down to the morgue and identify the body—"

"I already did that." I cut her off. "Venus had me do it at the crime scene." That was weird; why would they want Dad to go down there and do a second identification?

She shrugged. "Well, I'm just telling you what Detective Tujague said when he called. Your father decided it was better for him to go than me—the sexist." She sniffed. "Like I can't handle seeing a dead body?"

"True." I smiled faintly. Everyone in my family has seen their fair share of corpses.

"And that's where your father is," Mom went on. "He's going to make the arrangements with the funeral home while he's there. Since there's apparently no family—"

"I thought he had a sister in Vicksburg."

Mom shrugged. "Apparently that's not true, after all. He always told me her name was Blanche Segal, but there's no Blanche Segal in Vicksburg."

"That's weird."

"Apparently, son, Doc was not who he said he was," Mom replied. "Do you want to tell the story, Colin?"

"And what happened to your arm, anyway? Who shot you?"

"In good time, Scotty." Colin got up and started pacing. "Benjamin

Garrett wasn't his real name. He changed his name when he came back from Vietnam back in 1968. His real name was Benjamin Moon."

"Moonie," I breathed out. I closed my eyes. I was pretty sure I wasn't going to like where this was going.

Colin just gave me a brief look, and then continued. "He and two of his best buddies from college all enlisted, in 1965. The other two were Marty Gretsch and Matt Harper. They were all three from Biloxi, students at the University of Mississippi. They grew up together, went to college together, and enlisted together. Some of the other guys in their unit said they were inseparable, like three brothers rather than friends. And they always managed to arrange it so they had leave all at the same time. They traveled all over Southeast Asia. They went to one place more than once."

"Where was that?" I asked.

"A small independent nation sandwiched between the borders of India and Nepal, called Pleshiwar."

"Pleshiwar? I've never heard of it." I looked from one face to the other.

Mom inhaled sharply, and we both turned to look at her. She shook her head. "I've heard of Pleshiwar." Her face was grim. "It's a horrible place, ruled by a theocracy that's perverted the Hindu religion. Their primary deity is Kali—but not the same Kali the Hindus know. Their version of Kali is, well, evil." She swallowed. "Their ruler is the high priest, and the ruling class is the priesthood. The people are little better than slaves. It's a barbaric place, still trapped somewhere in the Dark Ages."

Colin nodded. "That's right, Mom." It rubbed me wrong to hear him call her that. As far as I was concerned, three years ago he'd lost the right to call her anything other than Mrs. Bradley. "Anyway, during one of their visits, a valuable relic disappeared from the Temple of Kali. It was one of the most holy relics, if not the holiest. In the center of the temple is carved ivory statue of Kali. It's about three feet tall, and is supposed to be an incarnate statue—that means Kali's spirit lives inside of it. The craftsmanship is unbelievable. This Kali looks so real it's like she is about to take another breath. This temple, this statue, is the absolute heart of their religion—and therefore their country. It is decorated with incredible jewels. In the center of her forehead was a large blue sapphire with a flaw in the center. The cut of the sapphire, along with the flaw, made it look like an eye."

"The eye," I breathed. The man who'd stabbed me—he looked subcontinental Asian. His English had been accented.

"The stone was called the Eye of Kali, and the cult believed the Eye was actually Kali's eye, and she saw through it into the temporal realm. You have no idea how sacred the stone is to the Pleshiwarians."

"Think of how much the gold plates mean to the Mormons—well, the idea of the gold plates," Mom said, "or the tomb of St. Peter means to the Catholics, then multiply it by about a hundred."

"It was stolen," Colin continued.

"How is that possible?" I asked. "I would think they would have it guarded. Heavily."

Colin shook his head. "Mom was right when she said the country is stuck in the Middle Ages. The cult leaders believed that Kali herself protected the temple, and would strike down anyone who defiled her. There were guards, of course, but that night, all the guards went to sleep. When the Eye was stolen, the high priest was torn to pieces by a mob of angry Pleshiwarians. The new high priest claimed Kali had put the guards to sleep and allowed the Eye to be stolen because she was displeased that the former high priest had not allowed modern technology into the country, and the stone would not be returned until the country had proved itself worthy of Kali, to spread her glory throughout the rest of the world."

I shuddered. "Sounds like a horrible place."

Colin nodded. "The three GIs, though, were in the country when the Eye disappeared, and left that same night for Vietnam. As Pleshiwar gets very few tourists, the priests figured that it was the Americans who stole the Eye. Shortly thereafter, Matt Hooper was found dead in a back alley of Saigon. He had been butchered, and his eyes were taken as well. Shortly after, the other two mustered out and returned to the United States, and disappeared."

"So, you're saying Doc and his friends stole the Eye, and then came back to the U.S. and changed their names and went into hiding." I pondered that for a moment. I shook my head. "I don't know if I buy this. Obviously, they couldn't sell the Eye of Kali, so why did they take it?"

Mom shrugged. "Maybe they didn't realize when they took it they wouldn't be able to unload it. Greed makes people do stupid things."

"And you think all this time, Doc has had the Eye?" It didn't make sense to me. "If they knew the Pleshiwarians were looking for them, and would kill them to get it back, why didn't they just return it?"

"They were dead even if they returned it," Mom replied. "Right, Colin? They had defiled Kali. The Pleshiwarians couldn't let them live. Kali is a vengeful and bloodthirsty goddess. She would want revenge."

"What doesn't make sense to me is the how and why of it," I replied. "I mean, does it make sense to you? Three GIs from Mississippi, serving in Vietnam—how did they even know about this jewel? What did they think they were going to do with it once they stole it?"

Colin shook his head. "We might not ever know the reason. But once I was able to figure out what they changed their names to after they came home from Vietnam, I did find some interesting things."

"Such as?"

"Well, they came back with a lot more money than they had when they enlisted." Colin shrugged. "Marty was able to buy a farm, and pay cash for it."

I remembered the bankbook in Levi's drawer.

"And Ben Garrett bought property here in New Orleans," Colin went on. "Several buildings here in the Quarter. No mortgages, just bought them outright. Now, where did they both get the money from?"

"Someone hired them to steal it?" Mom mused. "Paid them some of the money up front, the rest on delivery? And they never delivered it…probably because after Matt was murdered in Vietnam they got scared and went into hiding."

"So it may not be just the Pleshiwarians who are looking for them." Colin's voice was grim. "There's someone else, an unknown factor."

"And now all three of them are dead," I breathed. "And no one knows where the Eye is. They took the secret with them to the grave."

Colin looked at me, his eyebrows going up. "How did you know Marty Gretsch is dead?"

"I'm psychic, remember?" I replied sarcastically.

He looked at Mom. "I thought you said he didn't have the gift anymore?"

"Mom!" I glared at her.

She shrugged. "Well, it's true, isn't it?"

"It's none of his business," I said, my teeth clenched. "And besides, it seems to be coming back. I had a vision this afternoon." I glared at Colin. "And no, I didn't know Marty Gretsch was dead because of the gift." I swallowed. "His grandson hired me this afternoon to find Ben Moon, and—"

Colin interrupted me. "That's impossible."

"I am a private eye, after all." I snapped. "I may not work for a huge international investigation corporation—one that occasionally stoops to killing people, I might add—but it is my job."

Colin sighed. "Will you stop being so defensive? It's impossible because Marty Gretsch only has one grandson, and that child is only twelve years old."

Chapter Six

THREE OF WANDS
There is a tendency to scatter one's energies

I thought about it for a moment. I only had my client's word that he was actually Levi Gretsch. I hadn't asked for ID or anything, but maybe Millie and Velma had. The bankbook, though, had been in that name. I found it hard to believe the Whitney Bank would have allowed him to open an account without any identification.

But of course, identification could be forged, and I somehow doubted the new accounts clerk at any bank branch would be trained to spot fake papers.

"He came downstairs and hired me to find someone named Moonie," I went on, deciding not to say anything about the bankbook, or searching his apartment. "He had a letter from his grandfather, and a picture taken in Vietnam of three GIs. On the back of the photo were written the names Marty, Mattie, and Moonie. The letter didn't give any names…it just said one of them died over there, and the other lived in New Orleans and was called Moonie. It also said that Moonie had 'what they were looking for.'" I frowned. "If this guy wasn't Levi Gretsch, how did he get the letter?"

"Maybe he was the one who killed Marty Gretsch," Colin said, his face grim. "Maybe all Marty would tell him was that Moonie had it, and he lived in New Orleans." He started pacing. "Yes, that makes sense. So, after Marty died, he came here and pretended to be Marty's grandson, as a cover. It would work—no one here would doubt his story. They'd have no reason to." He shrugged. "People here tend to take strangers at their word."

"Yes, they do," I heard myself saying. Mom gave me a dirty look, and I was sorry I'd said it.

Colin had the decency to blush. "So, he comes here pretending to be Levi and starts looking around for Moonie. He doesn't have any luck, so he decides to hire you to find Moonie for him."

"If that's true, then he didn't kill Doc." I thought about it for a moment. "Because I didn't know Moonie was Doc until after he was already dead—and I still haven't told Levi." I explained how I'd found the picture of Doc in his military uniform on the floor and recognized him from the picture Levi had. "Venus and I went back to my house to talk to him about it, but he wasn't there. But the gate was open—"

"The gate was open?" Mom interrupted me. "That's very weird."

"I know, Mom, it worried me." Mom was well aware of Millie and Velma's fixation on security. "Levi's apartment door was open, but he wasn't there. Venus seemed to think he may have just gone out or something and forgot to lock his door, or thought he had and it hadn't caught, or something like that. I didn't have a really good feeling about it."

"I don't like the sound of this at all." Colin's voice was grim. "What else did he tell you?"

"He told me his mother went to school with Millie—"

"That can't be true," Mom interrupted. She'd gone to McGehee with Velma; they'd been classmates. Millie had also gone to McGehee, but was a few years ahead of them. "If the child of someone we went to school with had moved into Millie's building, she would have told me. He's been here for about a month, and I have met him a few times over there. Millie never said a word about him being the son of one of our classmates. Why would he tell you that? It's a stupid lie, because surely you could verify that with Millie or Velma."

"Maybe Millie just forgot to tell you, Mom," I replied, but had trouble believing it myself. It wasn't like Millie. She'd been active in the McGehee alumni association. She was proud of having gone there—as opposed to my mother, who considered it a disgraceful symbol of her overprivileged upbringing. If the grandchild of someone she'd gone to school with had moved in upstairs from her, Millie would have told everyone about it.

And even more to the point, it *had* to be a lie. If Levi's grandmother had been from New Orleans, as he'd claimed, then he had *family* here. It was possible he might not know his New Orleans relatives—but Millie would have. She would have access to records through her involvement with the alumni association. "Maybe he didn't want anyone to know about it?" I went on, but the words sounded hollow to me. "Maybe he asked Millie not to say anything?"

"Even if he had, it wouldn't matter to her," Mom pointed out. She was right. Millie wasn't good at keeping secrets, and the grandson of a long-lost classmate was just too good a story for her not to share with friends. If she hadn't said anything to Mom—then there was nothing to tell.

"Marty Gretsch's wife was from Ohio," Colin said, after punching some buttons on his cell phone. "She wasn't from New Orleans. She died about ten years ago."

"Why would he risk telling such a lie? It was a huge risk to take. It doesn't make sense." I scratched my head. "It would have completely blown his cover..." But come to think of it, I hadn't seen either Millie or Velma all day. "Mom, do you know where Millie and Velma are?"

Mom shook her head. "I asked them to ride in the parade, but last night at dinner they told me they were just going to stay in today. Velma had a rough week..." She narrowed her eyes. "Why do you ask?"

"I haven't seen either one of them all day." My heart started racing. I stood up. "Venus and I knocked on their door—there was no answer. I think we need to get back over there as fast as we possibly can." The gate had been open. No answer when I'd knocked on their door. A stupid lie told by someone who wasn't who he said he was. I swallowed. "He told me that lie *because he knew I wouldn't find out about it.*"

Which meant Millie and Velma... I stopped that thought in its tracks, before it could take hold. It was possible they were fine. It was possible they had been asleep and not heard us knocking on the door. Not seeing them all day didn't mean anything. Sometimes I could go for days not seeing them, or hearing any noise from their apartment. There was absolutely no need to panic or worry.

Easier said than done—I could feel the worry creeping up my spine.

Don't panic. Millie and Velma are more than capable of taking care of themselves. They are two tough ladies. Remember, Millie clobbered Frank that time with a frying pan when he was holding a gun on you.

But it wasn't very reassuring.

"Let me call first." Mom picked up her phone and dialed quickly.

After a few moments, she turned the phone off. "It went to voicemail." She bit her lower lip and crinkled her forehead.

That wasn't good, and we both knew it. Velma *always* answered her phone. She was a lawyer, and no matter what time of day or night it was, she woke up and answered the phone by the third ring. She always claimed the first ring woke her, the second ring cleared her mind, and she was wide-awake and alert by the third. If she didn't answer, she either wasn't there or wasn't able to get to the phone.

At this hour, she should have answered.

"Maybe we should call the police—" Mom started, and cut herself off when she looked at Colin.

I made a decision. "The police won't go over there just because they aren't answering their phone. Calling them would be a complete waste of time." I closed my eyes. "Colin and I can go over there," I said, hating the very idea of it. I still didn't completely trust him. I wasn't sure I believed his explanations about the Mardi Gras case—it all seemed a little too pat to me. *I can't tell you about it* was an incredibly convenient line. But I didn't want to go over there alone—who knew if the Pleshiwarian with the knife was out there waiting for me—and one good thing about Colin was he was really good in those situations. The guy was great with weapons, had been trained in hand-to-hand combat by the Mossad, and was fast. I was just going to have to trust him—for now. "For all we know they may have gone out of town for the night." Even as I said it, I knew it wasn't true. Any time they left town, they asked me to feed their cat. That cat was their baby; they wouldn't leave him overnight without making sure I was going to feed him.

Mom grabbed her purse, but Colin stopped her. "You aren't coming with us, Mom. You need to stay here and wait for Dad to get back from the morgue."

"I am not about to let you—"

"He's right, Mom." I hated that he still called them Mom and Dad. I could feel my face starting to flush. *I can worry about that later,* I decided. "We'll call you when we get there." She started to protest again, and I cut her off. "We need you to be *here,* in case something over there goes wrong." I glanced at my watch. Ten minutes or so to walk back to my place, another five or so to unlock the gate and get upstairs. "If you haven't heard from us in twenty-five minutes, call Venus. Tell her everything." I hoped Venus would listen to her...but at least she already knew some of what was going on. Besides, I grinned to myself, I knew my mother. She wouldn't get off the phone until a squad car was on its way—she'd threaten to sue everyone from the mayor on down until Venus moved on it. I stood up, and started to head for the back door.

"Wait a minute," Mom said. She walked over to a cabinet. She opened a drawer and pulled out a Glock. She checked to see if it was loaded, and tried to hand it to me. "You'd better take this—just to be on the safe side."

I shook my head. "Thanks, Mom, but I'd better not. I don't have anywhere to carry it."

"I have a gun." Colin slipped a shoulder holster over his left arm and pulled a black wool blazer on over it. He kissed her on the cheek. "Remember—no call in twenty-five minutes, and you call the cops."

She nodded. "Please be careful, boys."

We went out the back door and I made sure it was locked behind us. I let Colin lead the way down the back stairs, since he was armed. He opened the door to the street, and checked both ways. "Looks clear," he said, standing aside to let me go past out to the sidewalk. He shut the gate and made sure the latch clicked. He gave me a crooked grin. "Since when has Mom kept guns in the house?"

"Papa Diderot gave her that Glock after the levees failed," I said as I started walking up Dumaine toward Decatur. "When she and Dad came back to the Quarter, we were still worried about looters. She still objects to guns on principle, of course, but she's not crazy."

He didn't say anything until we reached the corner at Chartres. He motioned for me to stay back as he checked both directions, but it was deserted. "I'm sorry I wasn't here for that," he said softly. "I almost went crazy with worry about you and the family. The news footage—it was so awful."

"It wasn't exactly pleasant to live through," I said tartly.

"I wanted to jump on a plane—"

I cut him off. "I appreciate the sentiment, Colin." We rounded the corner at Decatur. There were some people milling about on the sidewalks in the bright lights of the bars. I breathed a sigh of relief. There were too many people around for someone to try anything. I started walking faster. "And we can talk about all that some other time, okay?" I hated making the concession. I didn't want to talk to him about anything. I knew it was a childish mentality, but seeing him again had opened a wound I'd thought closed long ago. It still hurt. And that made me angry with myself.

The truth was I would never have closure until we talked. There were things I needed to say to him.

"You've changed," he said as we walked past a group of gutter punks squatting in front of a secondhand store with their dog.

I bit back a sharp retort. *Finding out someone you love is a paid assassin will do that to you.* I forced down the hurt and anger and swallowed. "I know," I said quietly. "I've changed a lot since the last time you saw me, and I don't like it. I miss the person I used to be. I want to be that person again. But I don't know if that Scotty can ever come back. Too much has happened." And I added, "Frank's changed, too, you know. I'm not the only one you've hurt. I can't believe you haven't even asked about him."

"Mom told me he was out of town," he said quietly.

"Lucky for him," I said.

He had the decency to not reply.

We reached my building, and I pulled out my keys. I unlocked the gate, and he stopped me from going in. I nodded as he pulled out his gun and headed through the darkness. I watched him check the courtyard, and he motioned me to come forward. When I reached him, he whispered, "I'll go up first, you follow, okay?" I nodded, and he started up the stairs without making a noise.

It was creepy how he could do that.

I followed him. We stopped in front of Millie and Velma's door. I took a deep breath and began pounding on it. There was no response, no sound of movement inside the apartment. I could hear my heart pounding in my ears. "Go up and see if Levi's in his apartment," I hissed at Colin as I fumbled through my key ring for the key to their apartment.

Colin nodded. "Wait for me before you go in."

"Okay," I replied. He started up the stairs, again not making any sound. I smiled to myself. I wasn't about to wait for him.

He reached the midpoint landing. Once he was out of sight, I turned the key in the deadbolt and swung the door open. I reached for the light switch just inside the door. The hallway lit up, and their big gray tabby, Scout, began weaving around my legs, howling. He did that when he was hungry—which meant he hadn't had his evening meal. "Just a minute, Scout," I said. I left the door slightly ajar so Colin could follow me in. "Millie? Velma?" I called. "Anyone home?"

I heard a muffled sound coming from the living room at the end of the hall. It sounded—it sounded human. For a moment I thought about waiting for Colin and his gun, but the sound came again. Hoping I wasn't walking into some kind of trap, trying to convince myself that I was being ridiculous, and sorry I hadn't taken Mom's Glock, I crept down the hallway and reached around the corner to flip on the lights.

"Damn it!" I burst out once the room flooded with light.

Millie and Velma were gagged and tied to dining room chairs. They were facing me, and both of their heads bowed with relief when they realized it was me. Their wrists and ankles were duct-taped to the chairs. Velma started making urgent noises. I hurried over to her and said "sorry" as I grabbed one end of the duct tape and ripped it off her mouth. She howled.

I turned to Millie, who closed her eyes as I ripped the tape from her lips.

"I didn't think you were ever going to come," Millie whispered hoarsely.

"I'll get a knife," I said, dashing into the kitchen. I grabbed a steak knife from the knife stand on the counter and ran back into the living room.

"Get me free," Velma demanded. "I have got to go to the bathroom."

I sawed through the tape on her wrists. Once they were free, I went to work on her ankles. It seemed to take forever, but finally she was loose. She stood up as I moved over to Millie and started sawing at her tape. "My damned legs are asleep," Velma cursed as she somehow managed to flop her way over to the wall and, holding on to it, groped her way to the bathroom.

"What happened here?" I asked as I finished freeing Millie's arms.

"That damned new tenant!" Millie said, her lips compressed in a tight line. She shook her head. "Before you get my legs free, would you be a dear and get me a glass of water?" I nodded. Her voice followed me out of the room. "It was around three, wasn't it, Velma? We were reading the *New York Times,* and I heard you moving around upstairs.

I wanted to ask you about something—I can't think now what it was—and your door was open, so I walked in, and that young bastard was going through your desk!" She was trembling with barely contained anger. "I demanded to know what he was doing in your apartment, and I picked up the phone to call the police, and that's when the bastard pulled the gun on me." I handed her the glass and she downed it in one gulp. I knelt down and started working on her ankles. "He marched me down here and tied us up."

"If I ever get my hands on that young prick—" Velma growled from the kitchen. I heard the faucet turn on. She walked back into the living room carrying two glasses of water. She handed one to Millie and started sipping from the other one. "I'll make that little punk sorry he was ever born." I suppressed a grin. Velma was a woman of her word. For Levi's sake, I certainly hoped he was on his way out of town with a one-way ticket.

"He made me tie up Velma, and then he did it to me," Millie went on, taking another sip of water. She stood up, stretched her arms, and wiggled her legs to get the circulation going again. "I thought for sure the little prick was going to rob us, but he didn't. He didn't do or say anything." She shuddered. "All he did was whistle while he was doing it, like it was something he did every day, you know, like it was no big deal…and then he just left."

"We were lucky." Velma sat down on the couch. "He could have raped and killed us." Her voice was grim. "But you're wrong, Millie. He did take something—you just didn't see it." She pointed to a row of hooks on the wall by the kitchen door. "He took a set of keys." She shook her head. "We're going to have to have all the goddamned locks changed."

So he wanted a set of keys to every door in the building, I mused. I was only half listening to Velma as she went on a tirade about what she was going to do to Levi if she ever got her hands on him. *Why? He didn't want access to this place, he has his own keys for his own apartment and the gate—the only keys left are the carriage house, the coffee shop, Millie and Velma's, and—*

My apartment.

But why would he want a key to my apartment? He'd already been inside.

He wanted to be able to get in and out as he pleased.

I thought back as Velma continued her rant. She was really letting her imagination run wild, and it was a little disconcerting to know how dark the vengeful corner of her mind could be. I hadn't been paying attention when I got home from either the parade or Tea Dance. I wouldn't have noticed if anyone had searched my apartment. But why would he want to search my apartment?

What was he looking for?

It didn't make sense. He'd taken the keys *before* he'd hired me, before I'd known anything about Moonie. If he was after the Eye of Kali—and it stood to reason that he was—he had to have known it wasn't in my apartment.

Hiring me to look for Moonie had to be a ruse of some sort. He wanted to find out how much I knew.

But how could he have thought I'd known anything?

"His grandmother wasn't an old schoolmate of yours, Millie, by any chance?" I finally interrupted the tirade. Unabated, Velma could have gone on for hours. I wanted to be sure Colin's story held up.

"Schoolmate?" Millie looked at me like I'd lost my mind—which I was beginning to believe myself. "Of course not. I advertised the apartment on craigslist. He answered the ad, paid the deposit and the first three months' rent in cash. Where would you get the idea I went to school with his mother?"

"That's what he told me," I replied. "This afternoon, when he hired me to find someone for him."

Velma's eyes looked past me and narrowed with anger. "What the hell is *he* doing here?" she hissed.

I looked back over my shoulder as Colin walked into the room. "No sign of him up there just like you said, Scotty. His clothes and everything are still there. But I think it's safe to assume he's gone." He looked around the room. He gestured to Millie and Velma. "He tied them up, I gather?" He shook his head.

Millie smiled a horrible smile. She walked over to him, reared back, and slapped him as hard as she could. It was loud, and it had to hurt.

"That, you miserable son of a bitch, is for breaking Frank and Scotty's hearts," she said grimly.

I tried unsuccessfully not to smile. Millie and Velma didn't know the real story of Colin's departure; we'd kept that within the immediate family. It was a bit much, frankly, to get into with everyone. The story we'd given Millie and Velma was he'd reconnected with an ex over Mardi Gras and decided to go back to him. They'd been furious.

Colin gave her a rueful smile as he touched the red handprint on the side of his face. "Okay, Millie, I deserved that."

"You deserve more," she replied coldly. "Now, what the hell is going on around here? Obviously, Levi is some sort of criminal. Didn't you run a background on him, Velma?"

"Of course I did. Nothing came up." Velma shook her head. "He had good credit, references, and no arrests. I knew we shouldn't have rented to a stranger." She slammed her hand down on her leg. "Damn it to hell! I didn't call his references. What the hell was I thinking?"

"No sense beating yourself up about it now, dear." Millie got up and headed for the bathroom. "It's a little late for that now. And wait until I get back—I don't want to miss anything." The door shut behind her.

Velma walked into the kitchen and opened a beer, offering me one and pointedly ignoring Colin. He bore the snubbing with good grace as I took my beer from her and took a drink. "Seriously, Scotty, why is he here?" she whispered to me. "Is he back for good?"

I shook my head. "Doubt it. He's here on a case, and it involves Levi somehow."

The toilet flushed, and Millie grabbed herself a beer from the kitchen before rejoining us in the living room. She plopped down on the couch. "Now, what the hell is all this about?"

"Doc was killed tonight," I said gently. Both of their mouths dropped open. "And it seems his name wasn't really Benjamin Garrett."

"It was Larry Moon," Colin interjected. "Apparently, he served a tour in Vietnam back in the sixties, and after he came back to the States he changed his name and moved to New Orleans."

"Levi hired me to look for Larry Moon," I went on. "I didn't know he and Doc were the same person at the time. Apparently, Doc and his friends stole"—Colin was gesturing at me frantically from behind them, but I ignored him—"a sacred jewel from a temple in some country called Pleshiwar. All of the guys are now dead, all of them killed. Doc's been hiding here in New Orleans for almost forty years. And somehow, Levi is involved in this. I think it's possible Levi may have been the one who killed Doc." But even as I said the words, it didn't seem right. It didn't add up. Whoever had killed Marty Gretsch had tortured him. Doc had been thrown from his balcony. Their homes had been trashed from one end to the other. If he'd killed them, Millie and Velma were lucky to be alive.

Once Millie had caught him in my apartment, his cover was blown. He knew he hadn't had much time to do whatever it was he needed to do.

He knew he couldn't stick around much longer…so he came down to talk to me, give me this story in order to hire me.

But what did he think I knew? What was he looking for in my apartment?

"But why tie us up?" Velma asked. "We didn't have anything to do with any of this."

"And why hire you, if he knew Doc was this Larry Moon already?" Millie chimed in.

"I don't know," I replied, thinking. Everything had happened so fast, I really hadn't had much time to think…

And Colin had been directing my line of thought ever since I got to Mom's.

I glanced over at him. *What game is he playing?* I wondered. Aloud, I said, "Well, when you caught him in my apartment, Millie, his cover was blown."

"I guess we won't know the answers until we find him," Colin replied.

"I'm sure he's long gone," I replied, watching Colin's face. I wasn't ready to trust him yet, no matter what Mom thought. I was certain Colin was deliberately clouding the issue. *He* was the one who said Levi wasn't related to Marty Gretsch; I only had his word for that. And sure, Levi had lied about his grandmother's relationship with Millie, and he'd had to get them out of the way once Millie caught him in my apartment. He'd tied them up to buy himself some time—but time to do what? What was he looking for?

And it was very possible Levi and Colin could be working together.

I only had Colin's word for it that Levi wasn't really Levi, after all.

No, that didn't make any sense. He wasn't the real Levi. He'd invented the connection between Millie and his grandmother to earn my trust—and with Millie out of the way for a while, the way was clear for him.

But why?

My head was seriously starting to ache. None of this made any sense.

And I still didn't know who shot Colin in the arm, and why.

"Do you two want to go to the hospital?" I asked. "or should we just call the police?"

Millie and Velma exchanged glances. Velma said, "No need for the hospital, or for the police."

I just stared at them. "Okay, why not?"

Velma yawned. "I have to be in court at nine in the morning. If we call the police, I won't get any sleep. And what will we tell them?" She shook her head. "No, we can deal with it in the morning. I'm exhausted." She frowned. "I'm a little worried about the key situation."

"I'll stand guard," Colin volunteered.

She gave him a sour look. "I feel better already."

He flushed, but didn't say anything. I kissed them both on the cheek, told them to call me if they needed anything, and hustled Colin out the door. I waited until I heard their deadbolt slide into place before heading upstairs to my apartment.

"Ah, what memories I have of this place," Colin said, plopping down on my sofa.

"Don't get comfortable," I said, checking the answering machine. Nothing. Angela hadn't called back. "You're supposed to be standing guard, remember?"

"I've missed you." He patted the sofa next to him. "You have no idea."

I crossed my arms and leaned against the wall. I shook my head. "Uh-uh. Not going to work. Tell me about your arm."

He stood up and stretched. "I was tailing someone when I got shot. I didn't see who it was, and I didn't want to go to the hospital—they would have had to report it to the police." He shrugged. "So, I called Mom. If she didn't want to help me, I'd have to do something else, but it was worth a shot. Besides, I wanted to see her."

"Stop calling her that!" I snapped. *And just how long HAVE you been in town?* I wanted to ask. *And if you hadn't been shot, would you have contacted us?*

"Are you going to help me now?" He checked his gun, slipped on the safety, and slid it back into the holster.

"I told you I'd decide in the morning. Now go." I yawned. "I want to get some sleep."

"I really have missed you and Frank," he said softly, just before the door shut.

Chapter Seven
THE MAGICIAN REVERSED
The use of power for destructive ends

I was completely exhausted.

After locking the door behind Colin—and propping a kitchen chair under the knob as a secondary precaution—I went into my bathroom and started the shower. I stripped off my clothes, and removed the gauze from my neck. I got close to the mirror and tilted my head back. The cut had scabbed over, and Mom was right—it wasn't much. Apparently, only the tip of the mugger's knife had cut the skin.

But damn, I'd bled like a stuck pig.

I cleaned it again with antiseptic, and climbed into the hot shower. It felt good on my skin. I relaxed and let the water drum the tension out of my muscles. The last twelve hours had been an insane roller-coaster ride—and it didn't seem like the car would be pulling into the station any time soon.

Of all times for Frank to be away...

I dismissed that thought as I turned the shower off. I felt much better, and I was a big boy. Sure, it would be great to have Frank around—he *was* a trained FBI agent—but he wasn't. I was on my own to deal with this entire mess, and I needed to step up and take charge of the situation.

Forget the emotional fall-out from Colin's reappearance, and focus on the case, I told myself as I toweled dry. *Emotion just clouds your mind and keeps you from thinking clearly. You've got a good brain. Use it. Get some good sleep, and tackle it with a clear mind in the morning.*

I climbed into bed and turned off the lamp on my nightstand. I closed my eyes and felt all my muscles relax.

But my mind wouldn't shut off. I kept tossing and turning, and the best I could achieve was that wretched state of half-sleep where your body is relaxed but your mind is still aware. Every little noise made me jolt awake. The wind was still whipping around the house. It started raining again, a steady downpour that usually helped me sleep.

No such luck this night, though.

I debated taking something to help, but finally came down on the side of *it's not smart to knock yourself out with a pill.* The last thing I needed was to be asleep should Levi come back—or anyone else for that matter.

Finally, at about five in the morning I gave up on sleep and got out of the bed. I put on a pair of sweatpants and made a pot of coffee. Bleary-eyed, I put some bread into my toaster. While I was waiting for everything to be ready, I turned on my computer and got out a new notebook. I like to keep all of my notes from a case in one notebook, and I always start a new one with every case. I flipped the cover and stared at the blank page while my computer started up.

Where to start? After a moment, I wrote down *Why did they steal the Eye of Kali?*

Frank always said understanding the motivation behind a crime was a great place to start. Once you understood that, other pieces of the puzzle would start coming together. The motivation had been nagging at me since Colin first mentioned the theft last night. They were three grunts from Biloxi, Mississippi. Pleshiwar was a small postage stamp of a country—backward and hard to get to. How had they known about the Eye of Kali in the first place, let alone decided to steal it?

Think, Scotty, think.

Okay, the most obvious reason for stealing it was its value. From everything I could recall about the Vietnam War, Saigon had been a hotbed of intrigue and corruption during the war. The American-supported government had been little more than a dictatorship. The black market had thrived. In such an environment, it wasn't hard to imagine black marketers from all over the world flocking there and looting treasures from all over southeast Asia. The majority of southeast Asians had been very poor. It would be easy to bribe people to look the other way while treasures were smuggled out of the country. American soldiers were risking their lives every day for the measly government paycheck—and were held in contempt by the growing anti-war movement back home. Under those circumstances, it wasn't hard to see why even the most idealistic American GI would look for ways to line his pockets. Most of the soldiers were from poor or rural backgrounds. It was the children of the middle and upper classes with their college deferments who were protesting back home, calling them baby killers and spitting on them when they came home. They were just doing their patriotic duty as American citizens, and they were reviled for risking life and limb every day. Even Mom, who thought the Vietnam War was an abomination, thought the way those who served were treated was a national disgrace, one of the "worst examples of classism in the history of the country."

"They served their country and were treated like garbage," she'd said once. "So many of them are now mentally disabled, homeless, and hungry. Our government and people all should be ashamed of ourselves."

Disillusionment was a powerful motivator.

But that didn't answer the question of how three soldiers from Biloxi planned on disposing of the jewel once they had it. I chewed on the end of my pen. That was the key. I doubted they would have committed the crime without knowing how to turn the jewel into cash. Colin had said Marty Gretsch had paid cash for his farm when he got back from the war, and Doc had bought a number of properties in the Quarter. They'd come back from the war a lot richer than they'd been when they'd gone over there—but they still had the jewel. Had they double-crossed the buyer, taken the money and not delivered?

That was also a powerful motive for killing them.

But why did it take forty years to track them down? Any private eye worth his salt would have been able to find Marty and Doc. Even with the name changes, there had to be a paper trail—the Veterans Administration and social security records, just for two. Doc had gone back to school and finished his PhD at LSU. He'd had to transfer his credits from Ole Miss in order to do that. Marty had married and had a family.

I leaned back in my chair and tapped my pen against the notebook. If killers were looking for you, why would you have a family to put at risk? Who would do that?

Doc had never seemed like someone hiding something, or in fear of his life. On the contrary, he was a pretty public person in his field. He had written highly acclaimed books, articles, and academic criticism, and had traveled all over the country speaking at conferences. He had been profiled several times in the local press. Someone trying to keep a low profile wouldn't have done any of that. Every appearance, every time his picture was in the paper he was risking being discovered.

Obviously, Doc wasn't too afraid of being found out—which meant he was certain no one was looking for him.

There was something there, but it kept dancing away from my consciousness into the darker, inaccessible parts of my brain.

Something must have happened recently—something that made the jewel more desirable and brought all of this bubbling back to the surface.

What could that be? What had set all of this back in motion again after being dormant for forty years?

There was more going on than just looking for the jewel.

But I also couldn't rule out the jewel's value. Any number of wealthy collectors had no scruples about buying something stolen and hiding it away from the world. Someone had undoubtedly hired these guys to steal it—had either paid them some money up front or paid them in full but never received the stone. That was the only possible explanation for the money Doc and Marty came back from Vietnam with—but at the same time, why had that person never tried to hunt them down?

It was also possible they actually had delivered the jewel to the buyer.

Assuming Colin was telling the truth, the man I knew as Levi Gretsch was not who he'd said he was. He was the piece that didn't fit into my scenario. I wrote down *Who is Levi Gretsch?*

Okay, that was easy enough to find out. I switched on the computer and pulled up a browser. There were any number of Web sites accessible to private eyes I could use to find out. I went to my bookmarks, and clicked on the first one there. I logged in, and once the welcome screen popped up, I typed *Levi Gretsch + Ohio* into the search engine.

I got up and refilled my coffee cup and put some more bread in the toaster. As I waited for it to pop up, I remembered that Levi had tied up

Millie and Velma because he'd been caught in my apartment—and had stolen their spare set of keys.

I'd been so fried last night I'd forgotten about that. I'd meant to look around and see if anything was missing.

I made a quick round of the apartment. If Levi had searched my apartment, he was good. I couldn't tell if anything had been moved, and nothing seemed to be missing from anywhere, either.

I went back to the computer. The site had found five Levi Gretsches. Colin hadn't been lying. Not one of them was the right age for the guy who'd hired me. And there was one who was twelve years old, currently living in Carthage, Ohio.

Okay, so he was telling the truth about that—but that doesn't mean I can trust him.

I heard the toaster pop up.

I walked back into the kitchen and munched my toast. I thought about the timeline. I'd left for the parade around two thirty. Levi had tied up Millie and Velma shortly after three. He'd come in here and searched my apartment, looking for something. But what could he have been looking for? Apparently, he hadn't found it. That was why he'd come down to hire me. I tried to remember our conversation, word for word. He hadn't seemed to be pumping me for information, though.

I was refilling my cup again when it hit me. *He was looking for information. He came down here and told me that whole story to see how I'd react to it. It was obvious I knew nothing about what he was talking about.*

And once he knew that, he cleared out.

But why did he leave the gate open?

Duh. He didn't need to leave the gate open. He had a key.

I felt nauseous. *Someone without a key left the gate open so they could get back in again.*

And that didn't bode well for Levi.

But I was also assuming Colin was telling me the truth.

I sat back down at my computer. I wrote down, *What if Colin is lying about the Eye of Kali?*

Outside of the mugger, Colin was my only source that this was about a Pleshiwarian holy jewel. Correct that—the man who'd mugged me had simply asked me about an eye, and I was also assuming he was a subcontinental Asian. For all I knew, he could have just been some lunatic high on crack.

For that matter, how did I know he wasn't working with Colin and this whole thing was some kind of crazy set-up?

Try not to let your emotions get involved. Look at this rationally and logically.

Okay, point one: Colin was more than capable of staging some incredibly elaborate story to cover up whatever he was really up to. Point Two: he didn't want to say who had supposedly hired him, and hadn't exactly been forthcoming with information. Point Three: his first loyalty was *always* going to be to whoever was paying him. If it was in his best interests to screw me over to achieve whatever his final goal was, he certainly would do so without batting an eye. Point Three: it wasn't beyond the realm of possibility Levi was working for Colin.

I took a deep breath. Along those same lines, I also had to consider the possibility that it was *Colin* who'd killed Doc. Even if I could put aside our jaded history, he *was* a killer. He'd confessed that to me. He'd been a trained Mossad agent, going out and killing enemies of Israel, infiltrating terrorist cells and killing their leaders. He claimed he'd left all that behind him when he'd gone to work for Angela Blackledge… and come to think of it, she hadn't called me back.

And his reassurances to the contrary, I still wasn't convinced he hadn't killed my uncles. He'd convinced Mom, but she loved him and would pretty much believe anything he told her, regardless of how preposterous it might be. So, if that were indeed the case, he would probably kill again if it were necessary for whatever his endgame might be.

Okay, Scotty, just go by facts, not what you've been told. For all you know, Marty Gretsch could be alive and well and living in Ohio, blissfully unaware someone is in New Orleans claiming to be his grandson. Scratch that: he might not know what someone who may or may not be his grandson is up to in New Orleans.

Easy enough to check—I typed *Martin Gretsch* into the search engine. This time, there were only two results—one in Idaho, another in Ohio. The one in Idaho was the wrong age. I clicked on the Ohio one, and his information came up.

He had died a month ago.

Okay, so that checks out. Score one for Colin's honesty.

To be on the safe side, I went to a generic search engine, and typed his name and added the word *murder*. Only one link, from the Carthage, Ohio, *Courant* seemed to be the right one. I clicked and scanned the article quickly.

Martin Gretsch had been brutally tortured and murdered, his home torn to shreds. Survivors were listed as a son, Matthew, and a grandson, Levi.

Okay, that too was true. But why hadn't Colin mentioned the son?

Whoever had killed Doc had been looking for something. Doc was definitely the guy in the picture called Moonie—but that didn't mean his real name had been Larry Moon. Moonie could have just been a nickname his friends called him. I didn't have any proof other than Colin's word. And if I was going to not count his word as fact, maybe Doc was who he'd always said he was.

I reached for the file folder marked *Levi Gretsch* and knew as soon I put my hands on it that it was empty.

The picture was also gone.

Wait a minute. They were here when Venus and I came looking for him. So if he stole them, it was AFTER that. So he was in the building, waiting for me to leave again, so he could use the keys and get back in here.

Or he'd come in while I was sleeping—no, Colin was standing guard out in the courtyard. He would have seen him. Therefore, after I'd gotten the call from Mom, Levi had come in here and helped himself.

Nice try, Levi, I grinned to myself. I'd scanned them and e-mailed them to Venus. But as I looked over the icons on my desktop, my smile turned into a scowl.

The files weren't on my desktop.

Someone had deleted them.

I opened my e-mail program and clicked on "sent mail." I laughed out loud in triumph. The e-mail to Venus was there, and I opened it and downloaded the attachments.

Gotcha, Levi. I thought to myself as I opened them. I read the letter again and frowned. It wasn't the kind of letter someone would write to a twelve-year-old. *Go to New Orleans and find Moonie.*

No one would tell a twelve-year-old that!

Maybe it was a forgery Levi had doctored up to show me. Maybe that was why he'd needed to get it back.

I was pretty sure now Levi, or whoever he was, was long gone.

My head was starting to hurt. None of it made sense. I only had Colin's word for any of it. There were no facts.

I turned the page in my notebook and wrote *FACTS* across the top of a new page and underlined it. Underneath I wrote:

> *Doc was murdered and his apartment searched.*
>
> *I was hired by someone to find Doc. That person left a letter and a photo with me.*
>
> *The person who hired me tied up Millie and Velma and stole a set of their spare keys.*
>
> *That person stole the letter and photo back, and deleted the scans I did of them off my computer.*
>
> *Someone stabbed me in the neck, wanting to know where "the eye" was.*
>
> *Someone shot Colin in the arm.*
>
> *Someone claiming to be Angela Blackledge left a message for me on my machine. I called back and left a message.*

I scowled at the list. I crossed out "that person" on Number 4, and wrote "someone." I didn't *know* that Levi had done that. For all I knew, it could have been Colin.

It wasn't very helpful.

I leaned back in my chair and pondered for a moment. *Okay, let's approach this from the premise that Colin is telling the truth.*

Some dangerous people were looking for a holy relic that Doc and his buddies stole during the Vietnam War. They'd killed Marty Gretsch and Doc, looking for it. They hadn't found it. One of them had attacked me on the street, held a knife to my neck—

It hit me like a lightning bolt in the forehead.

Why did he come after me?

Sure, by then Levi had already "hired" me, but no one could possibly know about that if Levi hadn't told them. And Levi, if he was after the Eye, had to know that I knew nothing about it. I hadn't responded to his story in any way other than curiosity. I hadn't recognized any of the men in the picture when he showed it to me. So, it couldn't have been Levi who sent the mugger after me.

So if Levi wasn't who he said he was, he wasn't working with the Pleshiwarians or whoever they were.

It came to me in a bolt from the blue. *Someone knew Larry Moon and Doc were the same person. They were watching his apartment, had it staked out. And they saw me not only go in there, but come out with something.*

Mr. Bunny.

If whatever it was they were looking for wasn't in his apartment, they would think he'd gotten rid of it. And it was entirely possible the only thing carried out of his apartment yesterday was Mr. Bunny.

He'd gotten that phone call that had upset him so much, and when he'd come back from taking it he had Mr. Bunny with him.

I felt really cold.

I gave the damned thing to Mom.

And coincidentally, Colin had shown up and wound up inside Mom's apartment, telling some cock-and-bull story about being shot. He wasn't above shooting himself if it helped him achieve his objective.

Surely, though, he wouldn't hurt Mom or put her in danger.

Or would he? He'd pretended to love all of us once before. He'd pretended we'd mattered, when all along he was just using all of us. He'd been able to just walk away without saying good-bye, without any word.

I glanced at the clock. Wow, it was already past eight! Mom and Dad were night owls, and usually stayed up until dawn, sleeping in until about one every day. I picked up my cell phone and dialed their number.

It went straight to voicemail.

They always turned the phones off when they went to bed, so that didn't mean anything. Their sleep time wasn't to be interrupted. How many times had Mom lectured me about the importance of unbroken sleep?

Maybe I should just go over there, get the stupid rabbit, and give it to Venus.

There was a lot going on here I wasn't aware of, and that didn't help my mindset at all.

I wished Frank were here.

"But he isn't here," I said aloud, shaking off the gloomy mood. "And if he were here, he wouldn't put up with this negativity." I walked into the kitchen and got another cup of coffee. I sipped it as I sat back down again and stared at the pad of paper. I wrote down, *Who knew they stole the Eye of Kali?*

I tried to put myself into their mindsets. Three young men from Mississippi, from relatively poor backgrounds who volunteered for service to their country—

I wrote down, *Check into their backgrounds. They may still have relatives who could answer some of these questions.*

One of them, according to Colin, had been killed—butchered—in a back alley of Saigon. Matt Hooper, that was his name. I sat down at the computer. I typed in *Matt Hooper murder Saigon* into the search engine and waited.

A link popped up; it was not to a Biloxi newspaper, but rather the *Fresno Bee*. I clicked on it, and swore when a pop-up window informed me that "archived articles cost $3.95." I grabbed my wallet and filled out a lot of ridiculous personal information, including the credit card number, and hit Enter.

The article, which was a scan of the original newspaper page, downloaded as a PDF file, and once it was finished, the file opened.

I started reading. Matt Hooper wasn't from Biloxi, he'd been from a little town outside Fresno called Hanford. He'd been killed in a random crime in a back alley, stabbed to death, and his killer had cut his eyes out.

Well, Colin hadn't been lying about that.

I stood up and stretched, my back cracking. I went into the kitchen and got another cup of coffee. I sipped it. Something was nagging at me, but I couldn't put my finger on it. I walked back into the living room and sat down on the couch.

I glanced at my coffee table.

Surely, it wouldn't hurt to do a reading.

If the gift was coming back, maybe I'd be able to get some hints as to what the hell was going on. Besides, my mind was all jumbled—doing a reading used to help clear my mind.

I got up and walked to my front door. I eased it open and looked out into the courtyard. In the dim light just before dawn, I could make out Colin sitting at one of the garden tables. The light from my hall caught his eye, and he looked up and waved at me. I waved back and shut the door.

I *wanted* to believe him.

I sat down at the coffee table and pulled my cards out from under the couch. I lit the white candles, and said a prayer as I shuffled the cards. I laid the cards out and started flipping them over.

Certain danger on the pathway ahead.

Lies will be uncovered by the shining light of truth.

The past continues to influence the future.

I sighed. That wasn't particularly helpful.

I swept the cards back into a pile and put them back in the box.

My phone started ringing. "Hello?"

"Scotty, this is Angela Blackledge." I recognized the voice as the same from the message she'd left earlier. "I'm sorry it took me so long to return your call. It's imperative that we talk."

"Thank you for returning my call, Angela Blackledge," I replied. "No offense, but I was really hoping I'd never hear your name again. Too many bad memories."

She let out a low laugh. "Yes, I'm sure there are. I am truly sorry for everything that happened three years ago, Scotty. It was never my intent to cause you pain." She cleared her throat. "I understand you've already made contact with Abram?"

"If you mean Colin, yes," I replied. I'd known Colin wasn't his real name for years, but I would always think of him that way. "He told me a bunch of stuff I suppose I am supposed to take on face value? Because of course he's never lied to me before. For that matter, I could say the same about you." As I talked I was typing Doc's name into a search engine. I hit Enter, and a list of links popped up. They were mostly links to papers and articles he'd written; some were links to talks at conferences. I started scrolling through them.

"Scotty, this case is very important," Angela went on. "I am prepared to wire fifty thousand dollars into your business account for you and Frank to work with Abram on this. Is that sufficient?"

"That's a lot of money—and Frank's not available. He's out of town," I replied, trying to keep my voice level. This woman was even less trustworthy than Colin. I went on, "Tempting as that is, Angela, I don't need the money. And I am tired of being lied to."

"Scotty, the case is the most important thing right now. I can't stress how important this is. The Eye of Kali has to be found, and it has to be found quickly."

"Why is it so important? Why now, when it was stolen forty years ago? You're not making sense, Angela."

"This is highly sensitive information, Scotty. You cannot share it with the police, or anyone in your family." She took a deep breath. "They've discovered uranium in Pleshiwar. Are you familiar with the political situation there?"

"No."

"The country was a theocracy, ruled by a renegade cult of the Hindu goddess Kali. I am not going to go into all the background—you can research that just as easily as I can tell you, and I don't want to waste any time. Suffice it to say that many governments and groups hostile to the Free World are very interested in a new source of uranium. The ruler of Pleshiwar right now is friendly to the Free World, and to your own government. However, there are those in Pleshiwar who believe the old ways of the theocracy were best—and they want to return to power. They are being funded by many enemies of the West—enemies who are interested in access to that uranium. That uranium is of a particular geological purity, and can easily be enriched. Do you know what that means?"

"Weapons of mass destruction."

"So you can understand how vital it is that that uranium is controlled by friendly hands."

"And what does the Eye of Kali have to do with that?"

"It is their most holy relic, Scotty, and it's been gone for forty years. Whoever finds it and returns it to them is going to be viewed very favorably by their people. A number of people are looking for it...there's also a power struggle going on over there behind the scenes. I understand you were attacked last night by someone of Indian descent?"

"Yes."

"It cannot fall into their hands. The man looking to overthrow their leader is being funded by al-Qaeda. Do I have to explain to you what it would mean to world stability and security if al-Qaeda suddenly had access to an almost endless supply of uranium?"

"No, you don't." I, like every other American, had very vivid memories of 9/11, the day our country came under attack and the Twin

Towers fell. Al-Qaeda was dedicated to the complete destruction of our country. If they had a source of uranium—and wasn't that one of the reasons we invaded Iraq? To supposedly keep uranium out of the hands of terrorists?

"Say the word and I'll send the funds. They'll show up in your account in a matter of moments."

I considered. Fifty thousand dollars was a lot of money, but how could I be sure I was being told the truth? But the best way to find out the truth was from the inside. "Okay, Angela, I will. On one condition."

"Name it."

"If I catch him in another lie, I am going to the police."

"Fair enough." There was a pause, and she said, "Check your bank account."

I pulled up my bank's Web site and signed in. I pulled up the business account. There was a fifty-thousand-dollar deposit sitting there, pending.

"Okay, the money's there."

"I am sure I don't need to tell you to be very careful. These people we are dealing with—they have absolutely no problem with killing. As your friend Dr. Garrett found out." She hung up the phone.

I sat there for a moment, and placed the phone back into its cradle. Working with Colin again.

I was in the kitchen getting another cup of coffee when there was a crash that shook the entire building. "What the hell was that?" I almost dropped the cup, but grabbed it in time—still, coffee splashed all over my counter.

The crash had come from my gallery.

I crept over to the French doors leading out there. There was no roof on my gallery—Levi's apartment didn't have a gallery. I pulled the curtains aside and looked out.

The sun was coming up in the east, and the gloom of the night was burning off. There was a man lying in the middle of the balcony, face down.

He wasn't moving.

I opened the doors and cautiously walked out there. I reached for his wrist. No pulse, and his skin was cold.

I looked at the face, and my blood ran cold.

It was Levi.

Chapter Eight
THE WHEEL OF FORTUNE, REVERSED
Luck has deserted the seeker for the moment

He was dead, no doubt about it.

I backed away from the body and stumbled back into my apartment.

Was his killer still up there on the roof?

I took it all in as quickly as I could. His clothes were soaking wet. He was wearing a pair of jeans and a Saints jersey. His hair was also wet, plastered to his scalp. There'd been no pulse, and his skin had been so cold. I shuddered.

I looked up at the sky and tried to remember. It had rained yesterday evening, and sporadically through the night, but I couldn't pin it down to times. I remembered it raining while I was trying to sleep. I stood up and remembered the noise I'd heard on the roof when I was coming out of his apartment.

Had the killer been up there then?

I swallowed and closed my eyes, holding down the panicky thoughts. *No sense freaking about it now, and besides, you don't know how he was killed, or when. All you know is he's dead, and his body is on your balcony—and it had to have been thrown off the roof. So the killer has to still be up there.*

I wondered if Colin was still down in the courtyard.

Or did he throw the body down to my balcony?

I hurried back into the house while hitting the speed dial on my cell phone for Venus. I went out my back door, and sure enough, Colin was still sitting down there in the courtyard at the table. I waved at him, beckoning him to come up as Venus answered my call. "Casanova."

"Venus, this is Scotty Bradley. I'm not sure how to tell you this, but there's a body on my balcony."

There was silence on the other end of the phone, and then she let out a huge sigh. "I might have known this was going to happen when you turned up at my crime scene. It was just a matter of time, I suppose," she said with an air of long suffering. "We're on our way."

I hung up the phone just as Colin let himself in my front door. I was about to snap at him that henceforth he needed to knock, but I wasn't in the mood to get into an argument with him. "What's up?" he asked, yawning. "I don't think Levi's coming back."

"Oh, he came back all right." I gave him a brittle smile. "His body is out on the balcony right now. Didn't you hear it land? The whole building shook."

I could hear a police siren in the distance, and smiled to myself. There was no getting out of this one for him. It's not like I could call them back and tell them not to come. His face remained expressionless. "You've called the police?"

"Yes. They're on their way." The siren was getting louder. I was expecting him to make his excuses and get away as fast as he could. He'd talked Mom out of calling the police last night, but there was no way out of dealing with them now. In a way, I was sorry I'd told him I'd already called them.

It would have been interesting to hear his rationale for not reporting the body to the police.

He gave me a funny look and hurried over to the balcony doors. He opened the doors. "Don't go out there—it's a crime scene," I called out after him. He turned around, his face an expressionless mask. "Venus wouldn't like it. And you remember what she's like when she's pissed."

I expected some reaction from him. His face didn't change. All he did was nod. "You're right. We shouldn't disturb the scene." He closed the doors again.

"You weren't up on the roof last night by any chance, were you?" I asked. I kept my voice casual even though my heart was racing.

"The roof?" He shook his head. "I didn't leave that chair in the courtyard all night—except for when it rained. I sat on the stairs until it stopped. Why?" Realization dawned in his eyes. "You think I killed him, don't you?"

I shrugged. "It's not like it would be the first time."

He looked at me for a few moments without saying a word. His shoulders sagged a little bit, and his head drooped forward almost imperceptibly. He nodded, biting his lower lip. "I think"—his voice was very muted—"it's probably better if I wait outside." He gave me a wide berth as he walked past me on his way to the front door.

"Angela called me back," I said when he was halfway down the hall. "She told me about the uranium."

He stopped walking, but didn't say anything or turn around.

"I'm not entirely sure I trust you—or her," I went on. "But I'm mixed up in the middle of this, and I might as well get paid for it." I gritted my teeth. "If what she told me is true—well, I guess it's my duty to help you. But I still don't understand why you—or Angela—think you might need my help."

"You knew Benjamin Garrett. You knew him well. He was practically a member of your family." He turned around and folded his arms. "You—and your parents—interacted with him a lot over the last forty years. You might know something without even knowing you know it."

"All right. That's believable. I'll work with you, all right?" He started to say something but I held up my hand. "But that's all it means, Colin. I'll work with you. It doesn't mean I've forgiven you, and it sure as hell doesn't mean I trust you." I walked over to my desk and sat down at my computer. "You said Levi was twelve? Angela also confirmed that. But why didn't you mention there was a son, Matthew?"

His facial expression didn't change. "Matthew Gretsch is dead."

"It's right there in *The Carthage Courant*. Survived by a son, Matthew." I folded my arms. "What else have you lied to me about?" I gestured to the bandage on his arm. "Was that self-inflicted?"

He walked over and leaned over my keyboard. He clicked on the search engine, and typed *Matthew Gretsch, Carthage Ohio* into the search box. He hit the Return key. After a few moments, a new list of links popped up. He clicked on the first one, folded his arms again, and took a few steps back.

I looked. It was a death announcement for Matthew Gretsch, dated two weeks after his father's. He'd been killed in a car accident.

I felt cold. Coincidence?

Before I had a chance to think of anything to say, the buzzer rang.

I pressed the Open button and went out the door to wait on the stairs for the cops. It was two uniforms I didn't recognize. I introduced myself to them, told them where the body was, and sat down on the steps to wait for further instructions. Colin came out and sat down next to me. "Scotty," he said in a quiet voice. "I would tell you the truth about your uncles if I could, but I can't. You have to believe me when I say I didn't kill them. I was trying to keep them alive."

"You failed." He put his hand on my arm, but I jerked away from him.

"I know I did." He went on, "I failed, Scotty. And it almost cost Frank his life, and it could have cost you yours. Don't you think I know that?" He swallowed. "I couldn't allow my cover to be blown, and so I had to get out of town. I thank God every day nothing happened to you and Frank—that you made it through that okay. I wouldn't have been able to live with myself..." His voice trailed off. "It killed me having to leave you and Frank, but the job wasn't done yet, and I couldn't allow my cover to be blown. So I had to leave the way I did." He swallowed. "I hated doing it. I hated letting you and Frank, the whole family, think I was a murderer, that everything about me was a lie. That everything we had was a lie. It wasn't, Scotty. You have to believe that."

"I don't know," I replied. It sounded good. It was what I'd wanted to hear for three years. How many times had I thought about this very moment, when he would come back and explain everything? I wanted to believe him. The Scotty I'd been three years ago *would* have believed him without a single question. That Scotty would have thrown his arms around Colin and kissed him, gladly welcomed him back into his life.

But I wasn't that Scotty anymore. That Scotty was gone, and no matter how hard I tried, no matter how much I wanted him to, that Scotty wasn't ever coming back. Too much had happened. Part of that Scotty had died during that awful Mardi Gras. A catastrophic man-made flood had killed another part of him just five months later.

"I want to believe you," I finally said as the silence grew between us. "You have no idea how much I want to believe you."

"Mom and Dad believe me." His voice was husky with emotion.

"I'm not them."

"I was so worried about you both when I heard about the hurricane," he continued. "I was scared for you both, for the whole family. But I got word from some of the first responders that you were all okay. If I hadn't, I'd have been on the next plane here, you can be sure of that. I wanted to come anyway. Angela said it was a mistake."

"Angela," I replied. I put my head down on my knees. "Of course, she'll back your story a hundred percent. And you'll back hers."

"I guess I can't blame you for not trusting me." He swallowed.

"Good."

"But do you think maybe that someday you might be able to again?"

I didn't know how to answer that. Fortunately, I was spared from answering by the timely arrival of Venus and her partner, Blaine Tujague.

Venus was wearing a gray wool pantsuit over a blue silk blouse. She looked like she hadn't slept, and she was holding a cup of coffee from CC's. Blaine looked like he was sleepwalking. He covered a yawn with the hand not holding a cup of coffee. His hair was messy, and he hadn't shaved. His clothes looked rumpled, like he'd been either wearing them a long time or slept in them.

"Well, well, well, look who we have here," Venus said, shaking her head as Colin rose. She held out her hand. "I didn't think we'd ever see you again, Agent Golden."

Whatever I was expecting to happen, that wasn't it. That small part of my mind that I didn't like had been hoping to see her cuff him, read him his rights, and lead him off to jail. I just stared at her, my mouth open. *What the hell did she mean by calling him* Agent? "Wait a minute. Aren't you going to arrest him? Isn't there an outstanding warrant for him?"

Venus and Blaine looked at each other first. Venus looked at me like I had just started speaking in tongues. Blaine smothered a smile. They both gave Colin a quizzical look. He just shrugged. "I've been trying to tell him. He won't listen to me."

"Not my problem," Venus said as she pulled out a notebook from her jacket pocket. "So, what's going on here? A body on your balcony?" Her voice was all business, but I got the distinct impression a smile was tugging at the corners of her mouth.

"Remember me telling you last night about Levi Gretsch, my upstairs neighbor, and how he'd hired me?"

Venus's face turned to professional stone. "The one whose grandfather was killed in a similar fashion to Benjamin Garrett? The one we came here last night to talk to?"

I nodded. "That's who it is, Venus. I was online, drinking some coffee when I heard a loud crash from the balcony. I went and looked, and saw Levi's body." I took a deep breath, and told her about finding out from Colin—who didn't say a word, just let me talk—that the *real* Levi Gretsch was only a child. "So, we came back here to check on Millie and Velma—I hadn't seen them all day, and we found them bound and gagged in their apartment."

If she weren't a cop, I think Venus would have gladly throttled me right then and there. "And you didn't call me?" Her voice was dangerously low.

"Millie and Velma didn't want to," Colin interrupted. "They'd been tied up all day, Venus, and they were worn out." He shrugged. "There wasn't anything you could have done about it last night anyway. Velma had to be in court this morning. They decided to go to bed and decide what to do about it in the morning. Since Levi had a set of keys, we thought it would be best if I just stood guard down in the courtyard."

"You two wait here," Venus said, motioning to Blaine. "We're going to take a look at the body."

"I'll make some more coffee," I offered, and Venus gave me a grateful, if out-of-character, smile. Colin and I followed them back into the apartment. Blaine gave me a funny look as they moved out to join the uniforms on the balcony.

I walked into the kitchen and started the coffee. Colin sat down on the other side of the counter. "You're sure you never went up to the roof?" I hissed at him. "Because if you did, now's the time to come clean."

He raised his eyebrows. "I most certainly did not."

"And you're sure Levi didn't come strolling along last night while the rest of us were sleeping?" I shot back. "You didn't see or hear anything?"

His face turned red. "I told you, I did not kill Levi," he said in a controlled voice, but he was gripping the counter so hard his knuckles turned white. He took a deep breath. "What would I gain by killing Levi, anyway?"

"Look, I'm sorry, but you have to admit I have to wonder." I glanced over at the French doors. "*You* didn't even try to talk Millie and Velma into calling the police. *You* volunteered to stand guard last night. And this morning, his body lands on my balcony." I thought for a moment. He wouldn't have had time to throw the body off the roof and then get back down to the courtyard. I'd gone to check on him moments after finding the body.

But all that meant was he wasn't the one who'd thrown the body off the roof.

And Levi had been dead for hours.

"Okay." I took a deep breath. "You have no idea who this guy really was?"

"All I know is whoever this guy really was, it wasn't Levi Gretsch." Now he folded his arms and gave me a look I didn't much care for. "I don't think it's a good idea to tell Venus and Blaine about the Eye of Kali."

"Now you're asking me to lie to the police?" I hissed. "The problem with lies, Colin, is that once you're caught your credibility is completely destroyed. And why did she call you *agent*?"

He smiled at me. "I'm working for your government, Scotty—like I was when I was trying to protect your uncles."

I shook my head. "That doesn't make any sense to me. You work for Angela Blackledge."

"I've told you, sometimes we're hired by governments who need to keep a certain distance from the delicate matters we work on for them." He shrugged. "I can't tell you any more than that."

"Of course not," I said sourly, pouring us both a cup of coffee. Out of habit, I added Sweet'n Low and creamer to his, stirred it, and handed it to him, like I always used to do. As soon as he took it from me, I realized what I'd done and my face burned.

He was grinning at me as he sipped his coffee. "You *remember* how I take my coffee?" He put the cup down on the counter. He leaned forward onto his elbows, every muscle in his arm contracting.

"I remember a lot of things that don't matter," I replied evenly, sipping my own coffee. "But how can we keep all this stuff from them, Colin? It's called *obstruction of justice,* and it's a crime—even if you are working for the government." I hopped up and sat on the counter.

"Uranium, international conspiracy, and espionage—Venus will love hearing about it, I'm sure." But when I said it out loud, it sounded pretty absurd. In spite of myself, I started laughing.

Why does this stuff happen to me?

"Scotty, this isn't funny." Colin's smile faded into a concerned frown. "The stakes are high. If the wrong people get their hands on the Eye—"

"Yeah, yeah, I get it. Armageddon. Angela was pretty clear on the phone." I refilled my coffee cup. "I don't see how we can keep this from them. But it does sound ridiculous, if you think about it." But on the other hand, so did identical Russian triplets—and Venus and Blaine had worked that case, too. I felt really tired. The lack of sleep was starting to catch up to me. I downed the coffee and poured myself another cup. "You didn't see or hear anything weird from the roof? He was obviously killed up there—no one could drag a body up that ladder." Just thinking about trying it made me queasy. "And someone had to drop it off the roof to my balcony."

"It dropped from the roof?"

"Well, how did you think it got there? Magic?" I shook my head. "You didn't hear the crash when it landed? The whole building shook. I went and looked through the curtains—saw him lying there, and called Venus, and waved you to come up here." I scratched my nose. "There are only two ways it could have gotten there. Either it was heaved up there from the street, or it was tossed off the roof. I vote for tossed off the roof. So how did they get up to the roof? And why my balcony? Convenience?"

"Maybe they were aiming for the street and missed," Colin joked.

I just gave him a look.

"Okay, well, it's not as difficult to get up to your roof as you'd like to think it is," Colin said hurriedly. "It's not a far jump from the buildings on either side of you. And if Levi was indeed inside when we went looking for him earlier, it wouldn't have been too hard for him to get up there."

Much as I hated to admit it, he was right. New Orleanians never worried about people breaking into the building by crossing the roofs. All the security protections we put into place were to keep people from breaking in from the ground level. And getting down from the roof was relatively easy if you didn't have a fear of heights. Someone coming across the roofs obviously didn't have such a problem. Someone could have come across, lured Levi up the back ladder, killed him—

And what? Stayed up there all night through the rain until the time was ripe to drop the body down to my balcony? And then fled back across the roofs?

It wasn't likely, but Levi himself could have easily gone up the ladder when we came looking for him. He could have been hiding out on the roof.

Who would have known he was up there?

Ugh, my head was starting to hurt again. I poured myself some more coffee.

The French doors opened, and Venus and Blaine walked back in. I poured them each a cup of coffee, and they sat down on either side of Colin at the bar. "No identification," Venus said after taking a drink. "I'm going to need you to identify the body."

"It's Levi, or rather, the man I knew as Levi Gretsch," I said. "I don't need to look again."

"When was the last time you saw him alive?" Venus asked, pulling out her little notepad.

"Around five thirty yesterday afternoon." She made me go over the entire thing again. It was a little annoying, but I assumed she wanted to make sure there were no discrepancies, or if maybe I'd remembered something I hadn't thought about the first time around.

She turned to Colin. "And you, Agent Golden? When did you see him last?"

My eyes darted back and forth between the two of them.

"I never met the man," Colin replied. He shook his head. "All I know for sure is he isn't Levi Gretsch. Marty Gretsch's grandson is only twelve years old."

She nodded. "We've confirmed that with the Ohio state police. He's living with some relatives in Chicago—apparently, his father was killed in a car accident a few weeks after his grandfather was murdered." She shook her head. "The poor kid's been through a lot."

"Was it really an accident?" I blurted out. I blushed when she gave me one of her patented you-are-such-a-dumbass looks. "I mean, Marty Gretsch was murdered and then two weeks later his son dies in a car accident. It's weird, is all."

"They did a thorough investigation into the accident. He was hit by a drunk driver." She looked at me, and her eyebrows went up. "Scotty, what did you do to your neck?"

I blew out a breath. "Um. I was mugged last night when I was on my way to my parents'." I quickly ran through the whole incident, leaving out the mugger's mention of "the eye."

A muscle twitched in Venus's jaw.

"You didn't think," Blaine said quietly, his face turning red, "that might be important to our investigation?"

"Get off my back," I replied. "So I was mugged and didn't report it. Arrest me. And don't you think that's a bit of a stretch? People get mugged all the time. I didn't think it was important."

"Someone stabbed you in the throat and you *didn't think it was important*?" Blaine literally looked like smoke was about to come out of his ears. "Is there anything else you haven't told us that you don't think is important?"

"I'm so sorry, Detective Tujague," I snapped. "Let me see, in the last day a family friend was brutally murdered, my landladies were tied up, a body wound up somehow on my balcony, and this one"—I gestured at Colin—"turned up out of the blue. So, yeah, being stabbed kind of seemed a little unimportant." I held out my hands. "Cuff me and take me in, Mr. Detective."

Blaine had the decency to look a little sheepish. "Sorry," he mumbled.

"Cut the drama, Scotty," Venus said mildly. "Can you describe your attacker?"

I recounted what happened, beginning with Mom's phone call. I described the attacker as best as I could remember—which wasn't much, since I'd never gotten a look at his face—and wound up with arriving at Mom's. The whole time I was talking, Colin didn't say a word. He just sat there, his face expressionless.

"And your arm? What happened to your arm?"

"I shot myself." He didn't look at me. "I needed to get inside Cecile Bradley's apartment. So I shot myself. It's no more than a flesh wound, I aimed so that it wouldn't be really painful but would be really bloody. I wasn't sure if she would let me in if I just called her, but I knew her well enough to know if I was injured, she would."

I felt my blood starting to boil. I *knew* he couldn't be trusted. My hands were starting to shake. "I knew it," I said, my voice trembling. "I knew you couldn't be trusted!" I was furious. I don't think I've ever been that angry in my life. "You shot yourself! Oh my *God!*"

"Scotty, please." Venus held up her hand. "I said cut the drama—I'm not interested."

I started pacing around the kitchen. "Was anything you told me true?" I seethed. "Or Angela? You really enjoy making a fool out of me!"

I knew I was losing it. I tried to get a hold of myself, but nothing was working. I tried to take deep breaths, closing my eyes and trying to find a prayer for strength and calm, but no words came to me. Nothing he said could be believed. He was a liar, pure and simple.

"Scotty—" He reached out and grabbed my hand.

The words started pouring out of me. "Uranium, right? This whole thing about world security and terrorism and the stupid damned Eye of Kali was all just a bunch of bullshit, wasn't it?"

Colin's face went white.

And just as quickly as it came, the anger drained out of me. My legs became wobbly. Out of the corners of my eyes I could see things turning gray, and the gray crept across my sightline. I tried to grab hold of the counter but there wasn't any strength in my hands. *No, no, no! Not in front of the cops!*

"And just why did you need to get into Cecile Bradley's house?" I heard Venus ask. Her voice sounded like it was a million miles away, like someone had turned the volume on a television down to an almost inaudible level.

Everything was starting to spin.

"I believe Benjamin Garrett was murdered," Colin replied, "because for the last forty years he has been in possession of a stolen artifact from a small country called Pleshiwar. I believe he knew that agents unfriendly to the current Pleshiwarian government were getting close to him, and he had to get rid of it. I believe he put it inside a stuffed rabbit, which he in turn passed along to Scotty, who then gave it to his mother." His face was grim. "As long as that rabbit is inside her home, Bob and Cecile Bradley are in mortal danger."

Everything was getting foggy and I tried to keep it at bay.

Mom...

Dad...

And everything went dark.

I was falling through a cloud.
I wasn't afraid, because I felt surrounded by love and peace.
I drifted down through the cloud.
I came to rest on a soft bed of grass, and felt warm, loved and at peace.
"Scotty!" a voice called from my right.
I got to my feet and looked around for the voice. "I'm here! Is that you, Goddess?"
"It is I."
There were so many things I wanted to ask Jer. So many questions, so many things I wanted to know the answers to. "Why did you leave me for so long?" was all I could find the words for, and I sounded like a spoiled child, ready to stamp his little foot in rage.
"I never left you, Scotty. I was always with you, but I couldn't speak with you," she replied from the mist. "Your heart was closed to me." Her tone was gently chiding. "But I watched over you, as I always watch over you."
"But—"
"You are human, Scotty. It is not for you to understand the ways of the universe, how everything works and how everything is connected together. You will understand all one day, but that day is far into the future as you understand time." Her voice sounded hollow, different somehow than it used to. "But I am with you again, and you need never be afraid."
"But I don't know what to think, what to believe!"
"Your heart knows the answers, Scotty. The answers lie within your heart. You think your heart has been broken, but it is not possible for a heart to break. It can hurt, and it can harden, but it can never truly break."
"But—"
"Everything is a test, Scotty. The question is, are you brave enough to trust in your own heart again?"
The mist began to dissipate, swirling around me. The feeling of peace and love began to fade away, and the light in the distance began to grow brighter, and I started floating toward it, moving faster and faster as the light grew brighter...

...and the last thing I heard as I moved into the light again were the words "trust in your heart, Scotty..."

I opened my eyes.

My head was resting in Colin's lap. I looked up and saw Venus and Blaine staring down at me. Their eyes and mouths were wide open. Blaine was white as a ghost, and Venus looked like she was going to throw up.

"See?" I heard Colin say. "I told you he'd be fine. I've seen this happen before."

"Jesus fucking Christ," Venus said, her voice shaking.

"What did you see, Scotty?" Colin asked softly. He was stroking my forehead. "What did She tell you?"

"She—" I looked up into his eyes, and in that instant, I knew.

He had lied. He had lied to me and broken my heart. My heart, and Frank's, and my family's. But no matter how good an actor he was, he couldn't fake the love for me I saw in his eyes.

He hadn't lied about that, and looking at him, I knew I'd always known that in my heart.

I felt the tears welling up in my eyes, but I wasn't about to cry in front of Venus and Blaine. I struggled to sit up, and wiped at my eyes.

I took a deep breath. "She told me to trust in my heart, and it would show me the way." I looked around at all of them. "Shouldn't we be getting over to my parents'?"

CHAPTER NINE
EIGHT OF WANDS
Approach to a goal

Venus and Blaine were conferring by the balcony doors. I couldn't hear what they were saying, but their whispers had an angry tone to them that was impossible to miss. I felt my assumption that Blaine thought stopping by my parents' wasn't necessary was probably correct. Venus might not like me, or my family, for that matter, but she was always willing to listen to me.

Blaine, on the other hand, could be a bit of a douche bag. He'd tried to play me once during a case. Trying to get information, he'd claimed we'd hooked up once when we were both wasted—which, I'm sad to admit, was always a possibility with me. He *was* good looking, and nicely put together—and when I was single, I was a bit of a slut. There were any number of hot guys out there I'd hooked up with that I didn't remember—the main drawback to having such a checkered past. His plan had almost worked, too. Fortunately, I'd caught on. Sure, he was just doing his job—but it was still a shitty thing to do, and I never could bring myself to trust him again.

"Did you really shoot yourself?" I whispered to Colin. "Wasn't that a little bit on the extreme side?"

He didn't take his eyes off Venus and Blaine. "Are you mad at me?" he whispered back.

"I should be, but I'm not." I was a little surprised myself. I was still feeling the calming influence of the Goddess. When it wore off, I'd probably be furious.

"I didn't shoot myself," he whispered, reaching out and rubbing my arm. "I just am not ready to involve them that deeply yet. I'll explain everything later."

That figured. It was always *I'll explain later* with him. Sometimes, *later* never came. It was frustrating, but I decided not to let it get to me. Instead, I sighed and gave him a long, hard look. His right eye closed in a wink. But before I could say anything, Venus and Blaine finished their discussion and walked back over to us. Her face was its usual unreadable stone—but he was pissed. His face was flushed, his lips pressed together into a taut thin line. A muscle in his jaw was twitching.

"All right," Venus said, glancing at Blaine. "Scotty, I'll drive you over to check on your parents. Agent Golden, would you mind staying here? Blaine has some more questions for you."

Agent. Her tone was deferential—which was most definitely not like Venus. Who the hell was he working for, anyway?

"That's fine," Colin replied with a gracious smile for Blaine. "I'd be happy to answer your questions, Detective Tujague. Scotty, call me and let me know they're okay?"

I bit my lower lip. *They must be okay, otherwise he'd never agree to stay here.* But how did he know? It was his idea in the first place for us to go over there…

He just wanted to get Venus and Blaine out of my apartment.

What was he up to? Did he know more about Levi's murder than he was letting on?

My head was starting to hurt again.

I followed Venus down the back stairs and out to her SUV. As I buckled myself in, I asked," Why do you keep calling Colin *agent*?" She started the engine, turned on her siren, and slammed it into drive. The tires squealed as the SUV roared out onto Decatur Street. "What was that all about? And why didn't you arrest him?"

"That's very simple, Scotty." Venus didn't look at me as she turned onto Barracks. The car almost went up on two wheels. "I didn't arrest him because I can't. There's no warrant out for him." She shook her head. We reached the corner at Royal and this time we did go up on two wheels. I grabbed the armrest and said a quick prayer. Her facial expression didn't change as she barely missed a bicycle delivery guy. He went down in a heap, waving his fist after us. "A few days after Mardi Gras, Homeland Security took over his case from us. You know all they have to do is say 'terrorism' and that's it—we can't say a damned thing about it. They took our files, the evidence, everything. We were told not to worry about it, and were told the charges against him were being dropped." She shrugged. "I thought we pretty much had him nailed for it, frankly, but you don't question Homeland Security. They notified us they had a new suspect, they had him dead to rights, and all charges against Abram Golden, aka Colin Cioni, were being dropped. Period, no questions asked—in fact, they made it very clear that any questions asked would put *us* in deep shit." She let out her breath in a deep sigh. "They don't have to explain anything to us. So, that's why. I wish I had more to tell you, but that's all I know—and will probably ever know." She gave me a sidelong glance, and added, "I think there was a lot more going on there than we'll ever know, frankly."

I took a deep breath as the implications sank in.

He'd been working for the U.S. government, I thought as she made the turn onto Dumaine. What had he told me once? "The Blackledge Agency often takes on governments as clients for work where they need plausible deniability. They can just deny that we were working for them. There's always a way to hide the money trail."

He'd even said so during that case. I'd just assumed that was another lie.

Which logically led to the question, was he working for the U.S. government now?

"I got the call this morning." Venus shrugged as she turned onto Dumaine Street. "We are to give Agent Golden whatever assistance he needs, and our full cooperation is appreciated." She made a face. "I hate working in the dark—especially now that I have two homicides on my hands."

"It's kind of like last time," I observed. I added to myself, *but this time I'm getting to the bottom of the whole thing.*

Venus pulled over onto the sidewalk in front of the gate to my parents' back stairs. She got out of the car and waved me off as I came to the gate. "Stay here while I go up and knock," she said, "and if everything's okay—"

"No need to knock." I fished my keys out of my pocket. "I've got keys."

She gave me a look and held out her hands. "You heard me. Don't argue with me, Scotty."

"Look, we don't know anything's really wrong," I insisted. "And I have keys. I have their permission to go in and out at will. You're not breaking any procedural rules by going in with me as a guest. And if there's nothing wrong up there, trust me, they'll be in bed. They'll never hear you knocking." I grinned at her. "And besides, the gate's locked. They disconnect the buzzer when they go to bed." I pointed to a note next to their bell. It instructed that any deliveries before noon were to be taken to the store.

Venus gave me a withering look and gestured to me to unlock the gate. With a sigh of relief, I slid the key into the gate and turned it. I ran up the back stairs. She was right behind me when I unlocked the back door and pushed it open, then shouldered past me. Pulling her gun, she made a sweep of the kitchen and waved me in. I followed her in as she checked the living room. All the shutters were closed, all the lights off. I flicked on the chandelier lights, flooding the room with light. Everything was the way it should be. There was an empty wine bottle on the coffee table, along with two glasses with little spots of wine in them. A volume of the encyclopedia was open next to the wine bottle. I walked over and glanced down. It was open to the *Pleshiwar* entry. "I think everything's okay," I whispered. I picked the book up. The entry was a short paragraph. There wasn't even a corresponding map of the country to go with it.

"Check out the bedrooms," Venus whispered back. "And if anything seems off—"

"Trust me, I'll scream."

The apartment was silent other than the ticking of clocks and the sounds of the street outside. I turned on the hallway light and checked out the bedrooms. Mom and Dad's room was at the very end of the hall. When I reached their door, I turned back and nodded to her, giving her the okay sign with my right hand. I reached down and turned the knob gently, and pushed the door open a little, just so I could get a look.

Mom and Dad were cuddled up into a ball, sleeping with a wool blanket over them. In the gloom, I could see they were both breathing. I pulled the door shut and walked back down to where she was standing. I shrugged. "They're asleep."

Her lips tightened. There was an undercurrent of annoyance in her voice. "Everything seems to be as it should be around here. Any thoughts on why he sent us on this wild goose chase, Scotty?"

Oh, I have lots of those, I thought. I smiled at her and shrugged. "Well, to be fair, he said they were in danger, not that we'd find bodies."

I walked back down the hall and took a deep breath. Nothing made my parents angrier than being woken up before noon. Risking their wrath, I started pounding on the door. *"Mom! Dad! Wake up!"* I yelled.

I heard movement inside the room. The door swung open. Dad stood there, stark naked, hands on his hips and fire in his drowsy eyes. "Scotty, what the hell are you doing here?" His eyes focused on Venus at the end of the hall. She averted her eyes and stepped out of sight into the living room. He dropped his hands strategically. He looked back at me, puzzled. "Why is Venus here? What's going on?"

"Mr. Bradley, would you mind getting dressed?" Venus called from the living room. "I need to talk to you and your wife. It's very important. I apologize for having to wake you."

Dad yawned and nodded. He closed the door, and I heard him whispering to Mom. As soon as the door closed, Venus stepped back into the hallway. She rolled her eyes and smiled.

I walked into my old bedroom, or as I called it, the Scotty Shrine. I flipped on the light and went back in time. I'd moved out permanently when I was eighteen, and nothing had been changed in the room since that day. Posters of a shirtless Marky Mark still hung on the walls, the bookcases still held my collection of Hardy Boys, and all my wrestling medals and trophies were displayed on top of dressers. All my childhood toys and games were on the shelves in the closet. It was a little unsettling—Storm and Rain's rooms were the same.

And sure enough, Mom had put the damned rabbit in the center of my bed. I walked over and picked it up. It was so surreal to me that this filthy, disgusting old relic of my childhood was something people were being killed for. I closed my eyes and said a quick prayer, but felt nothing unusual. I opened my eyes and turned it over in my hands. Mom hadn't washed it, the way she said she was going to—she probably hadn't had time. Things had been moving pretty fast since the parade ended. I held it up to the light. It still stank of dust and mold. I squeezed it in a couple of places. It didn't feel like anything was inside it. I shook it a bit, feeling a little stupid.

Why would Doc put the Eye inside this thing? I wondered. I was just starting to think Colin was wrong when I turned it over.

There was a place, just below the tail, where it had been stitched back together. The thread looked new.

I squeezed it, but felt nothing but stuffing.

Venus is going to be pissed—there's no jewel stuffed inside this thing, I thought as I carried it back into the living room with me. I could smell coffee brewing in the kitchen. Venus was sitting on the couch, her face unreadable as she was typing into her cell phone. She looked up and her lip curled. "That's the rabbit he was talking about?"

Before I could answer, Mom walked into the living room in her tattered robe, yawning. "Scotty, why on earth are you waking us up at this ungodly hour?" She was too sleepy to be angry—so far. She peered at the clock on the mantelpiece. "Why, it's barely eleven!" She rubbed her eyes. "Venus, is there anything new on Doc's murder? Is that what this is about?" She plopped down into a wingback chair and yawned again. "And what are you doing with Mr. Bunny?"

I was digging through a drawer in the coffee table, looking for scissors. "Venus, you explain it to her?" There was a lot of crap in that drawer. Mom was pretty fastidious, but the various junk drawers scattered throughout the house were disorganized messes. I pawed through electrical cords, vials of glitter, instruction manuals for electrical appliances, and batteries before I finally put my hands on a pair of scissors. Dad walked in carrying mugs of coffee as Venus was explaining to Mom Colin's theory about Mr. Bunny. I started cutting the thread.

"So Colin thinks this jewel is in Mr. Bunny?" Mom took a swig from her coffee mug. She shuddered. "I'm not sure how I feel about having that evil stone in my home." She looked at Dad. "We'll have to do a cleansing." He nodded back at her.

"The stone itself isn't evil," I pointed out. "But it makes sense, doesn't it?" I said as the thread snapped in two. I started pulling the stitches out. "If it wasn't in Doc's apartment, he had to have gotten it out of there somehow before." I got the last of the thread out, and pulled the tear apart, sticking my right hand into the nasty stuffing. The old material ripped some more.

"Be careful, Scotty," Mom warned. "I'd like to keep him, you know."

"Wait a minute!" Venus cautioned. "That might be evidence—"

"That's a bit of a stretch, Venus." My father adjusted his glasses. "It belongs to Scotty, and it wasn't present in Doc's apartment when he was killed. If you want it, you need a warrant." He folded his arms.

In that moment, I felt sorry for Venus. My parents are a royal pain in the ass to the authorities. "Fine," she said after a moment, "rip the damned thing to shreds."

I gave her a sour look, and she smiled back at me. I started pulling out the stuffing, tossing it aside on the table. Mom grabbed a plastic bag and started collecting it. I stuck my hand in as far as it could go, and felt nothing. I kept pulling out the stuffing until there was absolutely nothing left inside. I started to toss aside the empty skin in disgust when a small slip of paper fluttered out of the hole.

I picked it up. It was folded into a little triangle, like the paper footballs kids make to play table football. Holding my breath, I started unfolding it.

I smoothed it out on the table, and stared at it.

"What does it say?" Mom sat down next to me and peered at it. "Read it out loud—I don't have my glasses."

I took a breath and read it out loud:

"From Pleshiwar to the parish of the maid,
Who saved a city and was burned down to ash
To the park where so many still ply their trade,
Behind the spires of the saint, always asking for cash
Stands the fisher of souls with his arms open wide
Follow his left hand to the canopy of trees
Just beyond the orphan's friend, go alongside
The Muses line up, to sing with the breeze
Just find the place for the blonds from the seas."

"A *riddle?*" I exploded, tossing the paper down on the table. "You've got to be fucking kidding me." I glared at the rabbit. "It's not even good poetry." As I said it, Venus's phone rang. She walked into the kitchen to take the call.

"Doc loved puzzles," Dad said, yawning. "And riddles. He said it kept his mind sharp."

"Does this make sense to either one of you?" I sat back on the couch.

Mom picked it up and squinted at it. After a moment, she put it down with a shrug and walked into kitchen to get more coffee. I picked up my own cup and took a drink.

"This was exactly the kind of thing Doc loved—a treasure riddle that leads to where he hid the jewel," Dad said, examining the paper over the top of his glasses. "I can almost hear the old son of a bitch laughing." He sat down next to me. "Obviously, he would have made it hard, but he wouldn't have made it impossible to solve." He patted me on the shoulder. "Let's use our brains, shall we?" He laughed. "You know how Doc was about brainpower." He covered a yawn, and closed his eyes. "This shouldn't be too hard, really, if we put our minds to it. Hmm, *the parish of the maid*? That's New Orleans, obviously."

"Huh?" My mind had wandered a bit.

"Joan of Arc was called the Maid of Orleans. Don't you remember your history?" Dad said patiently, patting my leg. "So, *the parish of the maid* would be New Orleans."

"Oh, yeah." I closed my eyes. There was a huge gilt statue of Joan of Arc mounted on horseback, and carrying a banner, down on Decatur Street where it split into two one-way streets. It had been a gift to the city from Orleans, France. "Okay, the first line is referring to the Eye, obviously. It came from Pleshiwar to New Orleans." I sat up. "That was easy enough." I reread the second line. "But what the hell does the rest mean? And *the blonds from the seas*? Who's the orphan's friend?"

"It's a riddle—it's not supposed to be easy," Dad replied. He frowned as Mom walked back into the room. She sat down on the other side of me.

"I don't get it." I shook my head. "Let's come back to that one. The next line?" I cleared my head. *"The saint, always asking for cash?"* I sighed. "A saint statue? But which one?" There were literally hundreds of statues of saints in New Orleans.

"I need to get back to the crime scene," Venus said as she walked back into the room, slipping her phone into her jacket pocket. "Everything's under control here, right?" She looked over at the riddle. "What the hell?"

"This is all that was inside the rabbit," I explained. "A riddle."

Venus shook her head. "I swear, every time I get involved with this family, it's something crazy." She pulled out an evidence bag from her pocket. She looked at me. "Can I take this?" When I nodded, she slipped the rabbit skin and the stuffing inside it and sealed it. "I'm going to need to take that riddle with me, too."

"You sure you don't want some coffee to take with you?" Mom asked.

"Let me make a copy first." I grabbed a pad of paper and wrote it down. I scrutinized the handwriting, to see if there were any clues in it. But no, it was just Doc's usual precise lettering. I handed it to her.

"I'll be in touch," she said as she sealed it into another evidence bag. "You know how to reach me if you need me." She walked out the back door.

"This is hopeless." I sighed. "If Doc weren't dead, I'd cheerfully strangle him."

"Nothing is hopeless, Scotty," Mom reprimanded me. "And don't joke about killing people, even if they are already dead. You don't want to send that kind of energy out into the universe." She shrugged. "So it's not easy? It's something we have to do. Doc left this for you. He wanted *you* to find this Eye thing, maybe to return it to where it belongs."

"Why didn't he just return it?" I groaned. "Why did he keep it all these years? Wouldn't it have just been simpler to give the damned thing back?"

"Well, we can't very well ask him, can we?" Mom retorted. "We may never know what he was thinking, or why he did what he did." She got up and walked over to one of the windows, opening the shutters and letting bright sunlight spill into the room. "I can't even begin to tell you how disappointed I am in Doc." She shook her head. "All that crap he used to spout about colonialism and imperialism, the destruction of native cultures and its appropriation by white supremacists, was all just a bunch of garbage."

"What do you mean?"

She turned away from the window. "If he stole this jewel from that temple—a jewel that was important to an entire culture—it's more than just a robbery, Scotty, don't you see that? He basically spat in the face of an entire culture, robbing them of their heritage. It's no better than the way the Europeans stole this entire continent from the natives. And if he really believed the things he said, he would have returned it to where it belonged."

"We may never know what he was thinking," I replied.

She made a face at me. "Don't mock your mother."

I sighed and wrote out another copy of the riddle. "All right, well, I am going to head home and see what's going on around there. I left Colin to watch the apartment, and I don't trust him completely."

"Scotty—" This was my dad. "Don't you think everyone deserves a second chance?" He gave me a sad smile. "He didn't kill your uncles, we know that now."

I bit my lip. "He still went away and left us thinking he did." I swallowed. "Not a word in three years, Dad. Not an 'I'm sorry I left the way I did,' not a 'hey, I'm alive,' nothing." My voice broke a little bit. "You weren't the ones he left."

Dad put his arm around me and shushed Mom as she was about to splutter something at me. "Son, he did leave *us*, too. You always seem to forget that. He was a part of our entire family, not just your boyfriend." He kissed the top of my head. "I know it's hard. I know it hurt. But we didn't raise you to be so unforgiving. Just because he had to go away and not say good-bye, or because you haven't heard from him since, doesn't mean he didn't care. Have you ever considered he might not have been able to? Maybe he thought it would be easier on both you and Frank to just disappear. I mean, his job is *dangerous*."

"Every time he is on a case he could be killed, Scotty." Mom took over. "Even when he's not on a case, I am sure he's made a lot of enemies who would love to see him dead—or maybe they'd want to harm people he cared about to make him suffer."

"Stop making sense," I said, irritated. It did make sense, and it was an angle I'd never considered. "I know he loves us, okay? I just wish Frank were here. I don't like having to deal with this alone. It concerns him, too." My heart sank as that thought sank in. *How the hell am I going to explain all of this to Frank?*

"Frank will be fine," Mom urged. She held up her hand as I started to speak. "No, listen to me. You have every right to blast him, to tell him how hurt you and Frank were when he vanished like that." She smiled. "Trust me, he got an earful from me."

I decided it was probably not the best time to tell her he'd probably shot himself to get his foot in the door. I also realized there wasn't any point to continuing the argument. They'd forgiven him and would think I was an awful person if I didn't at least try.

I couldn't win.

"Okay, I'll talk to him." I threw my hands up.

Mom and Dad smothered me in a huge hug.

I broke away from them and headed down the back stairs.

I opened the gate, and peered up and down Dumaine Street. It was a sunny day, and the coast looked clear. I shook my head and shut the gate behind me, making sure it latched. I headed down to Decatur Street, figuring it would be safer for me to walk up that street. It was similar to Bourbon Street in that every block was lined with restaurants and bars. There were also little shops that catered to the tourists, selling all that crap People Not From Here always seem to be convinced is symbolic of the city: feather boas, beads, little masks, etc. Farther up the street, closer to my house, there were a lot of secondhand shops that always came in handy when trying to put a costume together.

The coroner's van was pulling away from in front of my house when I got there. The Crime Lab van was also gone. I unlocked the gate and walked back in. I climbed the back stairs. I walked into my living room, and moaned. Crime scene tape was stretched across my French doors. Colin was sitting at my computer, typing away.

"So, I gather the balcony is off-limits?" I snarled, starting a pot of coffee. "Did they say for how long?"

Colin smiled at me. "No, they didn't, but I doubt they'll need to come back and check anything out. I mean, he obviously wasn't killed out there."

As the coffee started, I walked over and peered through the curtains. There was a chalk outline of a body where Levi had landed. I felt a bit nauseous, and turned back to Colin. "Did she say anything else?"

He nodded. "He was killed on the roof—they found traces of blood up there. He was bludgeoned. The body was cold, so they aren't sure of the time of death. That's going to take an autopsy. But I think it's pretty safe to assume he was probably killed sometime last night." He gestured around the apartment. "When you got back here with Venus last night, you thought the place had been searched, right?"

I nodded. "But why throw the body onto my balcony?"

"Here's what I'm thinking." He turned around and faced me. "While you were at the parade, Levi searched your apartment. He came down here and hired you after you got back—he was probably waiting for you. He fed you that line of bull, hired you, and then you went back out again. I think he came down here and started searching—"

I shook my head. "Doesn't wash, Agent."

He frowned. "Why not?"

"Because, dumbass, there was no reason for him to search my apartment." I folded my arms and smirked at him. "He had no idea Doc was going to give me the stupid rabbit—no one could have known before it actually happened. No one could have known Doc would dump water on me. Nobody could know I was even going to walk that way on my way to the parade."

He picked up a pencil and started tapping the eraser against his front teeth. "Well, Doc was obviously planning on doing something with the rabbit." He smiled at me. "And was the Eye inside of it?"

I shook my head. "Nope. All that was inside that rabbit was stuffing. Ratty, rotting, dirty disgusting stuffing."

He made a face. "Then where—"

"Doc was a lot smarter than that." I plopped down on the couch. I was exhausted, and just wanted to go back to sleep. "He left a riddle inside the rabbit. I'm assuming the riddle is a clue to where he actually hid the Eye."

"A riddle?"

I nodded, and yawned. "I tried figuring it out, but my mind is fried. Maybe I should just take a nap."

"Why don't you do that?" He sat down on the couch. "Give me the riddle and I'll see if I can figure it out while you sleep." He held out his hand.

I just gave him a look. "Yeah. That's going to happen."

His face fell a little bit. "You can trust me, Scotty."

"Can I really?" I replied. "Tell me about it, Colin."

He took a deep breath. "Look, I know it was incredibly shitty of me to leave the way I did. But it's my life, Scotty. The truth is, when I first moved here I thought I could give up that life. I really did. And I thought that—" He paused, and glanced over at the balcony doors. "Did you hear that?"

"Hear what?" I followed his gaze. "I didn't hear anything."

"Shh." He pulled his gun and got to his feet, and started creeping toward the doors.

But when he reached the end of the couch, the center doors exploded open, slamming against the walls with a huge crash as the glass inside of them shattered.

"What the fuck—" I spluttered as two black-clad figures leaped through the doorway.

"Drop the gun," one of them said.

Colin's gun fell to the floor.

"Who the hell are you?" I gasped out.

Colin turned and looked at me. "It's the Ninja Lesbians."

CHAPTER TEN
STRENGTH
Love is always stronger than hate

Surely, I hadn't heard that right—I must be in shock.

He did not just say *ninja lesbians.* Did he*?*

Without moving my head, I stole a glance at him out of the corner of my eyes. Despite the fact my French doors had just been kicked in, my mind registered that he seemed relaxed—too relaxed, given the situation. Shouldn't we be ducking for cover? Shouldn't he be pulling his own weapon?

What the *fuck* was going on?

Eternal seeming seconds passed as we all stared at each other. I focused on getting control of my thoughts as the two black-clad figures kept their guns aimed at us. *Stay calm,* I said to myself as I slowed my breathing and tried to bring my heart rate under control. They hadn't fired right away, so maybe they weren't here to kill us, after all.

My eyes narrowed a bit as I watched the intruders. They were wearing tight hoods over their heads. Only their eyes were exposed. Their bodies were concealed in tight black bodysuits made from some material that hugged every inch of their bodies—and I realized they were most definitely women. There was no mistaking those curves. The one on my right was slightly shorter than the one on my left. Each was holding a gigantic-looking gun in her right hand.

I really hate looking down the barrel of a gun. It's something you never really get used to, no matter how often it happens. And no matter how fast I could dive, I wasn't faster than a speeding bullet.

There was no place to dive anyway. We were both standing in the open. Colin might be able to launch himself over the couch, but he wasn't moving.

I closed my eyes and braced myself for the shots I was certain were going to follow.

Instead, the one to my left said, in a thick Middle Eastern accent, "Abram? What the hell are you doing here?"

I sighed inwardly, resisting the urge to roll my eyes. *Of course they know each other,* I thought. *Can this day get any crazier?*

They both lowered their guns. The one on my right reached up with her free hand and pulled the hood off. Long, thick chestnut brown hair fell loose. Whatever I was expecting to see once the hood pulled free, it sure as hell wasn't one of the most beautiful women I'd ever seen. Her face was heart-shaped, with prominent cheekbones and a sharp chin that gave her a bit of a feline look. Her almond-shaped eyes were a gorgeous shade of green, and her lashes were long and thick. Her nose was petite and perfectly centered in her face. Her skin was smooth and creamy. Her red lips slowly spread into a delighted smile, lighting up her entire face. She tucked her gun back into a shoulder holster and she started moving with a squeal of delight. In four steps she bounded across the room and threw her arms around Colin in a bear hug, her legs going around his waist as she buried her face in his neck. Colin laughed and threw his own arms around her, spinning her around.

"Would someone," I said, exasperated, "explain to me what the hell is going on? Who the hell are you people, and what are you doing here?"

The other one yanked her own hood off. She was older, with a mop of brown curls cut short. She was more striking than pretty. Her face was rounder, and not as perfectly proportioned. But her brown eyes were larger, and became warmer as she smiled at me and rolled her eyes. "Pay them no mind," she said. She had an accent that sounded Middle Eastern to me, although she didn't look Semitic. "They do this every time they see each other." She wearily waved her gun. "It's becomes tiresome. They're like children. Try to get used to it." She sighed and holstered her gun. "Of course, it's been years and I am still not used to it."

"Oh, relax, Rhoda," the other said, kissing Colin on the cheek. She jumped off him lightly, landing without making a sound. Her English was flawless, although I thought I detected a bit of a Texas twang. She held out her hand to me. "So sorry about the entrance. I'm Lindy, and this is my partner, Rhoda." Her green eyes widened, and she turned back to Colin. "Oh my God, oh my God!" She gestured at me, bouncing on the balls of her feet, her voice bubbling with excitement. "Is this—is this *the* Scotty?" She looked back at me. Her smile was so wide it had to hurt. "Are you Scotty? Please tell me you're Scotty!"

Before I could say anything, Colin grinned at her. "The one and only."

In one gazelle-like bound she had her arms around me and kissed my cheek. She was squeezing me so tight I could barely breathe, and her large firm breasts were pressed against my chest. She smelled of Chanel, and I felt a little dizzy. It was a bit on the surreal side. Just a few moments earlier she'd been holding a gun on me and now she was squeezing the life out of me in one of the tightest bear hugs I'd ever felt. She was incredibly strong, even though she looked slender.

"I can't *breathe*," I finally managed to gasp out when it started to seem like she was never going to let go. I looked over her shoulder at Rhoda, who was also smiling.

"Sorry." She let me go, and I gulped in air. "I'm just *so* excited to *finally* meet you! My God, we've *heard* so much about you—I was starting to think Abram was making you up, no one could be that perfect, you know what I mean, and look at you, you're even cuter than he said, which I didn't think possible, you know he is kind of prone to exaggeration, and if I weren't a lesbian I'd—"

"Down, girl." Colin interrupted her. He was grinning from ear to ear. "Give him a chance to recover from that dramatic entrance." He gestured to my wrecked French doors. "Was that really necessary?"

"Sorry about that." Rhoda plopped down on the sofa. "We didn't know what we'd find here, so we figured no one would expect us to come in through the windows—" She shrugged and looked back over at the broken glass twinkling in the sunlight on my floor. "We'll replace them, of course."

"Of course." I shook my head, which was starting to hurt again. I walked over and closed the shutters, latching them. "At least it isn't raining." I grabbed a broom from the hall closet and started sweeping up the broken glass. Lindy bounded over and took the broom from me. She beamed at me with that thousand-watt smile. "Let me. It's the least I can do."

"She likes to clean," Rhoda said with a shrug.

As I watched her methodically get every sliver and splinter of glass into the dustpan, I thought, *When the shock wears off I'm probably going to be really, really pissed.*

I walked back into the living room. "So, what were you expecting to find here?" I collapsed into my armchair. The headache was getting worse. It didn't help that I was exhausted. "That warranted breaking in? And how did you get on my balcony in the first place?"

"From the roof," Rhoda replied. She exchanged a look with Colin I didn't like. "We've been following the Wolf—"

"The Wolf?" I interrupted. "Who is the Wolf?"

Colin whistled. "Levi was the Wolf! Of course! That makes sense!" He started pacing. "How long have you been following him?"

"We got a tip he was here in New Orleans." Rhoda gave him another strange look. "We'd followed him to Ohio a few months ago, but we lost him. So, we followed up on the tip and came here a few days ago, and spotted him on the street." She shrugged. "We followed him and found he was living in this building. We've kept an eye on him ever since."

"Did you kill him?" I blurted out.

They all three looked at me. Rhoda pursed her lips and said in a rather chilly tone, "Of course we did not. We had no reason to kill him. He was worth more to us alive than dead."

"But if you were following him, then you must know who killed him."

Rhoda shook her head. "No, we do not."

Colin's eyes narrowed and he gave me a look I think meant *let me do the questioning here.*

Irritated, I bit my lip and glared back at him. He ignored me, and said, "Why don't you start at the beginning? Why were you on his trail to begin with?"

Lindy winked at me and plopped down on the couch next to Rhoda, leaning into her. Rhoda put an arm around her shoulders and kissed her on the cheek. "What are you doing here, Abram?" Lindy ran her fingers through her luxuriant hair, changing the subject. "No one told us you were here. Are you working the same case as we are?"

"Hold on just a minute," I said, struggling to control the irritation and anger I could feel rising. "Just who exactly are you two, anyway?"

My voice was shaking. *Stay calm, Scotty.* "You can't just break in here, point a gun at us and—"

Colin threw his head back and laughed.

I wanted to slug him.

He wiped at his eyes. "Scotty, these are two of the best agents the Mossad has to offer. Rhoda Sapirstein and I went through Mossad training together," Rhoda inclined her head to me, "and Lindy Zielinsky—she was in my first class when I worked as a trainer for the Mossad."

"He introduced us to each other," Lindy kissed Rhoda's cheek again, "for which I will be forever grateful."

"In the business they're known as the Ninja Lesbians—"

"Don't listen to him, Scotty." Rhoda interrupted him. "He is the only one who calls us that." She gave me a wicked grin that chilled me a little bit. "He's a horrible tease—but you probably already know that."

I bit my lower lip and started counting to ten in my head. Colin saw the look on my face and winked at me. Surprisingly enough, that didn't make me any happier. "Why are the two of you here in New Orleans?" he said hastily. "Why were you on the trail of the Wolf?"

"Who the hell is the Wolf!" I exploded. "I want some answers!" I gestured to my shattered French doors. "You break in here, point guns at us—"

"Calm down, Scotty," Colin said in a patronizing tone that made me want to throw something at him. I closed my eyes and focused on my breathing. "No one knows his real name, or where he's from—where he was from. He's a master thief. Sometimes he works for someone else, sometimes he works on his own." He frowned. "You're certain he was the Wolf?"

"Reliable intelligence," Lindy replied, placing her right leg over Rhoda's. "We got the word that the Wolf had been hired to find Kali's Eye. And given what's going on in Pleshiwar right now—well, it is not in our national interests for Kali's Eye to fall into the wrong hands. We couldn't find out who he was working for—whether it was an individual who just wanted to possess the Eye, or if it was one of our enemies." She shrugged. "Our orders were to follow him and take the Eye from him if he found it." She smiled at me. "Such a small world—who knew he'd been living upstairs from Scotty?" I wasn't sure how I felt about being referred to as a thing, but just bit my lip and didn't say anything. "Had we known you were on the same trail, Abram, we certainly would have made contact. Better to work together, right? Since we have the same objective."

Colin's face was expressionless, and I raised an eyebrow. *They're assuming Colin has the same final objective as they do.*

I may not be a highly skilled agent trained by the Mossad, but even I could see that assumption could prove to be a costly mistake. "And what," I said, keeping my voice as calm as I could, keeping my eyes on Colin, "is that objective?"

"That control of the Pleshiwarian uranium is in the right hands, of course." Rhoda crossed her legs casually. "That is why you are here, right?" She winked at me. "Why else would there be all this international interest in the stolen eye of an idol from a remote little mountain country nobody has heard of?" She leaned forward. "Obviously, who has control of that uranium is of vital interest to our country, Abram. It cannot be allowed to fall into the hands of our enemies."

"Obviously," he replied. "Why else would Tel Aviv risk having agents operating within the United States?" He sat down on the arm of my chair. "Does Tel Aviv care who finds the sapphire, as long as it winds up in the correct hands afterward?"

"Politics." Lindy waved her hand. "They bore me. Scotty, would you mind if I made some coffee?" She punctuated it with a yawn. "I'm seriously under-caffeinated."

"Scotty can make it," Colin said, and as I opened my mouth to protest he pinched me—hard. I glared at him, and his only response was to move his eyes in the direction of the kitchen. Okay, he wanted me out of the room.

He better not have bruised my leg, I thought angrily.

Rubbing my leg, I stood up and walked into the kitchen. Lindy followed me and hopped up on my kitchen counter as I filled the pot with water from the tap. "Thank you." She smiled at me, yawning again. "I should probably break my caffeine addiction, but I haven't slept in almost twenty-four hours."

"I know the feeling," I replied sourly, scooping coffee into a filter. I poured the water in and switched it on.

"We're truly sorry about the doors," Lindy said, petting my shoulder. "But we knew the Wolf was killed and tossed down onto your balcony. We assumed there must be some kind of link between you and the Wolf—" She shrugged. "And the element of surprise always works."

"Give me a break," I snapped as I got two mugs down. "If you were watching, you had to see Colin come in with me. You knew he was here all along." I smiled at her. "And I don't believe for a minute you believe he's on the same side as you."

She inhaled sharply, and her eyes narrowed a bit. A smile began to spread across her face. "He was right, you are sharp." She punched me lightly in the shoulder. "And good looking. I can see why he's so crazy about you."

I ignored that and smiled back at her. "So, tell me, who killed the Wolf? Was it you two?"

She shook her head. "No, it wasn't us. We didn't see it happen. But we did see whoever it was dump the body." She closed her eyes and inhaled the smell of the brewing coffee. She reached over and filled her mug. "Even with our binoculars—we were on a roof nearby—all we saw was someone climb up onto your roof. They lugged something over to the edge and tossed it over." She took a gulp of the coffee and sighed with bliss. "This is good. Anyway, we could see it was the Wolf's body. Whoever was up there was a man, we could tell that much, but he was wearing a stocking cap over his face, and all black." She shrugged. "It may have been Abram, for all we know. Whoever it was climbed back down from the roof behind your building."

I inhaled sharply. *Then if it wasn't Colin, he had to have seen who it was. He was down in the courtyard—*

I cut off that thought before it went any further. There was a half-smile on her face as she took another drink.

I was being played.

"Divide and conquer" was the oldest trick in the book—so was splitting off the weakest member of the herd. I bristled a little inwardly. Obviously, I wasn't a trained agent like Colin, but I wasn't exactly a fool. As I watched the coffee streaming down into the pot, I realized two things—they'd been watching us so they'd known Colin was here, and their dramatic entrance was carefully designed to throw us both off balance. Or maybe just *me*—and she was trying to drive a wedge between Colin and me.

Well, two can play at that game, I thought, pouring myself a cup of coffee and allowing a confused look to appear on my face. *Let's see what you're up to, Agent Zielinsky—I bet I can get some information out of you.*

After all, nobody can play dumb better than I can. I opened my eyes a little wider and turned to face her. "You aren't serious, are you?" I allowed a little horror and uncertainty to creep into my voice. "You don't think..."

She shrugged. "It's possible, after all. He works for Blackledge now, and you know they're capable of anything." She shivered. "The stories I've heard"—her eyes glinted—"make things we do look like child's play. But at least we work for the security of our country, and our people. They work for whoever pays them the most."

"I worked for them, too."

She dismissed that with a wave of her hand. "You were just part of their cover. You never really worked for them, Scotty." She hopped off the counter and refilled her coffee cup. "You're not capable of what they require."

"I don't know what you mean." Now I wasn't playing dumb—I really didn't know what she was talking about.

"You and the other one—Frank, right—never did any research on who you were working for?" She patted the side of my face. "Not that there would be anything to find. They are much too good for that—it is necessary for their success for them to operate completely under the radar. If people knew—" She made a face. "I wish Abram would stop working for them and come back to us. He was the best, you know, which is why none of us can understand why he works for such awful people now." She clinked her coffee mug against mine. "Have you heard of Blackwater?"

"Who hasn't?" Blackwater was a private company of mercenaries for hire, and had worked for the U.S. government in Iraq. My mother had raged against Blackwater as more of their atrocities and criminal conduct had become public knowledge over the last few years.

She leaned in close and whispered, "Blackledge makes Blackwater look like amateurs. I love Abram like a brother—but I wish he didn't work for those awful people." She turned and walked out of the kitchen.

I gulped down the rest of my coffee and refilled it. I leaned against the counter and closed my eyes.

She's playing you, just like you thought. She's trying to drive a wedge between you and Colin—Abram, whatever the hell his name is. The Ninja Lesbians are working their own angle here, and whatever it is, the endgame is different than the one he's playing for. And you already don't trust him. Why should you believe anything she says? You don't know her, either. And the Mossad—remember what Colin told you about why he left the Mossad? He had to kill a young boy who was a suspected terrorist. But is that true?

And what she said made a certain kind of sense.

Frank and I had simply taken his word all those years ago that the Blackledge Agency—which was how he'd always referred to it—was just an international investigation company, with offices all over the globe. I'd certainly never thought to do any research, even after the Mardi Gras case. Angela Blackledge had denied all knowledge of Colin and us.

How could we have been so stupid? And after Colin was gone— we hadn't bothered to do any more checking. I hadn't wanted to know any more than I did.

Maybe Lindy was right. My mind just didn't work that way.

It is necessary for their success for them to operate completely under the radar.

Angela had lied back then, to protect their agent. She'd already admitted as much on the phone.

You're assuming that was actually Angela Blackledge you spoke to this morning—it could have been anyone, really—someone working with or for Colin, someone he put up to it. No, that doesn't make any sense. Angela Blackledge ran Blackledge, that's been verified. And if Colin is working for her…it makes sense.

My head was starting to hurt again.

I plastered a smile on my face and walked back into the living room in time to hear Rhoda say, "Okay, then. We will touch base with you later this evening here—and compare notes." She stood up and held out her hand to Colin. "It's a pleasure to be working with you again."

Hugs were exchanged, and the two of them left by my front door this time. I escorted them down the stairs and out the gate, and just as I was about to shut it, Lindy smiled at me and whispered, "Remember what we talked about."

I nodded, gave her a brittle smile, and shut the gate behind her.

I climbed the steps. Colin was pacing in my living room. I stood and watched him for a moment, then folded my arms and leaned against the hallway wall. "Okay, so now we're working with them?"

Colin looked at me. His face was grim. "No, we aren't." He sat down on the couch, and patted the cushion next to him. "Sit down, we need to talk."

I ignored him and sat down in the armchair. "Wasn't that what was decided?"

"Scotty, I don't trust Rhoda and Lindy as far as I can throw them." He shook his head. "You forget, babe, I *trained* them. They are very good at what they do." He smiled at me. "No doubt when you were in the kitchen with Lindy, she told you some things that made you wonder if you could trust me."

I kept my face impassive. "She suggested you might have killed Levi—I mean, the Wolf." I gave a nonchalant shrug. "It wasn't like I hadn't wondered about it myself."

His eyes narrowed for a moment. Finally, after a few moments he said, "They killed him," he mused aloud. "But why? He wasn't close to finding Kali's Eye, and supposedly he was their only lead. And I don't believe for a minute they didn't know you were my Scotty. As soon as they had an address, they would have found out everything about the building—who owns it, who else lives in it. I trained them, remember, and that's what I would have done—what any agent worth his pay would have done." He pulled out his cell phone and punched in some numbers. "Excuse me for a moment." He got up and opened the shutters, stepping out onto the balcony.

I got up and walked over to my computer. I logged into the Internet and pulled up a search engine. I typed *Blackledge Mercenary* into the search box, and clicked Enter. A number of links popped up. I leaned forward. The first one was an article from *The Times* of London. The headline read: GOVERNMENT PAID MERCENARIES, MP CHARGES.

I clicked, and started reading.

In 1968, mercenaries paid by the British government stole a valuable religious symbol of a small country called Pleshiwar, charges Charles Driscoll, MP.

"A full investigation is called for," Driscoll went on to say in a press conference. "How long has our government

been employing mercenaries to conduct covert operations in violation of international law?"

Driscoll alleges that the UK government hired an international mercenary company called Blackledge to steal Kali's Eye, a sapphire of deep religious significance, in the small country of Pleshiwar in 1968. The theft resulted in the collapse of a theocratic government that had ruled the country for centuries. Driscoll also charges that operatives in the country were involved in the revolution that followed. The end result was the installation of a government friendly to the Western powers.

"I do not know, as of yet, why this was necessary," Driscoll went on to say. *"The country has no apparent strategic value, in either its location or in resources. But I demand a full investigation be launched into this matter— and into this company, known only as Blackledge..."*

The article didn't really say anything else of significance.

But there it was, in black and white.

I smiled to myself. MP Driscoll would be very interested to know there was uranium in Pleshiwar.

It made sense. Doc and his buddies had been hired by Blackledge to steal Kali's Eye—to trigger the overthrow of the priests who'd ruled the country for centuries.

It explained the financial windfall Gretsch and Doc had enjoyed after their tour of duty was up. It also explained the question of why they'd done it. They'd been paid to do it. It also explained Colin's presence in New Orleans. Former employees of Blackledge were being murdered. They'd probably been paid to steal it, hide it away, and now the trail had finally led back to them.

I heard the shutters close, so I minimized the program and spun around in my desk chair. I smiled.

"What are you doing?" Colin slid his phone back into his pocket.

"Checking e-mails." I put the computer to sleep and stood up. My heart was beating quickly, and I hoped my face didn't give me away. "What do we do now? Who did you call?"

"Just letting Angela know about this new complication." He yawned.

"I have a question for you." I folded my arms.

"Shoot," he replied.

"You trained them for the Mossad?"

"No, I trained Lindy." He smiled. "Rhoda and I went through training together."

"Why didn't you tell me the truth about Blackledge?"

His eyes narrowed. "What exactly did Lindy say to you in the kitchen?"

"Don't lie to me, Colin," I replied. "It doesn't matter what she said to me. I can use a computer—anyone can." I gestured back at my computer.

He sighed and sat back down on the couch. "You weren't checking your e-mails, were you?"

"No." I sat down next to him. "Look, you're back. For whatever reason, you're here. All I want you to do is tell me the truth."

He looked down, and started drumming his fingers on his knee. "I tell you what I am allowed to tell you—and sometimes, and I know you don't want to hear this, but sometimes I didn't tell you things because you were better off not knowing them."

"I get it." I took a deep breath. "I really do, Colin. But I just read an article about Blackledge being paid by the British government to steal the Eye of Kali, which triggered a revolution that wound up overthrowing the Pleshiwarian government. I'm not going to get into the morality of self-determination, or whether or not the old government was a bad thing or not. But is that true? Were Doc and the others working for Blackledge when they stole the Eye?"

He leaned back and closed his eyes for a moment. "I honestly don't know, Scotty. I don't know. But if I had to hazard a guess, I would say it's highly likely." He shrugged. "I had access to a lot of information about Doc before I got here—information that could have easily been gathered, but it also seemed pretty handy." He sighed. "I honestly can't tell you one way or the other. I'm sorry. That's the best I can do."

I hadn't expected that much, to be honest. I smiled at him. "Thanks, Colin, I appreciate that."

He yawned again, and stretched a bit. "Man, I am tired. You mind if I take a little catnap?"

I feigned a yawn myself. "Not a bad idea." He got up and started to walk down the hallway. "Not so fast, mister. You can sleep on the couch."

He looked hurt. "I thought—"

"You thought wrong." I grabbed a blanket and a spare pillow out of the hall closet and tossed them to him. "Make yourself comfortable."

"Scotty—"

I ignored him and walked down the hallway, slamming my bedroom door for effect.

I was tired, but I wasn't going to be able to fall asleep.

I got my laptop out of the closet and turned it on. It was all starting to make sense to me now.

Man, I wished Frank were here. He'd know what to do.

But for now, I was going to do some more research on Blackledge and Pleshiwar. And wait till Mom and Dad found out Colin was working for a company worse than Blackwater—that overthrew governments and who knew what else.

I sat down on the bed and leaned back against my pillows, propping the laptop on the bed next to me. I yawned again as I waited for it to boot up. As soon as the little icon popped up showing I was connected to the wireless, I opened the search engine again. This time, I just typed in *Blackledge*.

But just as the list of links started to come up, I saw the grayness coming around the edges of my vision.

I just managed to put my head back against the pillow as everything faded to black.

CHAPTER ELEVEN
ACE OF WANDS
A creative beginning

I was drifting downward through a fine mist, cushioned as if on a cloud. As always, there was no sense of time or place. There was just awareness, a sense that I was in some nether-place, not a part of one dimension or another but somewhere in between. But this time felt different from the others.

The air was cold, and I felt goose bumps rise on my arms as I floated. From what I could remember of the previous times, it was temperate and comfortable. I also felt uneasy rather than relaxed. I didn't have a sense of peace, the way I usually did when I went into a trance like this, when the Goddess called me to Her side. Instead, I sensed turmoil, violence, and anger. It disturbed me, and made me nervous and tense. Thunder roared deafeningly close, and the mist lit up with flashes of lightning that blinded me. The smell of burnt ozone filled my nostrils as I continued my descent. The farther down I went through the mist, the greater the feeling of unease. Soon, I was terrified to the core of my soul.

It didn't make sense to me. The Goddess had never inspired fear. It went against everything I believed.

When my feet touched down, the sense of terror was so strong that I started trembling. The mist swirled and cleared away as if it had never been there. I was standing on the edge of a sheer cliff that dropped away behind me. My stomach lurched—heights have always terrified me. I quickly backed away from the edge, but not before I caught a glimpse of a river and a thick jungle on its opposite bank thousands of feet below me. I turned my back on the drop, closing my eyes and praying. When I had calmed a little, I opened my eyes and realized that the cliff was actually a wide ledge on the side of the mountain. About *a hundred feet away from me the mountain began to rise again up into the clouds, its peak hidden. The ledge itself was smooth, as though the stone had been worn down over the years by the footsteps of thousands of feet over centuries. Where the mountain began to rise again I saw a gazebo-like structure with three stone steps leading up to its platform. Stone columns supported the onion-shaped dome, which looked like it was made of gold. An unearthly light glowed beneath the dome, and I felt terror growing inside me. I knew I was supposed to walk up those steps into the glowing light, but I didn't want to.*

This was a manifestation of the Goddess I had never seen before, and one I wasn't so sure I wanted to experience.

The cold wind began to pick up, and heavy drops of rain began to fall. I heard a low rumbling sound from beneath me, as though the ground itself was afraid.

"COME BEFORE ME!" a female voice roared from inside the structure.

I didn't move. My terror was so strong my body couldn't move. I was frozen in place. I did not want to face Her.

The rumbling sound from beneath me grew louder, and the ground itself began to tremble beneath my feet. I heard a cracking sound from behind me, and I turned in time to see the ledge begin to crack at the edge. My eyes widened as a large piece of the ledge crumbled and fell away. Another crack began to split and started to spread toward me. I began to back away from it as it approached where I was standing. Finally, I turned and began to run toward the stone steps. I finally reached them, and jumped up onto the bottom step. The wind howled as it whipped so strongly around me that I almost lost my balance. I rubbed my arms with hands, trying to warm them. The chill was penetrating, piercing through my body.

I could feel it in my very soul.

"COME BEFORE ME!" the voice roared again, and reluctantly I climbed up onto the next step. The fissure that had opened began to close as I watched, and I turned my eyes back to the glowing light under the golden dome. The rain began falling harder, striking my skin with such force that it stung. I climbed up to the final step and into the glowing light.

As soon as I did, it faded away until all that was left was a blue glow in the shape of an eye on the opposite end of the platform.

I closed my eyes and prayed.

My prayer was answered with a laugh.

It was a horrifying sound, a laugh so bloodthirsty and evil that I began to fear for my very soul.

I fell to my knees.

"That's right, grovel before Kali," a voice whispered into my ear.

Kali! The Great Mother of the Hindu religion, the Great Goddess who had created the earth and all living things! She was a goddess of love, of creation, but she also had another face. She was also Kali the Destroyer, who killed gleefully and happily, because creation can only come from destruction. Her dual nature was both wonderful and terrifying. One must never anger Her.

"Come before me," the voice purred softly, echoing around me in the shadows. "Rise and walk."

Somehow I managed to get to my feet and forced myself to walk toward the glowing blue eye. As I drew nearer the torches, the darkness seemed to fade. The glowing eye grew brighter, casting off a powerful light that I could not take my own eyes away from. It drew me nearer, and as I got closer I saw the form of a woman, seated cross-legged on a stone platform. She had four arms, and her large breasts were bare. Long thick tangled black hair hung around her head. She wore a large gold crown sparking with small diamonds. A necklace of skulls hung around her neck, large gold hoops adorned her ears. One of her eyes was closed, the other glowed blue. In one of her four hands she held a long, ugly sword. Another held a human skull.

I dropped to my knees, but could not avert my eyes. Her countenance was beautiful yet terrifying.

"Yes, kneel in my presence," she said through bright red lips that barely covered teeth filed to sharpness. The glowing eye narrowed. "You are the one?" She threw her head back and roared out laughter. It echoed in the room and inside my brain. It was a sound I knew I would never forget, and would most likely hear in my nightmares for the rest of my life. The glowing blue eye focused on me, and as I watched it, the blue faded and it became a normal eye, the white almost blinding in its purity, the brown center remarkably beautiful. "If you are the one, then you are the one. Are you strong enough in body, mind, and spirit to do my bidding?"

"I...I don't know, Great Mother," I whispered.

Outside, I heard thunder roar again.

"My eye must be returned," she said. "This sacrilege can no longer be permitted to continue." The closed eye opened, and I bit my lip to keep from screaming. It was an empty socket, and blood streamed from it. It shut again.

"I—"

"SILENCE!" She roared again, and I winced, clapping my hands over my ears in pain. "I did not give you permission to speak! How dare you, insolent human! I should strike you dead!"

I dropped to my hands and knees, putting my head down in obeisance as my entire body began trembling in terror.

"You quake with fear in my presence, as you should. An eternity ago I danced this world into existence," she went on. "And forty years ago, as you measure time, I was defiled. I have tired of waiting for this sacrilege to be rectified by believers. They have failed me, and they shall be punished. My patience has been exhausted." All four arms waved, reaching heavenward. "Kali will be avenged, make no mistake about it, human. I am the creator and the destroyer. If I am not appeased, I will rain destruction down on this insignificant world." I looked up as she smiled. The sharpened teeth were dripping with blood. "It will bring me great pleasure to hear the screams of the suffering. Let them suffer as I have suffered from this affront to the Goddess! Let the streets run with blood! Let the air reek with the smell of burning flesh! Let the oceans turn to fire, the creatures of the air burn! Only then will my anger be appeased!"

The air crackled with energy. Blue sparks flew from Her fingertips.

And the skull necklace began to move.

My stomach lurched as the skulls gained flesh and lips. Eyes appeared in the once-empty sockets. Streams of blood ran from the severed necks. And as I watched, I began to recognize the faces.

Mom. Dad. Colin. Frank. Millie. Velma. Storm and his wife Marguerite. Rain and her husband. David. The head of everyone I'd ever loved or cared about was hanging around Her neck. Their mouths opened in silent screams, their eyes moving from side to side in agony.

I closed my eyes. I could not bear to look at them. My stomach roiled in terror. My skin was covered in goose pimples, and I began to shake again.

"Please," I whispered. "No, Great Mother." As soon as I said the words I braced myself in terror, waiting for the killing stroke. Yet She did not swing Her terrible sword. She did not roar Her anger again at my insolence.

I opened my eyes.

The streaming blood pooled at Her feet and began flowing toward me in a single stream.

"I must be avenged," She said again, and the eye began to glow blue again.

The river of blood reached my hands. It was warm and sticky. It began flowing heavier, and up my arms.

"Look into my eye," She purred again, "and see what I am capable of."

Against my will, my eyes were drawn to the intense blue glow. As I looked, all I could see was blue—

—and then I saw the mushroom clouds expanding over cities I recognized, one after another. London. Paris. New York. Chicago. Sydney. Rio de Janeiro.

I heard the screams of the dying, of the terrified.

Blood, everywhere death and destruction, all living things being consumed in that horrible atomic fire.

I started screaming, and over it all, I could still hear her maniacal laughter…

I sat up in my bed with a start, shivering.

I was cold, so damned cold. I pulled my blankets around me. I'd never had such a horrifying vision before in my life. The Goddess had always come to me with love, even when She had a warning for me. I had always known that there were many faces, many incarnations of the Great Mother, but this? There had never been anything like it before. I was terrified. I could not get the image of the necklace of dripping and dripping heads around Her neck out of my mind.

Please, Great Mother, please do not do this.

But She had been insulted, defiled, and She was angry. Kali would not be denied.

And with control of a source of uranium at stake, it would be so easy for Kali to make good on Her threats. It would be all too simple. There were so many men in this world that would relish obtaining the power of the uranium, unleashing its forces of death and destruction on the world without a care for the outcome. There were so many who would welcome the purifying fire, see themselves as holy martyrs cleansing the world by unleashing the power that would lead to its end.

Time, as we measure it, means nothing to the universal powers. It might not happen tomorrow, but Kali was angry, and She did not make empty or idle threats.

She was the Creator, but She was also the Destroyer.

Thunder roared as I sat there, almost making me jump out of my skin. My laptop screen glowed in the darkness, next to me on the bed. I'd forgotten it was there, but it no longer mattered. It no longer mattered who had killed any of the people who had died thus far because of Kali's Eye. All that mattered was finding that damned sapphire and returning it.

Kali must be appeased, or Her vengeance would be terrible to behold.

Rain began to fall, hard and heavy. I could hear the wind whipping and howling around the house. I tried to calm my heart rate, tried to get my terror under control. *Stay calm, Scotty,* I told myself over and over again. *You must stay calm.*

I swallowed. The fate of the world might very well rest in my hands.

Me. Scotty Bradley, who used to shake his ass on bars for dollar bills to pay his rent.

The universe certainly had a strange sense of humor.

It was not for me to question Kali. It was not for me to understand Her reasons, or why She had chosen me. It was now up to me to find the damned sapphire. And to do it, I had to be calm. I had to be rational. I had to solve Doc's stupid riddle, and to do so, I had to have a clear head and focus.

I took a deep breath, cleared my mind, and said a quick prayer for strength.

I pushed the blankets off, and started to get out of my bed when I heard something just outside my window. I froze as my heart rate went back up, and listened closely.

Someone was coming up the stairs.

It might just be Millie, I tried to reassure myself, but in my gut I knew it wasn't her. I'd heard Millie climb those stairs a million times, and unless she'd gained some weight, it wasn't her. I kept listening, and cursed to myself when I remembered my gun was locked safely in my desk drawer. There wasn't enough time to get it before whoever it was reached my door. *You might not need it,* I reassured myself, and besides, Colin was sleeping on the couch in the living room—and surely he had his gun within reach.

But the storm was loud. Colin most likely couldn't hear someone coming up the back stairs in the living room—and he was sleeping.

I slipped out of bed and crept noiselessly to my closet. I reached inside and grabbed my baseball bat.

I had just put my hands on it when I heard my front door open.

Didn't I lock it? I swore at myself.

Thunder roared again as I heard someone moving in the hallway.

I crept over to my bedroom door and listened as the intruder walked past my door. I turned the knob slowly and let the door ease open. I stepped into the hallway quickly, raising the bat as I—

"Frank?"

He turned around with a huge smile on his face. "Surprise!" He dropped the suitcase in his right hand and took a step toward me. He stopped, and the big smile faded into a frown. "What are you doing with the baseball bat?"

I sagged against the wall in relief. The bat slid out of my hands and hit the floor with a loud crash. I launched myself at him, throwing my arms around him, and in spite of myself, I started laughing and crying at the same time. He hugged me back, stroking my back. His strong arms felt so good around me, and the warmth from his body seemed to chase the chill from my own.

"What's wrong, baby?" he whispered, kissing my forehead and squeezing me tighter. "Shh, it's okay, I'm here. What's going on?"

"Oh, Frank—I don't even know where to start." I let go and smiled at him, wiping at my eyes. "What are you doing here?"

He grinned down at me. "A pipe burst in the training room. It's going to be about two weeks before we can get back to work again, so I thought I'd surprise you and come home." His forehead wrinkled. "Now, tell me. What's going on?"

"Where do I even start?" I closed my eyes and rested my head against his strong chest. I bit my lip. *Oh dear, how am I going to explain*

Colin being here before he goes completely insane? Frank had a temper. He could keep it under control most of the time—that FBI training—but when he lost it, it was something to see. And he was sure as hell going to lose his temper the minute he saw Colin sleeping on the couch. "Um, I have a lot to tell you. Promise me you won't get mad or do anything crazy until I tell you everything."

His blue eyes narrowed. "Scotty—" he said. He took a deep breath, and I could tell he was counting to ten.

I took a deep breath, and said, "Colin's here."

His eyes narrowed, and he tilted his head to one side. "Oh, really? Where?"

I grabbed his hand and pulled him down the hallway. "Please, please don't lose your temper. Stay calm, okay?" I said, reaching over and flicking on the light switch. The chandelier filled the room with light—

—and it was empty.

"What the hell?" I said, turning in every direction just to make sure. He was gone. The kitchen was empty. I left Frank standing there and opened the door to the spare bedroom. It, too, was empty. *Now, what is—* Realization dawned on me.

Shit, shit, shit! I thought, dashing over to my desk. I pulled open the center drawer.

I sighed in relief. The riddle was still there.

"Now, where the hell did he go?" I scratched my head. His habit of disappearing was really quite annoying. I turned back to Frank. "He was here."

"I believe you. Somehow I always knew he was going to turn up again." Frank folded his arms and shook his head. "Okay, I'm listening." He was wearing a black sweater over a pair of jeans. Frank had always been in amazing shape, but pro wrestling training certainly agreed with him. His muscles were thicker, and his waist had narrowed a bit. The sweater was straining at the shoulder seams, and it looked like his upper arms were going to rip through the wool at any moment. He was also a lot darker—he'd told me he'd been using a tanning bed every day since he'd left.

He looked incredible. After all this was over, we were going to have some *fun.*

I put my lusty thoughts aside. "You better sit down. You want some coffee or something?"

"I don't need anything, thanks." He walked into the living room and sat down on the couch. "I'm fine. Come on, just tell me everything and get it over with." He crossed his legs. He patted the sofa next to him, and gave me a wink. "Come on, Scotty, sit down and tell Hot Daddy everything."

He's certainly taking this better than I thought he would, I thought, taking a deep breath and sitting down next to him on the couch. "Well— it all started yesterday"—*Goddess, was it just yesterday?*—"when I was on my way to the Gay Easter Parade…"

His facial expression didn't change at all as I went over everything that happened since I left the house yesterday in that ridiculous bunny costume. As I listened to what I was saying, the whole thing sounded preposterous. His jaw was clenched the entire time, and a muscle twitched just below the scar on his cheek—but other than that, he didn't react at all. His lack of reaction made me nervous and I started talking faster and faster. "And then you came in—and he's not here," I concluded.

He frowned and didn't say anything for a few moments. He bounced his right fist on his leg, and said, "So, your visions have come back?"

What? That was it? I stared at him. I'd been expecting an explosion, and this unnatural calm was a bit unnerving. "Um, yeah. I've had two for sure, and that maybe one yesterday during the parade." I shuddered. "The one I just had—Frank, I can't even begin to tell you how awful it was." I closed my eyes and wrapped my arms around myself. "I've never had one like that before."

He grabbed my face with both hands, and tilted my head back. "And this is where that guy stabbed you?" His voice was calm and soothing. "Thank God that was all he did." He kissed my throat just above the scab. "Good thing I came home." He then kissed me on the lips. "I've really missed you."

"You have no idea how many times I've wished you were here." I snuggled up against him. Oh, he felt so damned good. "And Colin? You're okay with him being in town? You're not going to try to kill him or something, are you?"

He looked deep into my eyes, and shook his head. "What good would that do?" He shrugged. "I decided—I thought we *both* decided—a long time ago that no matter what, we weren't going to let him or what he does change us in any way, or affect who we are as people." He shrugged. "Would I prefer he never came back? Sure. I'd prefer not to see him again, or ever speak to him. But it sounds to me like"—he hesitated for a moment—"he might need our help this time, and if all this stuff about the uranium…" He slid his arm around my shoulders and I leaned down into him. "Man, I thought I was done with this kind of shit when I retired from the FBI." He kissed the top of my head. "And that's really what's important here, isn't it? Finding that Eye sapphire and making sure terrorists don't get a hold of that stuff?" He squeezed me again, rubbing my shoulder as he did so. "We can put our personal feelings aside until we have this whole thing wrapped up."

"Oh, I don't know that he needs our help all that much," I said. "I know he's not telling me everything. And I'm not positive he didn't kill Levi, or the Wolf, or whoever he was." I closed my eyes and listened to his heartbeat. It was soothing. Man, I'd missed him.

"Why don't you get the riddle and we can try to solve it?" He stroked the top of my head.

"All right." I got up and retrieved it from the desk drawer, sitting back down on the couch with my legs across his lap. "Okay, the first line is *From Pleshiwar to the parish of the maid…* It's pretty safe to assume that refers to the Eye—it came from Pleshiwar to New Orleans." I frowned as I looked at the next line. "Okay, *Who saved a city and was burned down to ash*—I mean, obviously that's Joan of Arc—the Maid of Orleans. But we already know the Eye is here, so why bring her up again?"

"It's a second clue, maybe." Frank started stroking my shoulder. "Obviously, the riddle is directions to where Doc hid the eye—and he intended for you to be able to figure it out. So, my guess would be it's intentional, not a repetition—maybe the St. Joan statue on Decatur Street is the starting place."

"That makes sense," I said. "So, if the statue is the starting place…" I thought for a minute. "*To the park where so many still ply their trade*—that's got to be Jackson Square." I smiled to myself. The statue of Joan of Arc was on Decatur Street where it split. Right up the street from the statue of St. Joan was Jackson Square. The pedestrian mall on the other three sides of the square was always full of artists, mimes, and fortunetellers.

The spires of the saint.

St. Louis Cathedral, of course. I grinned. *Always asking for cash.* That was Doc, all right. About ten years earlier, the cathedral had needed a facelift. The Archdiocese had gone on a fund-raising tear and appealed to the citizenry of New Orleans for help. The basis of the appeal was that the cathedral was perhaps the most famous landmark of the city, and it really belonged to the whole city. Ergo, the city had a responsibility to help keep it up.

Doc had been *furious.*

"The goddamned cathedral *does not* belong to the city," he'd raged one night over bourbon and cigars at my parents'. "It's a working Catholic church, and why is it the responsibility of the city and the people who live here to pay for the upkeep on a goddamned Catholic church? Why don't they just ask the pope to sell a fucking painting? I am sure the Vatican could spare one of its treasures to keep up the Cathedral. But why should the goddamned church pay for it when they can beg the people to do it for them? They should be *ashamed* of themselves. It's all they do—ask for money. Maybe someday they'll get a pope who actually reads the Bible and will drive the money changers out of the temple."

I smiled. Whatever else he was, Doc had certainly had some opinions.

"Okay," I said out loud. "You start at the statue of St. Joan, move up Decatur to Jackson Square, and then behind the cathedral is a statue of Jesus—*the fisher of souls*—and his arms are spread wide. So *Follow his left hand to the canopy of trees."*

The canopy of trees—what did that mean?

I concentrated harder.

"Uptown." I opened my eyes and jumped off the sofa. In my desk drawer, I had a map of the city.

"Uptown?" Frank got off the couch and watched me dig through my drawer. He grinned. "Of course, the canopy of trees!"

St. Charles Avenue was lined on either side with massive live oaks.

Their huge branches reached over the street creating a canopy of trees. And the park behind the cathedral with the statue was on Royal Street, which became St. Charles Avenue when you crossed Canal Street on the way uptown.

I unfolded the map, but looked down at it and frowned as I looked at it. All the streets in New Orleans followed the river—and there was a bend in it just past the Quarter. All the streets made about a forty-five degree turn on the other side of Canal Street. I traced a straight line from behind the cathedral uptown. "Prytania Street," I said out loud. Prytania Street started on the other side of I-90 and ran uptown, ending near Audubon Park. It started in the lower Garden District, and the cross streets that ran toward the river were named after the Muses: Polymnia, Terpsichore, Euterpe, Clio, Urania...I followed Prytania Street with my finger as it crossed each street named after a Muse...

The Muses. There was a line in the riddle about the Muses.

I grinned and looked at the riddle again.

"The Muses line up, to sing with the breeze," I said, sitting down in the chair. Frank came up behind me and started massaging my shoulders, digging his strong fingers deep into the tight muscle tissue. It felt amazing.

Like St. Charles, Prytania was also lined with live oaks on either side. I *always* drove up Prytania when I was on my way uptown—there wasn't as much traffic as there was on Magazine Street or St. Charles, because both of these streets ran to Canal Street. Magazine became Decatur when it crossed into the Quarter, St. Charles becoming Royal.

And almost its entire length Prytania had a canopy of trees.

"The riddle wants us to go to the lower Garden District," I said out loud.

"And then what?" Frank asked.

"I guess we'll have to go and see." I looked at the riddle again. "I have no idea what he means by *the blonds from the sea.*"

There was a blast of nearby lightning and thunder shook the entire building. The lights went out.

"Great." I swore under my breath as I headed for the kitchen in the dark. I grabbed some candles from my storage cabinet and lit them. Lightning again lit up the entire apartment as I carried them back into the living room. I set them down on the coffee table.

Frank held the riddle close to one of the candles. He squinted at it, and shook his head. "You know, Doc always was a bit of an asshole."

"That's what Mom said," I replied.

"Do you think this riddle really leads to where he hid the Eye?" Frank put the riddle back down on the coffee table. He sighed. "This whole thing seems a bit much to take—uranium, international espionage…and our very own Colin working for an international mercenary business." He shrugged and grinned at me. "But I guess it's no crazier than some of the other adventures we've had."

"Well, Doc wanted me to find it—and Kali certainly made Her wishes pretty damned clear to me," I replied. "And the sad thing is we don't really know who all the players are in this. We don't know who killed Marty Gretsch or Doc—or Levi, for that matter—and we don't even know who to turn the thing over to if we do find it." I stood up. She would not be ignored. "Come on, let's go find the stupid thing." It sucked that it was raining, but maybe the rain would slow down the other players in this crazy game.

Frank nodded. "I don't want to just sit around here in the dark." He hugged me again. "Come on, babe, let's go find a sacred sapphire."

Chapter Twelve
NINE OF WANDS
Eventual victory, but more fighting must be done

We grabbed our raincoats and umbrellas. We each slipped our guns into inside pockets of our coats—better safe than sorry—and headed out into the downpour.

New Orleans has always been at the mercy of the weather, and I don't mean just hurricanes. As so many pointed out after the levees failed and ninety percent of the city filled with water, much of the city is either at sea level or below. When a lot of rain comes down in a short period of time, the streets and gutters fill with water. This was one of those rainstorms. As I went out the back door, the rain pouring off the roof made it look like the back stairs were inside a waterfall. The cold wind had picked up and it howled as it roared around the building. I thought about suggesting we wait for the storm to pass—but decided against it.

As awful as the weather was, I figured it would protect us—who'd want to try to follow us around in such a downpour?

And it wasn't a bad thing to get a jump on everyone else.

We kept Frank's car in a parking lot a few blocks away, in the Faubourg Marigny. The gutters were so full of water the sidewalk's edge was starting to submerge. I flipped up the collar of my raincoat. The balconies were leaking, and the wind was blowing the roaring water from the roofs on us. Before we even got to the corner, the part of my jeans exposed below the bottom of my coat was soaked through. My sneakers and socks were also sopping wet. The light at Esplanade was red, and the passing cars were driving slowly, their windshield wipers desperately trying to keep up with the downpour. We stood back a little from the corner to avoid the walls of water thrown up by tires. Finally the light changed and we dashed across the street. Just past the fire station, Decatur made a sharp ninety-degree turn to follow the bend in the river. The parking lot was on the next block, across the street from the Lesbian and Gay Community Center. The wind kept trying to rip my umbrella out of my hands, or to flip it inside out. I tucked my head down to try to keep the rain out of my eyes. My hair was sopping, and water was dripping down my back. Decatur was filling with water, and lightning forked through the dark sky. The deafening roar of thunder followed almost immediately. We finally made it to Frank's little classic red MG convertible and climbed in. Frank revved the engine, and he zipped out of the parking spot and headed for the gate. He swiped the parking pass, and the gate rose. He swung out onto Decatur Street.

"Follow Decatur through the Quarter," I directed. The windshield was fogged up. Frank turned the defroster to high, clearing a space at the bottom of the windshield. My teeth were chattering from the cold. Decatur was clogged with cars, all driving about five miles an hour. I hummed with impatience. We reached the statue of Joan of Arc. Just ahead was Jackson Square, and I craned my head to see—and yes, there was a break in the buildings where you could see the spires of the cathedral.

I looked at the riddle again and grinned. Okay, the first few clues were easy—but it was nice to confirm my deductions. "We're on the right track," I said over the roar of the defroster, "but who's *the orphan's friend*?"

Frank shrugged.

We finally made it through the Quarter and stopped at the light at Canal. "Go ahead and cross Canal," I ordered. "Then when you get to Poydras turn right, and then left at the next light—that's Magazine Street."

I sighed as Frank followed my instructions. The little car sped through the rain, and Frank maneuvered around cars driving at a crawl. "The way people drive, you'd think it never rains here," Frank complained as we waited for the turn signal at Magazine and Poydras to turn green.

Magazine Street's gutters were under the water, which was rising almost to the bottom of the parked cars. Traffic was moving at a crawl, and instead of using both lanes, the cars were moving in the center— straddling the white line to avoid the deepening water on either side.

"Turn right on Calliope, and take the first left after that," I said.

Calliope was the feeder road that ran alongside I-90—and was also, come to think of it, one of the Muses. "Magazine in the lower Garden District always floods." And sure enough, when we got caught by the light at Calliope, Magazine Street looked like a river on the other side of the underpass.

The light changed and Frank turned, swinging out into the left lane. We got caught again at the next light, and I looked to my left. "You don't think Prytania is going to flood, do you?" he asked, concern in his voice. He'd gotten caught in one of our flash floods in the car once and it cost almost seven hundred bucks to get it running again.

"Well, I don't think Prytania floods," I replied, trying to remember. I hadn't owned a car since I dropped out of college and moved back to New Orleans, so I never paid much attention to that sort of thing. "I think it's a high street."

Camp Street and Prytania met underneath I-90, merging into one street on the downtown side. The light turned green and he turned. There was a small little park right there, shaped like a piece of pie as the two streets drew nearer to each other. "Stop!" I shouted.

Frank slammed on the brakes and pulled to the side of the road. "What are you doing?" He looked at me as I opened the car door.

I reached behind the seat for the umbrella I'd stashed back there. "I know I'm right," I grinned at him, "but I need to look at the park to make sure."

He sighed and opened his car door once I had the umbrella open and walked around to that side. The park was small and surrounded by an iron fence. At the rear stood a huge live oak, its branches dripping water on the flowers and bushes inside the fence. There was a statue of a matronly looking woman sitting in the park, with her left arm around a little girl who stood at her side looking up at her. There was a historical marker plate mounted on the fence. *Urns in Margaret Place to honor Waldemar S. Nelson, donated by his employees July 8, 2000.*

That wasn't helpful, but there was another one on the other side. I splashed through the water over to it.

It read: *For a gracious lady, fence donated by Waldemar S. Nelson and Company, Incorporated 1994.*

"Damn it," I cursed under my breath. This was no help. I was just about to suggest we just get back in the car when I noticed yet another marker on a stand at the edge of the pie shape where the two streets joined at Calliope. I dashed up the granite walk edged with red bricks, with Frank on my heels.

I gave a fist pump and shouted "Yes!" after I finished reading it.

MARGARET'S PLACE AND WALK

Margaret's Place and Walk honors Irish immigrant Margaret Gaffney Haughery (1813–1882), who devoted her life to orphaned children and the needy. An orphan herself, Margaret lost her husband and baby to illness. Although illiterate, Margaret established a bakery and a dairy and became quite wealthy. Her wealth funded seven orphanages, which she founded with her friend, Sister Regis and the Daughters of Charity. The names of her orphanages are shown in the pavement leading to her statue, sculpted by Alexander Doyle of New York in 1884. The funds for the statue were raised by subscription after Margaret's death. The statue was located within sight of the New Orleans Female Orphan Asylum (demolished 1965) and the Louise Day Nursery, which she helped to found.

"The orphan's friend." Frank grinned.

I was fairly dancing with excitement by now. *"And the Muses lines up to sing with the breeze?"* I pointed up Prytania Street. "They're right up there."

Frank looked and shook his head. "What are you talking about?"

"This neighborhood is the lower Garden District, that's what most people call it," I explained. "But haven't you ever noticed the weird street names whenever you head up St. Charles?"

Realization dawned in Frank's eyes. "The Muses."

The first streets on the uptown side of I-90 were named after the Muses. Clio, Erato, Melpomene, Euterpe, Terpsichore, and Polymnia. "I know we're going the right way, Frank," I said as we walked hurriedly back to the car. My feet and legs from the knees down were soaked, and the wind kept trying to rip the umbrella out of my hands.

He checked for oncoming traffic, and we started up Prytania. I grinned as we passed the streets of the Muses—but once we passed Polymnia I told him to pull over. "I *knew* we were going the right way,"

I said. "*The blonds from the sea*! There they are!" The Norwegian Seamen's Church was a small, nondescript building with the Norwegian and American flags hanging out front. "Pull over."

Frank pulled over into a space on the side of the road. "This is it," I said. The three flags in front of the small building were hanging limply in the pouring rain. "The sapphire must be hidden inside the church."

"You know, for a riddle, this is pretty easy," Frank replied as he waited for a car to drive past. A torrent of water splashed across our windshield. "I mean, think about it, Scotty. Don't you think this is kind of easy?"

"It isn't easy," I replied. I opened my door and shut it again immediately. The water in the gutter was almost to the bottom of the car. There was no way I was getting out on that side—and we couldn't leave the car here for long. I looked out the window.

A huge brick complex about five stories tall took up the entire block—but there was a paved area behind it—maybe for deliveries. "Pull up there—we can leave the car there for a little while."

"I don't want the car to be towed," Frank protested.

"Frank, who is going to call a tow truck in this mess? Besides, tow trucks are going to be busy for a while with swamped cars," I insisted. "But if you want to stay here with the car—"

He pulled up into the paved area and switched the car off. "I'll stay here and keep an eye on the car," he said. "You go see what you can find out there."

I got out of the car and opened the umbrella. The wind almost took it out of my hands, but I got a better grip. The road was clear so I splashed across the street. There were two red doors about five yards apart. The one the right had a window in it, so I assumed that was the main entrance. I walked up the stairs. There were some windows running between the doors, and I peered into them. There were a few tables inside, glass cases on the walls, but I didn't see anyone. I turned the knob and pulled.

It was locked.

Right next to the door, inside a glass case, was listed the name of the pastor and the hours.

It was closed on Mondays.

"Damn it, damn it, damn it!" I swore. I stood there for a minute, thinking. There was no doorbell—but next to the windowless door I could see one. I dashed across the well-manicured lawn and up the steps and pressed the bell. I could hear it ringing inside. I pressed it again, and was just about to give up when the door opened.

"I'm sorry, young man, but we are closed." The older man who was standing just inside the door spoke with the singsong intonation of Scandinavians. His skin was very pale, and behind his spectacles his eyes were a very light blue. His hair was completely white and cut short. He was wearing a Tulane sweatshirt and a loose-fitting pair of jeans.

"I'm sorry to bother you—"

His eyes widened and he smiled. "You're Scott, aren't you?"

My jaw dropped. "Yes, but how—"

"Please, come in. I've been expecting you."

I closed the umbrella and stepped inside. He was already walking down the hallway in his house shoes. He stopped when he reached a door, and gestured for me to enter. I stepped into a small room that was set up as an office. An ancient PC was sitting on the desk. Shelves of books lined the walls. There was a cross hanging on the wall directly behind the desk. "Tch, tch, you are soaked through," he said. "May I get you something warm to drink?"

"No, thank you." I unbuttoned my coat. It was very warm in the room. "How did you know my name?"

"I am Oleg Sjowall." He shook my hand. "We have a friend in common." He sat down behind the desk. "Benjamin." He peered at me over his spectacles. "He sent me a rather cryptic e-mail yesterday morning, along with a photograph of you." His eyes twinkled. "He wanted me to give you a message." He chuckled. "No explanation, of course, but that was Benjamin all over." He opened a desk drawer and started rummaging through it. "I would imagine he is playing some kind of joke on you—he loves that sort of thing, but then if you know him you already know that—oh, yes, here it is." He handed me a folded slip of paper. "I was to give it to you, and you only. He said others might come asking—but if someone I didn't recognize asked about him, I was to deny I knew him." He leaned back in his chair. "That Benjamin! I am of course happy to do a favor for a friend, but so mysterious." He shook his head.

I swallowed. Obviously, he didn't know Doc was dead. "I'm sorry to have to tell you this, Mr. Sjowall, but Benjamin died yesterday."

"Ah." He leaned back in his chair with his eyes closed. "I am very sorry to hear that." His lips moved silently, and I bowed my head when I realized he was praying. After a few moments, he said, "I hope he finds peace. He was a very troubled man. Is there going to be a service?"

"I'm sure," I replied, realizing as I said it how lame it sounded. "Do you have a card? I'll have my parents get in touch with the information."

He smiled sadly and handed me his card. I slipped it into my pocket. "Well." I stood up. "Thank you for giving me the message."

He also stood, and shook my hand. "Benjamin often spoke of you," he said as he escorted me down the hall. "He thought of you as a son, you know."

Unexpected tears filled my eyes. So much had happened—I hadn't really had a chance to mourn, or even think about the fact I'd never see Doc again. "Thanks," I murmured again, opening my umbrella and running out into the rain again.

I was sobbing when I got back into the car. "Scotty!" Frank grabbed me and put his arms around me. "What's wrong?"

"Nothing," I blubbered. I pulled away from him and wiped at my eyes. "Sorry, it just hit me that Doc is dead…" I took a deep breath and got my emotions under control. "Okay. Whew. Sorry. Doc e-mailed the pastor—he was a friend—a message for me." I pulled it out of my pocket and unfolded it.

It was another riddle. I read it out loud.

"A president where so many were laid in their graves
Where the wings of the angel reach up for the sky
Follow the finger of the shepherd who saves
Those who gave their lives fighting the fire
Lead the way to a maiden whose own very eye
Looks where you will find what you most desire."

I closed my eyes and leaned my head against the window.

"Lafayette Cemetery Number One," I said after a few moments. *"A president where so many were laid in their graves*—it's on the corner of Washington and Prytania."

Frank started the car and pulled back out onto Prytania Street. The rain hadn't let up, and Frank had to drive slowly because the visibility was so bad. I pushed all my sad thoughts about Doc out of my head—there would be time to mourn him later, once we had the damned sapphire in our hands and this was all over.

The light at Washington was green, and I told Frank to park on Prytania. The main entrance to the cemetery was on Washington Street, but directly across the street was Commander's Palace. Even with this storm, parking would be a mess on Washington. It always kind of amused me that one of the city's best restaurants was across the street from a cemetery.

We got out of the car and opened our umbrellas and crossed the street, running down the brick sidewalk. The gates to the cemetery were open. Despite the rain, which was undoubtedly keeping visitors away, it was open. It was getting colder, and the rain continued to pour down. Lightning flashed nearby, and the thunder was deafening. We darted through the gates. A steady stream of water about two inches deep was flowing out of the main walkway through the gates, and my feet were freezing. "Maybe we should wait out the rain," Frank shouted.

I glanced at my watch. It was almost four. I shook my head. "They lock the gates at five," I insisted, "and if we're going to find the thing we should do it now. I'd feel a lot better if it were in our hands rather than his."

Frank nodded as we made our way through the cemetery, and I sighed.

This was where it got hard.

I wasn't familiar with Lafayette Number One—it wasn't where either side of my family had their tombs. Originally, my Creole ancestors were buried in St. Louis Number One, just outside the French Quarter, and there was a Diderot mausoleum there. But about a hundred years ago, for some reason the Diderots had started being buried in the cemetery out near Metairie, at the end of Canal Street. The Bradleys had always used that same cemetery. This was my first time ever setting foot in Lafayette Number One.

Legend holds that the original French settlers had tried burying their dead below ground, but the first rains had brought the bodies up to the surface. This was why they started building small mausoleums, with spaces for multiple coffins to be put in at once. Once the mausoleum was full, the next body was simply shoved into the oldest crypt, and the former occupant and their coffin was shoved into the back, where a receptacle was built for the old bones and decayed coffins. The cemeteries were like cities for the dead, with the mausoleums looking like little houses and the pathways between them laid out like streets. Lafayette was really the old American cemetery, from the olden days when the descendants of the original French looked down their noses at their new neighbors and refused to mix with them. The cemeteries were filled with beautifully sculpted statuary either in front of the door or on top of the mausoleum. The more stern Protestants simply adorned their mausoleums with a huge cross on the top, not going in for that Catholic idolatry.

"I see at least five angels just from here," Frank said through chattering teeth. "Which one did he mean?"

I shook my head. "We could be here all night," I replied. I was feeling a little discouraged. I thought for a moment. "The next line has to do with those who gave their lives fighting the fire." My own teeth were starting to chatter. We took shelter from the wind in the doorway of a mausoleum marked *McQuay*. "I wonder if there's a—" I stopped talking, and pointed directly ahead of us.

JEFFERSON FIRE STATION was carved across the top of a mausoleum. Beneath the words, a horse-drawn fire truck was carved into the marble. The mausoleum directly to the right had a giant angel standing in front of it, carrying a sword.

"This is too damned easy," Frank said. He was shivering. "I mean, come on, it's even in the same street from the damned gate."

"I don't know, Frank," I snapped. "Maybe Doc just thought I was too stupid to find it if he made it hard."

"That isn't what I meant, and you know it," Frank said.

"Well, he did want me to be able to find it," I replied. "And he pretty much fixed it so that Mr. Sjowall wouldn't give the last riddle to anyone but me."

But I was beginning to doubt myself when I got this eerie feeling like we were being watched. I looked back to the gate, which was still open. A car drove past on Washington Street, creeping slowly in the rain but still splashing up a stream of water. I looked the other way, but couldn't see anything through the sheets of rain and the gloom. Lightning forked through the sky nearby, so close the air smelled burnt. The deafening thunder followed almost immediately. I was soaked through to the skin, and shivering with the cold. But I couldn't help but feel we weren't alone in the cemetery.

"Frank," I said, swiveling my head from side to side, "I've got a bad feeling—"

I felt the bullet whiz past my ear and embed itself into the stone behind me. A chip flew out and hit me in the back. Frank grabbed me and tossed me to the ground. A geyser of water splashed up as the impact knocked the breath out of me. The water was moving pretty fast and the dirty cold water filled my mouth and nose. I sputtered and gasped as Frank hit the ground next to me, throwing up yet another spray of water into my face.

"We've got to find cover," he shouted over the rain.

Well, duh, I thought, the shock wearing off. I looked up and scanned the area. I hadn't heard the shot, which meant whoever it was had a silencer. There was a splash next to me as another bullet missed. *Damn it!* In a split second I figured that the shooter was in front of us, most likely to our left and firing from above. "Come on!" I shouted at Frank and rolled through the water to the right and slightly backward. Just as I moved, another little geyser sprayed up as a bullet hit where I'd been just a moment before. Frank moved back, and after what seemed like an eternity we were shielded by the mausoleum. I grabbed Frank's arm and pulled him down so I could say in his ear, "Come on, babe, we've got to move."

Frank nodded, his lips pressed tightly together.

I looked around the corner, and through the gloom could make out a shadowy form leaping from the top of one mausoleum to the next, getting closer to us. I pulled out my gun, carefully judged the speed of movement, aimed, and fired just as the form landed on a mausoleum about ten yards from where we were hiding. The form fell backward and vanished from view. "I think I got him," I shouted to Frank. He winked at me, water running in a steady stream down his face. "Let me go be sure."

Ducking down just in case, I ran across the flowing water to where I'd seen the form go down. I peered around the corner of the mausoleum and saw a body lying on its back in the water. Still crouched, I crab-walked over to it. He was dark-skinned, and there was an eye tattooed in the center of his forehead. His eyes were open and staring.

He was dead. But was he alone?

I stood up and looked around. I didn't see anyone—but to be on the safe side, I crouched down and ran back to where I left Frank.

"He's dead," I shouted over the rain.

Frank nodded.

I motioned to go around the back, and we made our way to the street behind the mausoleum. I wondered again if the guy was working alone—just as another bullet went past me. Frank ran ahead of me, splashing until he reached a mausoleum with a door rather than drawers. The name on it read *James*. He kicked the door in and ducked inside. I jumped in behind him and shut the door.

It was dark inside, and as my eyes grew accustomed to the gloom, I saw that we were inside a narrow room that ran the length of the tomb. The wall behind me was where the drawers for the coffins were located. I shuddered and knelt down, putting my head down and taking deep breaths.

"We can't stay in here forever," Frank whispered, moving to the door and peering around the corner. Lightning lit up the inside of the room, followed by the ubiquitous thunder. "I don't see anyone—do you have your phone?"

"Yeah." I fumbled for it inside my jacket pocket, and flipped it open. I scrolled through the stored numbers and pressed Call when I reached Venus's. The phone started ringing, and just as she answered, Frank fired.

"Venus, this is Scotty Bradley," I said. "Frank and I are in Lafayette Number One and we're being shot at." Frank fired again.

"On my way," she said and hung up.

That was one thing I loved about her—she didn't waste time.

"I got him!" Frank exulted.

I breathed out a sigh of relief and pushed past him. I gave him a big kiss on the cheek. "I wonder if there's anyone else out there?" I looked out and saw another body lying in the water about four yards away. He was face down in the water. Frank grabbed me by both shoulders and dragged me back inside.

"Are you crazy?" he hissed at me. "You don't know if there's anyone else out there."

"I'm going to go look for the Eye," I replied. "I don't feel like there's anyone else out there—and once the cops get here, we're going to be tied up for hours, and we can't risk someone else finding it."

I shook his hands off and boldly walked back out into the rain. I scanned in every direction and didn't see anyone. And that creepy feeling of being watched was gone, too. I splashed through the rising water and walked back around to the main alley.

"Those who gave their lives fighting the fire lead the way to a maiden whose own very eye points the way to find what you most desire," I muttered to myself. I stared at the firefighters' tomb. Lead the way? How—

I looked at the engraved carving of the horse-drawn fire truck. The team of horses all faced forward, except for the one in the lead. His head was turned slightly and looked out into the alleyway at about a forty-five degree angle. I turned and followed the direction of his head. It pointed to a passageway between the Fontenot and Delahaye tombs. I splashed over. The rain was starting to lessen a little and the sky was lightening. I heard Frank behind me. Once I was out into the alley behind those two tombs, I saw it.

A statue of a young woman was standing in front of a tomb. Her arms were spread wide, and she was wearing a long, diaphanous gown. Her head was tilted to her left, her head looking down at the bottom of the structure. It took everything I had not to scream out in delight.

The name carved at the top of the building was Garrett.

I dashed across to the front and looked at the stone in the lower left corner and caught my breath.

BENJAMIN GARRETT

APRIL 28, 1947–AUGUST 3, 1968

Underneath the dates were carved the words *He gave his life for his country.*

I closed my eyes. Larry Moon had taken the name of a New Orleans soldier who'd been killed over there. What better identity to assume than that of a dead man?

I knelt down and felt around the edges of the stone. It was loose. "Frank!" I yelled as I shoved my fingers into the small crevice. Frank knelt down beside me and we pulled.

The stone came out.

And just in front of the coffin was a small metal box.

My hands shaking, I reached forward and pulled it out. There was a lock on the front—but that wasn't a big deal. It would be easy enough to cut that off—

"Please to hand me the box," a voice said from behind us.

I turned. Two dark-skinned men in long trench coats with hats pulled down over their foreheads were standing there. Each held a gun in their right hands.

"Please to hand me the box." The one on the left gestured with his gun. "I will shoot you."

"How do I know you won't shoot anyway?"

"By the name of Kali I pledge not," he replied.

"Give it to him," Frank said.

I held it out to him. Keeping his gun still pointed at me, he stepped forward and took the box, slipping it under his arm.

"Kali thanks you," he said. "Now, please, go back to tomb where you hid?" He gestured in the direction of the James tomb.

Glumly, Frank and I put our hands up and walked back inside the tomb. The door shut behind us. I heard something snap shut, and then hurried splashing. I tried the door.

It was locked.

In the distance, I could hear the wail of police sirens.

CHAPTER THIRTEEN
THE WORLD, REVERSED
Success yet to be won

I have to give you two credit," Venus said with a shrug as she shut the door of her SUV. She handed Frank and me each a cup of coffee from the shop across the street from where she'd parked. "Whenever you come around, there's always an impressive body count."

I opened my mouth to deny it, but thought better of it and said nothing. I couldn't argue the point with her. She was right. The bodies in the cemetery were the third and fourth corpses I'd been around in a little less than twenty-four hours. I doubted anyone else in New Orleans could say that. "I can't take credit for Doc," I said after taking a sip from the steaming coffee. "You were already there."

We were sitting in the backseat of her black SUV, wrapped in NOPD blankets. She had the heater on full blast, and I was finally starting to feel warm again—though I couldn't wait to get home and get out of these wet clothes. But at least my hands weren't shaking as I took another big drink of the steaming coffee. I closed my eyes and leaned back against the seat. *It's all over,* I thought with relief. The storm had passed, but the sky was still covered by dark clouds. We'd already being grilled about what happened inside the walls of the cemetery.

Venus hadn't been happy to find out some of the things Colin had kept from her—but without him to direct the interrogation, I'd seen no reason to keep anything back from her.

I couldn't wait to get home and take a hot shower.

The front passenger door opened and Blaine Tujague climbed in. Venus handed him some coffee. "Thanks, Venus." He took a drink and turned back to us. "They had their passports on them." He shook his head. "Pleshiwarian nationals; apparently they entered the country through Houston. They came in with two others—I've put out an APB on them." He sighed. "I wonder how long before the Feds take this over?" He glanced at Venus and added angrily, "We might as well not even bother to start an investigation. I'm surprised Homeland Security hasn't already arrived here with an army of Feds."

She shrugged resignedly. "We do our jobs until told otherwise." She gave me a faint smile. "And you have no idea where Abram Golden is?"

I shook my head. "No. Like I said, I took a nap. When I woke up, he was gone—and I haven't heard from him since." *And trust me, I have a lot of questions for him myself.* "I've tried his cell a couple of times, but he isn't answering." *No surprise there, either.* I didn't want to think he'd sent the assassins after Frank and me, but it was a possibility.

The one thing I couldn't understand was why the first two had shot at us—the other two could have easily have shot us rather than locking us in the James mausoleum. But they hadn't.

I guess we'd find out when they were caught.

I looked out the window just as the Crime Lab techs were carrying a body out on a stretcher. I winced and looked away.

No matter how many times I see death, I never get used to it.

"You two are free to go for now," Venus said. "We'll get your statements typed up, and just come by the station house to sign them later tonight or in the morning. And try to stay out of trouble?"

"All I want to do," I said wearily as I opened the back door, "is take a hot shower and go to bed for a week."

We got out of the SUV and walked over to where Frank's MG was parked. The coffee was definitely helping. I'd begun to think I'd never feel warm again. We got into the MG and headed back home.

Frank was silent until we got to the light at Camp and Canal. "I have a confession of my own to make," he said slowly. "Don't be mad at me."

"I'm too tired to get mad," I replied, finishing the last of the coffee. It was true. I felt drained, both physically and emotionally. It was all over. The Eye was in the hands of the Pleshiwarians, Colin was gone again, and as far as I was concerned, the police or the Feds or whoever the hell wanted to could handle the whole mess from now on.

"I knew what Blackledge really was, and I didn't tell you," he said as he turned right onto Canal. There wasn't much traffic, and he whipped the car into the U-turn lane just past Decatur. "When Colin said Blackledge wanted to open a branch office in New Orleans and hire us...well, I'd heard of Blackledge. Not much, but what I'd heard wasn't good. Sure, I went to their Web site—you saw it—but I..." His voice trailed off as he turned onto Decatur in the direction of home. "Their Web site was just innocuous, like you saw. An international investigation company, but I knew it was probably just a cover. So I checked with some of my buddies at the FBI."

"And what did you find?" I closed my eyes and leaned my head against the car window. I wasn't so sure I wanted to hear any more of this.

"I found out what Blackledge was." He gripped the steering wheel so tight his knuckles turned white. "Oh, there was nothing concrete—they're much too good for that, of course. They've been operating worldwide since the end of the Second World War, doing dirty jobs governments want done but don't want tied to them, you know? It was all mostly rumor and conjecture." He sighed. "So I confronted Colin about it."

"And you didn't tell me any of this?" I closed my eyes. I was too tired to be angry or outraged. All I felt was disappointment.

"Colin—" He hesitated. "Colin told me that it was true, that there was a branch of the company that did that kind of work, but he assured me that we would never get involved in that, we'd be working for the investigation side." He shook his head. "I believed him because I wanted to believe him."

"And you didn't tell me."

"Colin thought it was better that way, and I agreed with him." We stopped at the light in front of Café du Monde. The gilded statue of Joan of Arc was directly in front of us. I looked away, out the window at the empty tables and chairs under the green and white awning. "It was a mistake—I realized that once..." He swallowed. "Once we knew Colin had killed your uncles. But then, I was...I didn't know what to do, Scotty."

"You figured it was just easier not to tell me then." I felt empty inside.

"I mean, by then we all knew what he was." He stole a glance at me, but turned his head back to the road. The light turned green and the MG jumped forward. "I didn't think—well, I didn't think it much mattered at that point whether I…"

"Stop beating yourself up," I said, sharper than I'd intended. "Right now, I am so tired and drained I can't be mad. I don't have the energy for it."

"I just don't want you to hate me."

"I could never hate you." I closed my eyes and put my head against the window. It was true. "I'm disappointed you didn't tell me. I'm disappointed that you actually thought it was better to keep it from me than tell me the truth. I don't know what that says about what you think about me, but right now I am too tired to get into it, okay?"

We drove the rest of the way to the parking lot in silence. I felt betrayed, but couldn't summon up any emotion. We got out the car and walked back to the apartment. I unlocked the gate. Now that the storm had passed, the temperature was starting to go back up. We stripped out of our wet clothes on the second-floor landing and tossed them in the dryer and went on up to our apartment. I didn't say anything as I walked into the bathroom and turned on the shower. As the steam from the hot water started filling up the room, I walked back into the bedroom. Frank had put on a robe and was sitting on the bed.

"Can I join you?" he asked.

"You go first," I said, and walked out of the bedroom. I went into the kitchen and started a pot of coffee. As I watched the coffee brew, I tried to remember the last time I felt so tired, so drained, so *defeated*.

You didn't fail, Scotty. The whole point was for the Eye to be returned to Pleshiwar. They have it, it's probably on its way back to the temple right now, so Kali has been appeased. She won't destroy the world now that Her Eye is being returned to Her. Colin is probably on a plane out of the country even now. And does it really matter if Frank knew what Blackledge was all along and didn't tell you? He was just sparing your feelings.

It didn't make me feel any better, though.

I filled a mug with coffee and walked into the living room. I sat down on the couch.

I looked at the clock on the mantelpiece. It was shortly after five. Just twenty-four hours ago, Levi was sitting in here telling me his tale of woe. It was all lies, of course, and now he was dead.

Everyone lied to me.

Doc's entire life had been a lie. He wasn't Dr. Benjamin Garrett from Biloxi, he'd just been Larry Moon—he and his buddies had been hired by Blackledge to steal the Eye in the first place, for some reason known only to whoever had hired Blackledge.

And now they were all dead, and the mess they'd started all those years ago was finally over. The Eye was on its way back to Pleshiwar, where it belonged. Maybe it was in the right hands, maybe it wasn't. It wasn't my problem anymore.

I closed my eyes and leaned back.

I heard the shower turn off.

"Scotty?" Frank said. I didn't open my eyes, and felt him sit down on the couch next to me. "Are you mad?"

"I'm not mad, I'm just tired," I replied. I leaned against him, and he put his arm around my shoulders. "I know you think you were just trying to protect me—although I can't imagine why."

"You were so hurt," he whispered. He put his head down against mine. "We both were—the whole family. Everyone was so hurt by what he'd done. I just didn't see any reason to make things worse. I was wrong, I know that—I've regretted it ever since. I should have told you from the start...but—" He paused for a moment. "When I found out, it didn't seem to matter. I know I shouldn't have believed him—especially given what happened later—but we were all so happy...I've never really been happy before."

"I know, Frank."

"And I didn't want to mess that up. I'm so, so sorry."

"It's okay." I stood up. "I'm going to go get in the shower." I leaned down and kissed him. "I love you, Frank. That's not ever going to change, okay?"

He nodded.

I walked back into the bathroom and turned the shower back on. I climbed in and let the hot spray flow over my body. The hot water felt incredible. I closed my eyes and leaned my head against the side of the shower. I mechanically went through the motions of soaping my body and washing my hair. It felt good, rejuvenating me. My mind was waking up, and all the tiredness was draining out of me. I turned off the water and grabbed my towel.

Poor Frank, I thought, *it must have been rough keeping that from me all these years, feeling guilty.*

There was a loud crash from the living room, and a howl of pain. *What the hell?*

There was another crash, and a loud thump. I wrapped the towel around my waist and, still dripping, ran out into the hallway. What I saw in the living room stopped me dead in my tracks.

Frank and Colin were rolling around on the floor.

"Stop that!" I screamed at the top of my lungs.

They both looked at me. Frank was on top of Colin, his right fist cocked in the air. Colin's hands were on Frank's throat. His lip was swelling, and a trickle of blood was running out of the left side of his mouth. "Get off of him, Frank," I demanded, my teeth clenched.

Frank punched him again, but Colin moved his head and the blow glanced off his cheek. Frank got up, and Colin got to his hands and knees, shaking his head from side to side. "Hell of a way to say hello, Agent," he said, rubbing his jaw.

"You're lucky I didn't kill you," Frank replied, crossing his arms angrily.

"There's been enough killing," I replied. "Colin, what the hell are you doing here?"

Colin got to his feet. A bruise from Frank's last punch was forming on his right cheek. "I thought we could plan our next move." He looked at Frank. "I wasn't expecting to see Frank."

"Our next move?" I shook my head. "There is no next move, Colin." I plopped down on the couch. "It's all over."

"What are you talking about?" He looked at Frank, then back at me. "We need to solve the riddle and find the Eye."

I couldn't help it. I started laughing. "You're a little behind, Colin. We've already found it, no thanks to you."

Colin's face was a study in shock. *Damn, he's a good actor,* I thought to myself. He said, "What are you talking about?"

"Like I said, you're behind the times," I replied wearily. "I woke up from my nap, and you were gone. Frank came home unexpectedly, and we solved the riddle. We went out and found the damned Eye."

"You found it? But that's great." He looked from me to Frank and back again. "I had a lead on the Pleshiwarians I wanted to follow up—a dead end, I might add—you were sleeping so soundly I didn't want to wake you up…where is the Eye?"

"We don't have it anymore. It was taken from us." I waved my hand. "But we solved the riddle, and we did find it." I rapidly went through the whole thing. "So, they have the Eye. It's over."

"Damn it!" he roared, slamming his fist into his leg. "It's *not* over, Scotty—we've got to find them and get the Eye back."

"Are you insane?"

"Scotty, the *wrong* Pleshiwarians have the Eye." He started pacing. "Okay, listen to me. I didn't tell you any of this because I thought—"

"I couldn't handle it?" I glared at him, then looked at Frank, who wouldn't meet my eyes.

"No." He bit his lip. "Because it was on a need-to-know basis, and you didn't need to know."

"We're listening." This was Frank. I shot him a glance. That muscle was twitching in his jaw, and a couple of veins were pulsing in his forehead. This wasn't a good sign.

"Okay." Colin sat down on the couch. "I'm going to tell you the whole story." He started talking.

In the early 1960s, a British anthropologist named Valerie Stratton had gone to Pleshiwar to study their unique culture for her doctoral dissertation. At first, the Pleshiwarians were resistant to her, but her knowledge of Kali and their religion—and her familiarity with their dialect—won their begrudging respect. She was there for three years, studying. But when she wrote her dissertation, a section about their sacred mountain triggered some interest at MI6. She was recruited by them, and she returned to Pleshiwar with two men—one an agent, the other a geologist. The three of them disappeared, but not before the geologist had sent a cable back to the home office in London: *Sacred mountain suspicions correct.*

"The suspicion, of course, was that the sacred mountain was a source of uranium," Colin went on. "As you can imagine, that created quite a stir among the Western nations. At that time, India had not become a nuclear power—nor had China, and right here on their borders was a tiny country that had a source of uranium. And no one was sure what had happened to Stratton and her team."

It was determined that control of Pleshiwar and its uranium source was of vital interest to the Western nations. The United States, however, was currently involved militarily in Vietnam; and any other Western venture into south Asia was a card that could easily be played by the Communist powers. It was determined that deniability was crucial.

"So, they came to Blackledge, and hired us," Colin continued. "We assembled a team. Five of our best young agents—one of them a native Indian who spoke Pleshiwarian. We sent him into the country to prepare the way. The other four—one a helicopter pilot, the other three trained agents—were to wait for his signal. He infiltrated the cult of Kali and determined that the current high priest was unfriendly to the Western powers. He wasn't exactly friendly to the Communists, but the American presence in Vietnam wasn't viewed with favor. The undercover agent determined that the best way to bring about a regime change in Pleshiwar was to steal Kali's Eye. Our undercover operative inside the country would spread the word that the Eye was stolen because Kali was displeased with Her high priest."

"That's disgusting," I replied.

Colin shrugged. The three agents—Larry Moon, Marty Gretsch, and Matt Hooper—went to Saigon to wait for the operative moment. When the whispering campaign against the high priest had reached critical mass, they got the signal to move. The undercover priest drugged the temple guards, the three agents went in, stole the Eye, and got out. Once the alarm about the Eye went out, there was a bloody uprising that resulted in the priest being killed, and his replacement was someone more friendly to the West. But unfortunately, something went wrong. We weren't the only ones with agents operating in the country. When Matt Hooper was murdered in Saigon—and the helicopter pilot disappeared, we pulled Larry and Marty out and hid them inside the United States. We gave them new identities."

"What I don't understand," I interrupted, "is why you let *them* keep the Eye. Why wasn't it put in a bank vault somewhere? I mean, seriously, Colin. Blackledge certainly took a risk there."

He shook his head. "I don't make those decisions, nor do my superiors tell me why they do things the way they do, Scotty."

"It does seem kind of stupid," Frank said. "In fact, this whole thing sounds like a goddamned fairy tale."

"I know, I know," Colin replied. "When I was briefed on this whole thing, I said the same things. Need to know, and I didn't need to know." He took a deep breath. "Anyway, there's a new movement in Pleshiwar, to try to unseat the high priest who is friendly to the West and replace him with one who isn't. What better way to do so than to find the Eye? This is why we needed to retrieve it, to return it and show that Kali favors the current leadership. The Pleshiwarians here now, they are the enemy. They tracked down Marty Gretsch and Ben Garrett, and killed them both. The Wolf was also working for them."

"Well, it doesn't matter now," I replied. "They took the Eye from us, and it's probably already on its way back to Pleshiwar now."

Before Colin could respond, my cell phone beeped. I picked it up and flipped it open. I had a new text message. I clicked it open and my eyes widened in horror.

A picture of my parents, bound and gagged, filled the window.

The phone rang. "Hello?"

"Meet me in the coffee shop downstairs, alone," an accented voice said. "Or your parents die."

Chapter Fourteen
TEN OF SWORDS, REVERSED
Overthrow of evil forces

The phone dropped out of my hand.

"Scotty?"

I didn't know which one of them said it, and didn't really care.

I got up and tossed my phone at Colin. "Thanks for keeping an eye on my parents," I snarled and ran down the hall to my bedroom. I tossed the towel into the bathroom. I didn't bother with underwear, pulling on a pair of discarded jeans from the floor. I was pulling my Saints sweatshirt over my head when I heard Frank say, "Scotty, what are you doing?"

I sat down on my bed and pulled on my sneakers. "Whoever has my parents is waiting for me in the coffee shop downstairs." I tied the laces, but my hands were shaking so hard I messed up and had to start over.

"I'm coming with you."

"He said to come alone," I replied, finally getting the laces tied. "It's a public place, so I guess I'll be okay."

"What does he want?"

"I guess he'll tell me when I get down there." I got off the bed, but Frank was blocking the doorway. "Get out of my way."

"Scotty, think," Frank pleaded. "You can't go down there without backup."

"Get out of my way, Frank," I said in a low voice. "I'll go through you if I have to."

Frank bit his lip and moved. I ran out the back door and took the stairs at a breakneck speed. There was a back door to the coffee shop underneath the stairs, and I unlocked it with my key. I stepped inside and walked past the bathrooms, the office, and the storeroom. The coffee shop was empty, other than the girl working behind the counter and a man sitting in a booth with his back to me. Obviously, he was expecting me to come in from the front. I wished I'd brought a gun with me.

I don't know what it says about me, but I wanted to put a bullet through his head.

Since I was unarmed, I walked up behind him and said, "You wanted to see me?"

He didn't jump. Instead, he swiveled his head and looked up at me. "Have a seat, Mr. Bradley." He gestured to the other side. "Or would you prefer a drink first?"

"I'm not thirsty," I said, sliding into the booth across from him.

He was tall and thin, with dark skin and hair. His brown eyes were narrow, and in the center of his forehead was a small tattoo of a third eye—a blue eye. He was wearing a three-piece brown suit. The jacket was open, but the vest underneath was buttoned. He was wearing a white button-down shirt with a red tie. His hands were long and spidery, free of jewelry. His nails were long and manicured. His lips were narrow and thin. He held his right hand across the table to me. "I am Rajneesh Abhwesar," he said, pulling the thin lips back into a smile, revealing crooked yellow teeth. "It is a pleasure to finally make your acquaintance."

I didn't offer my hand, keeping them both flat on the table. It was all I could do to not grab him by the throat and choke him. "I wish I could say the same," I replied after a short silence.

He didn't stop smiling, but put his hand down. "So it is going to be like that, is it? I was hoping we could negotiate like gentlemen."

"Gentlemen?" I narrowed my eyes. "It's not exactly *gentlemanly* to hold my parents as hostages."

He closed his eyes and inclined his head. "Touché."

"If anything happens to my parents, I will hunt you down like a dog," I said pleasantly. "There's no place on this planet you'll be able to go where I won't find you."

"Tut, tut, there's no need for that." He held up his hand. "I understand your distress, of course. I assure you your parents are quite well, and in good health. Nothing will happen to them. I will take very good care of them." He smiled. "Your mother is quite spirited, I must say."

"You're lucky she's tied up," I replied evenly. "And your men better hope she doesn't get loose—she'll make them sorry they were born. What do you want?"

"I need your assistance," he said, reaching into his pocket. "Just a few hours ago, you discovered this in the cemetery." He held out something wrapped in a handkerchief to me. I took it from him. "My men took it from you. Go ahead, unwrap it."

I carefully unfolded the handkerchief and found myself looking at a beautiful blue stone in the shape of an eye. There was a fault in the center that looked like a retina. I stared at it. "I don't understand."

"It was inside the small box you found," he went on. "It looks like Kali's Eye, does it not?" He reached over and picked it up. He held it up to the light for a moment, and then set it down on the table. He pulled out a small pocketknife, flicked it open, and then ran it over the surface of the stone, leaving a deep groove.

"What are you doing?" I stared at him.

"Sapphires are hard stones, Mr. Bradley." His smile faded. "A knife cannot cut a sapphire. Sapphires are as hard as diamonds. This stone is a fake. A very good one—its resemblance to the real thing is extraordinary—but it is a fake." He closed the pocketknife and slid it back into his pocket. "The real stone is hidden somewhere else." He reached inside his jacket pocket and removed a folded piece of paper, which he slid across the table to me. "This was also inside the box."

I opened it. It was in the same handwriting as the riddle.

To whom it may concern:

You have made it this far, but your quest still has another step before you find what you truly desire. The stone in this box is but a clever reproduction; it is not the holy stone that you seek. Consider this a reward for a job well done.

But where is the real Eye, you are asking yourself. Where, indeed, could it be? It was taken for a reason. It was not stolen to be sold, or given as a gift. It was not stolen for power, it was not stolen for riches. Rather, it was stolen in order that a people might be able to be free.

Freedom is something to be fought for, to spill blood for. It is not something to be held in your hands, but something intangible to always strive for. It is a state of mind, but even

should the shackles be taken away, it is not a guarantee that
other shackles will not take their place.

The Eye should not be returned until there is more than
a promise of freedom. Promises can be empty words spoken.

The Eye will not return to Pleshiwar until the shackles
are gone for good.

Slowly, I looked up at him. "What does this mean?"

He shook his head. "It makes no sense to me." He waved his hand. "You knew this man. You know how his mind worked. Solve this, and return the Eye to me, and I will let your parents go, unharmed."

"How do I know I can trust you?"

"I swear to you on the sacred Eye of Kali."

"Not good enough."

His smile faded a bit. "You have no reason to trust me, and you are wise not to trust a stranger. The Mother was right when She sent me to you." He closed his eyes and leaned back against the back of the booth. "There are those in Pleshiwar who would kill you rather than try to bargain with you." He waved his hand again.

"Like the assassins you sent to the cemetery?"

"They were not ordered to kill you." His eyes flashed angrily. "But as I said, there are Pleshiwarians who look at you and see unbelievers who defile Kali. Their instructions were to simply liberate the Eye from you and to leave you alive. The Great Mother can be bloodthirsty, but too much blood has been shed already in Her name. Their deaths were regrettable, but their companions knew what to do when they started shooting at you."

"I don't understand." I looked at him. "Are you saying—"

"The two fools who disobeyed orders and shot at you were exterminated by the others, who know better than to disobey me."

If that's true, Venus is going to swear a blue streak when the ballistics reports come back, I thought.

He went on. "I regret the inconvenience of having to take possession of your parents, but I—and the Pleshiwarians like me— have had enough of killing." His lip curled. "We do not wish to move our back into medieval times as those in power believe. We no longer see the Great Mother as a creature of darkness who swims in rivers of blood and demands death. There are those who think that any of the modern changes that have been brought to our country since the Eye was taken are abominations, that our country must be returned to what it has been for centuries—backward, isolated, and superstitious. But the modern innovations—could they not be seen as gifts from the Great Mother, to ease our lives and make them more comfortable? But I, and those who follow me, do not believe that the Great Mother should be ignored, treated as a relic of our superstitious past." He leaned forward, his eyes narrowing. "With the Eye's return, the veneration of the Great Mother can begin again. There is room for the modern world and for Kali both in our nation."

"You are backed by evil men," I replied, not caring if he got angry. "Evil men who want to plunder the natural resources of your country in order to destroy the rest of the world."

"Bah." He waved his hand. "We take their money, but once we are back in control of our country we will then decide which the right path to take. For our country, and for Kali."

"So, you're telling me you're one of the good guys?" I couldn't help but laugh. "I find that rather hard to believe."

"It is immaterial to me what you, an unbeliever, believe." He gave me a sad smile. "What do you think happened when those men originally stole the Eye and defiled Kali? Do you think that the transition was peaceful and bloodless?" He shrugged. "Pleshiwar swam in blood for years."

"And now you propose to drown the country in blood again." I shook my head. "The Great Mother may be the Destroyer, but She is also the Creator. She cares not for the follies of humans, Mr. Rajneesh. She is eternal. She wants Her defilement avenged—but doesn't care who rules Pleshiwar."

"What do you know of the Great Mother?" he snapped.

"She has spoken to me." I leaned forward. "I have seen Her sacred shrine in Pleshiwar. She came to me in a vision. Your mission will fail, Mr. Rajneesh." I kept my voice steady as I formed the lie in my mind. "She told me so Herself. She has threatened to destroy the world if Her Eye is not returned. But if it is returned, She will again become Durga, the Creator, and all will be harmony."

"Then it matters not who brings the Eye back to Pleshiwar, does it not?" His eyes burned into mine. He gestured to the paper. "Find the Eye, and bring it to me." He slid a card across the table to me. "My number is on that card. Find the Eye, and your parents will go free. There will also be a reward." He stood up. "Kali can be most generous when the mood strikes Her."

He walked out of the coffee shop.

I sat there and looked at the items on the table, finally folding the paper back up and pocketing the phony eye. I walked out the back door and up the stairs. I let myself into the apartment. I could hear Frank talking on his phone in the living room. I walked in, and he gestured to me to sit down. "Okay, keep me posted," he said into the phone and turned it off. "Well?"

"I have to find the Eye," I said, my voice hushed. "He says he won't harm Mom and Dad, but he won't let them go until I do and turn it over to him." I buried my face in my hands.

"What was in the box we found?"

"A phony stone." I pulled it out and placed it on the table. "And this." I tossed the paper next to it. Frank picked it up and read it. He put it back down.

"That doesn't make any sense to me," Frank said.

"Me, either. Where's Colin? Or should I ask what you did with the body?"

Frank had the decency to blush. "Okay, I shouldn't have hit him, but when he walked in, like he still lived here—I kind of lost my head." He hung his head down. "But he went down and is following the guy you met with. He made a call, too—to the people who were supposed to be watching your parents." He made a face. "He called them the Ninja Lesbians."

"Oh, Rhoda and Lindy." I picked up the paper and started reading it again. "What did they say?"

"He didn't get them—just their voicemails."

I looked at him. "Neither one of them answered their phones?" That wasn't good.

"No." He looked at me. "Seriously, Scotty? Ninja Lesbians?"

"It's true," I replied. "They work for the Mossad. He trained them. They're supposed to be on our side. Israel doesn't want terrorists having access to that uranium any more than Uncle Sam does." I waved at the broken French doors. "They did that when they announced themselves."

"Oh."

My cell phone started ringing. I answered. "Hello?"

"Scotty, this is Lindy."

I glanced at Frank. "We were just talking about you."

"We just got Colin's messages. But he isn't picking up." She went on. "His message doesn't make any sense, Scotty. We're watching your parents' building right now."

"What?"

"You heard me," she said patiently. "I am telling you. No one has gone in or out of your parents' apartment since we took up our positions. We are on the balcony across the street. We have a very clear view of the entrance. No one has gone in or out."

I could feel a headache starting. "I thought you two were supposed to be crack agents," I snapped. "Are you watching the staircase in the back?"

"Yes."

I struggled to control my temper. "Didn't you know there is an entrance to my parents' apartment from inside the store?"

"Yes, Scotty, we know that," Lindy responded. "I am telling you, your parents have not left their building. If they are being held—they are being held *inside*."

"I'm on my way." I hung up the phone. I picked up the note and folded it, placing it in my jeans pocket. "Come on, Frank. We're going over to Mom and Dad's."

Frank grabbed his gun. "Let's go."

It was starting to get dark as we walked quickly over to the corner of Royal and Dumaine. Rhoda and Lindy were waiting for us across the street in their black outfits. I introduced them to Frank, and they quickly filled me in. They'd been in position since they'd left my apartment. Colin had instructed them to keep an eye on my parents—he was afraid the bad guys would try to use them somehow to get the Eye from us once we found it. "He didn't tell you because he didn't want you to worry," Rhoda explained in her thick accent.

"I'm really really tired of not being told things for my own good," I said, giving Frank a pointed look. He blushed. "So, you're saying no one went in or out since you got here?"

"No," Lindy said. "Some customers came into the store, but they were all accounted for—they all left. Your parents—we saw them right after we took up position, but we haven't seen them since. They went up the back stairs with some bags—like they'd been shopping. No one else has gone up those stairs."

"Then how did they get in?" I shook my head. None of this made sense.

"Over the roofs?" Frank asked.

We all looked up.

"Please tell me you watched the roofs," I said quietly.

Rhoda and Lindy looked at each other.

The headache was coming back. "You mean to tell me," I said, trying to keep my voice level, "that after someone killed Levi and dropped his body off of *my* roof, it never occurred to either of you that they might come after my parents the same way?" I wanted to scream at them.

"Of course we watched the roofs," Rhoda said, her voice showing her offense. "No one came onto the balconies. Isn't that the only way into their apartment from the roofs? Onto the balconies?"

I sighed. "I'm afraid not."

"There is a door?"

"There's a deck in the very center." I groaned. It was in the middle of the second floor, and was completely invisible from the street. Mom had turned it into a little garden area, complete with misters for the summer since it was blocked from breezes on every side. "Didn't Colin tell you?"

"Oh," Lindy said softly. "We did not know."

"If Colin didn't tell you, it's not your fault." I shook my head. I'd get mad about it later. Now we had to rescue Mom and Dad. "Okay, it's pretty safe to assume that they're being held inside their apartment. We don't know how many men are watching them, or how heavily armed they are."

I pulled my phone out and looked at the image of my parents again. The chairs were pushed up against a wall. As I looked, I saw details I'd missed earlier in my shock. The chairs were from my parents' kitchen table. The look in Mom's eyes was pure fury. Dad just looked resigned. I felt another surge of anger.

"We can't rule out the possibility they aren't being held in their apartment," Frank said. "Maybe they took them out over the roofs?"

"Only if Mom was completely unconscious. She would have fought them tooth and nail, you know that," I disagreed, trying to think.

I looked at the image again. "Besides, those are their kitchen chairs. They're inside the apartment, all right.

"We can go up the stairs from the store," I said. "If they didn't search the house—and they came over the roofs—"

"Then they might think the only way in or out is the back stairs," Frank said. "Makes sense. The door to the stairs in the hallway looks like just another door—if they didn't look…"

"We cannot assume that." Rhoda's lips set in a tight line. "Assuming is the first step into the grave."

"If they came in over the roofs," Lindy said, a smile starting to spread across her pretty face, "they won't expect us to come in from the balcony." She winked. "Rhoda and I can get up there easily."

"Without attracting attention?"

"Posh." She shrugged. "If someone calls the police, all the better."

Rhoda grinned. "Yes, the plan makes sense. Lindy and I go over the balcony, we can move like ghosts—they will never hear us."

"And Frank and I can go up the stairs." It was starting to come together in my mind. "The shutters are all closed, but you can see through them—there's enough room. Check all the windows and send me a text message."

"Agreed."

Frank and I went into the store. It was weird how normal everything in the store seemed, given that just upstairs my parents might be held hostage. Emily was working behind the counter. She looked up when the bell rang, and grinned. "Hey, guys!"

"Hey, sweetie," I said, as Frank moved over to the door to the stairs. "Talked to Mom and Dad today?"

She shook her head. "No, but I know they're home." She went back to her *Vanity Fair.* "I've heard them moving around up there."

"Great." I unlocked the door, and Frank and I moved up the stairs in the dark. When we reached the top, we paused and listened, not hearing anything inside.

My phone vibrated. I flipped it open. The screen lit up.

Two men, main room. Two minutes go in.

I watched the clock on my phone, sweat running down my face. The seconds seemed to last an eternity.

Finally, two minutes passed. I turned the key in the lock and kicked the door open just as there was the sound of breaking glass in the living room. Frank and I flew into the living room just as I heard the muffled spit of silenced gunshots.

I turned on the lights.

Mom and Dad were in chairs, up against the wall.

Two men lay on the floor in pools of spreading blood.

Lindy and Rhoda were grinning.

I ran to Mom and Dad. I took off Mom's gag as Frank took off Dad's.

"It's about time." Mom said. "What took you so damned long?"

I gave her a big kiss as I checked to make sure she wasn't injured. Relief flooded through me. "You know," I said, giving her a hug once Lindy cut her ropes off and she stood up, "we really need to have a talk about your tendency to be taken hostage."

Chapter Fifteen
THE CHARIOT
Victory, success through hard work

Venus closed her notebook and stood up. "Seems like old times, doesn't it?" she said with a vague smile as she stood up. "Bodies at the Bradleys'." She shook her head. "No offense, but I'd kind of hoped that wasn't ever going to happen again." Her phone rang, and she moved away from us.

We were all sitting around in the Devil's Weed. Emily had closed and locked the doors a few moments after we all trooped downstairs, while I called Venus. The Crime Lab was upstairs, doing their job, and the coroner's van was just outside, parked on the sidewalk. We'd closed all the shutters after we got tired of being gawked at by passersby.

We still hadn't heard from Colin, which gave me a weird feeling of déjà vu. This was how that horrible Mardi Gras case had wound up—Mom and Dad being held hostage, a shoot-out in their apartment, and then no word from Colin after the police arrived. He'd been long gone, and that had been the last we'd seen of him until I walked into Mom and Dad's last night—*was it just last night?*—and saw him sitting there in his bloody bandage.

I took Frank's hand and squeezed it just as Venus walked back in. "We've picked up Abhwesar," she said. "He's claiming diplomatic immunity, of course—apparently he's somehow attached to the Pleshiwarian embassy—but the State Department is contacting the ambassador, and he's safely behind bars." She whistled. "The two men upstairs are apparently the only thugs he had left in the country, so it looks like you're all safe."

I let out my breath in a sigh of relief.

"You think Colin's already on his way out of the country?" Frank whispered to me.

"I don't know," I replied. "I mean, who knows? They didn't get the Eye, and if that was his objective, his work here is done."

"Where is the Eye?" Mom asked. "I don't get it. Why did Doc go to the trouble of making that riddle that led to a phony stone?"

"I don't think we'll ever know, Mom." I reached into my pocket and pulled out the piece of paper Abhwesar had given me. "Abhwesar said this was in there with it." I handed it over to her and Dad. "Can you make any sense out of it?"

Mom read it and shook her head. "No, it doesn't really seem to say anything."

"Maybe he never had it here in New Orleans," Rhoda said slowly. "No offense, but that never made any sense to me. Why would he do that? Why wouldn't Blackledge take it and keep it safe somewhere?"

That had been bothering me all along. When it just seemed that three American GIs had decided to steal it, it sort of made sense that one of them would keep it. But now that we knew they had been Blackledge agents, it didn't.

"Probably the only person who can answer that is Angela Blackledge herself," I said slowly, "and I think it is pretty safe to assume we'll never know."

"Maybe the whole thing was a subterfuge of some sort," Dad replied. "Maybe the stone was never really stolen in the first place? Maybe the whole thing was set up to topple the theocracy, and Doc was a decoy, trying to draw out the enemies of the current Pleshiwarian government." When we all looked at him, he shrugged. "Hey, I enjoy a good conspiracy theory. I still don't think Oswald acted alone."

I took the paper back from Mom, and read it over again.

To whom it may concern:

You have made it this far, but your quest still has another step before you find what you truly desire. The stone in this box is but a clever reproduction; it is not the holy stone that you seek. Consider this a reward for a job well done.

But where is the real Eye, you are asking yourself. Where, indeed, could it be? It was taken for a reason. It was not stolen to be sold, or given as a gift. It was not stolen for power, it was not stolen for riches. Rather, it was stolen in order that a people might be able to be free.

> *Freedom is something to be fought for, to spill blood for.*
> *It is not something to be held in your hands, but something*
> *intangible to always strive for, It is a state of mind, but even*
> *should the shackles be taken away, it is not a guarantee that*
> *other shackles will not take their place.*
> *The Eye should not be returned until there is more than*
> *a promise of freedom. Promises can be empty words spoken.*
> *The Eye will not return to Pleshiwar until the shackles*
> *are gone for good.*

I shook my head again. It didn't make any sense to me.

"Whatever anyone wants to believe about the afterlife, I hope wherever Doc is, he's burning," Mom said. "All that talk about freedom—it sounds like some right-wing militia tract."

"But it says you have one more step before you find what you desire," Frank said. "So this message has to be a clue of some sort to where he hid the Eye."

I stood up. "Well, maybe after a good night's sleep, we can give it another try," I said. I started to put it in my pocket, but Venus snatched it out of my hands.

"Evidence." She smiled at me as she put it inside a plastic bag, and marked it. "You have the phony Eye?"

"It's back at my apartment," I replied.

"Well, I'll give you a lift over there," she said. "I need to take it in. It's evidence."

"All right." I gave Mom and Dad a hug. I said good-bye to Rhoda and Lindy.

"I suspect our paths will cross again," Lindy said with a wink. "It's been fun working with you."

I just smiled. "No offense, Ninja Lesbians, but I hope I never see you again."

"None taken." Rhoda winked at me. "But we can be quite fun when we aren't working."

I laughed. "There's no doubt in my mind about that."

Frank and I rode back with Venus in silence. When she pulled up on the sidewalk in front of our gate, she said, "I'll wait here." As I started to shut the door, she added, "But if you're not back down here in ten minutes I'm coming up with my gun blazing."

"Don't even joke about it, Venus," I replied. "If there's anyone up there, I'll throw them off the balcony myself." I slammed the door.

I unlocked the gate, and we went down the back passageway. Millie was folding the clothes we put in the dryer after we'd gotten back from the cemetery. "Scotty, how many times have I told you about leaving your clothes in here?" she snapped, but her features relaxed when she saw Frank. "When did you get here?" she asked, giving him a rib-crushing hug.

"It feels like a million years ago," he replied. "Sorry about the clothes."

I kept climbing the stairs. "Millie, we've got a lot to tell you. But one thing—I need to have some glass replaced in one set of French doors."

She just gave me a quizzical look.

"Later, Millie, I promise. I have to get something for Venus right now. She's waiting."

Frank gave her a kiss on the cheek. "Come on, Millie. Let's go inside and I'll tell you everything. And I am dying for a cup of coffee."

"Anything for you, Frank dear." I heard the door close behind them.

I unlocked the door and walked in to the apartment. It was blessedly silent, thank You, Goddess. I walked into the living room, and there it was, sitting on the coffee table where I'd left it. I put it my pocket and went back out to give it to Venus. I walked around to the driver's side. She put the window down, and I handed it to her. "Thanks for everything, Venus."

She took it and put it in her jacket pocket. "Well, I have to say, things aren't dull when you're around." She laughed.

"Well, no offense, but I'll settle for dull for a while." I started to walk around the front of her SUV when she called after me, "Nice work, Bradley."

I climbed back on the sidewalk and waved as she put the SUV into gear and winked as she drove off.

Maybe she's changing her mind about me, I thought, and laughed out loud. *Not a chance in hell.*

I stripped out of my clothes when I got to my bedroom, and collapsed into the bed. I was just starting to drift off when I felt Frank climb into the bed with me. He wrapped his arms around me. "I've missed you so much," I said drowsily, and drifted off to sleep.

I was standing on the cliff again, facing the pedestal where I knew the incarnate statue of Kali rested. The sky was blue and free of clouds. I felt no fear; rather, I felt the peace and love I always felt in the presence of the Goddess.

I could hear birds singing.

I started walking toward Her. As I drew near the steps, I could see that both of Her eyes were shut. The necklace was just skulls again. Her long tongue hung down from between Her red lips. When I was a respectful distance from her, I dropped to my knees and bowed my head.

I felt Her awaken, and felt Her gaze.

"You may rise," She said, Her voice soft and gentle.

I looked at Her and saw that Her open eye was brown and normal looking. "I failed you, Great Mother."

She smiled, and I saw that the teeth were no longer filed sharp. "It is true that you did not find my Eye, Scotty, as I commanded you. But I am a merciful Goddess, and have no doubt that you will complete your quest."

Her four hands began waving, undulating up and down. She was not holding a skull or a sword this time. The motion of Her hands was quite beautiful and hypnotic.

"I will continue looking, Great Mother."

"You will succeed," She replied. "As you succeeded in defeating those who would commit evil in my name. I am the Destroyer, but I am also the Creator. I danced this world into existence, and when I choose I will dance it into oblivion. But my hand will not be forced, and it will not be done in my name until I wish it to be done. And this creation of mine has much time as you measure it to continue to please me."

"As you wish, Great Mother."

"You may go now. Go and find my Eye, and see that is returned to me."

"But Great Mother—where should I look for it?"

She threw her head back and laughed. It sounded like music to my ears, it was a wonderful sound I could have listened to forever. "You already know, Scotty, in your heart of hearts. You have begun to remember to listen to your heart, and have let me back into it. Look into your heart of hearts, and you will know where to look."

I opened my eyes and looked over at the clock. It was just past seven. I felt completely refreshed—mentally, emotionally, and physically. I eased myself out from under Frank's arm. He was snoring softly. *I am truly blessed,* I thought as I watched him sleep for a moment. I leaned down and kissed his scarred cheek. I pulled on a pair of sweatpants and walked into the kitchen. I got the coffee started, and while it brewed I sat down on the couch. The copy of Doc's final note was sitting there on the table. I picked it up, remembering the dream.

Look into your heart of hearts, and you will know where to look.

Hmm, I wondered as I read it over again. *What did She mean by that?*

The note kept repeating the words *freedom* and *shackles* over and over again.

I puzzled over it for a while, and then it hit me in a rush. My heart started beating a lot faster. *Damn you, Doc!* I thought to myself as I ran back to the bedroom. *You were one tricky son of a bitch!*

And in the back of my mind, I could almost hear him laughing.

I tried to wake up Frank, but he just grunted and rolled over. I dressed and called Venus. "I think I know where the Eye is," I said quickly. "Can I meet you at the station house?"

"Yeah, I'm here," she replied. "Come on down."

I hung up the phone. Frank was still snoring, so I didn't bother trying to wake him again. I gave him another kiss on the cheek and headed out the door. It was a gorgeous day. I ducked into the coffee shop and got a coffee of the day to go, which I sipped happily as I strolled up Royal Street. The gutters were filled with debris from the storm, but I felt like singing as I walked.

I just *knew* I was right.

I said hello to every pedestrian I met. It was, truly, an incredibly beautiful day. There were no clouds in the sky, which was a brilliant shade of blue, and it was about seventy degrees with a cool, gentle breeze blowing. Finally, I reached the precinct house, which looked like an old plantation house and was painted a lovely shade of peach. I laughed as I climbed the steps. The last time I was in this building was on Lundi Gras, way back in 2005, when we were all trying to sort out the huge mess of my murdered half-uncles. I'd also been arrested for assaulting a federal agent, but the charges were dropped. That had been a hell of a night.

I checked in with the desk sergeant and made my way back to Venus's desk. It was everything I would have expected it to be— organized to within an inch of its life. She was wearing an LSU sweatshirt over a pair of black jeans. She smiled at me and put down her cup of coffee. I looked around. "Where's Blaine?" I asked.

"Day off." She shrugged. "I got some paperwork to catch up on, so I came in anyway. I've got your statement for you to sign." She pushed it over to me.

I read it over and gave a laugh. "Reading it makes it seem even crazier." I grabbed a pen from her desk and signed it.

"Every time I get a statement from you I feel like I'm in *The Twilight Zone*." She shrugged. "But it keeps me on my toes. So what are you thinking?"

"Do you have the phony Eye?" I asked.

"Got it out of the evidence room as soon as you called." She unlocked a desk drawer and pulled out the bag. "Right here."

I took it from her and removed the fake sapphire. I smiled at her. "Check this out. You got a pocketknife?" She gave me a weird look but got one out of her purse and handed it over to me. I laid the fake Eye down on her desk and opened the knife. I sliced into the front of the Eye.

"Hey, don't destroy evidence!" She grabbed my arm.

I shook my head. There was a groove in it where my knife had cut it. I rolled it over to the other side, where Abhwesar had cut it in front of me. "Look," I said, "the grooves are about the same depth."

"So?"

I put my knife inside the groove Abhwesar had cut, and tried to saw it. Nothing happened. With the knife in the thin groove, I twisted it. Flakes came off. I shaved at it, and more flakes came off.

"You mean—" Venus said, realization dawning in her eyes.

I nodded. "Where is the smartest place to hide something? Right in front of our eyes." I shook my head. "I should have remembered how much Doc loved puzzles and mysteries. This is the real Eye. He just encased it in some material, the same color as the original. So a jeweler or an expert would look at it and say it was a fake." I laughed. "And the real thing was there the whole time! What a great joke on everyone!"

"But how did you know?"

"All that stuff about shackles and freedom in that note," I said. "He was telling us the real Eye was shackled, *encased* in something. We had to 'free' it from its 'shackles.' I thought it was weird when Abhwesar cut the stone in front of me. I thought it was weird that the cut was so shallow—I mean, if it wasn't the real sapphire, he should have been able to cut it pretty deeply."

I heard someone clapping behind me, and I turned to see Colin standing there. He had a big smile on his face. "I knew if anyone could find it, it would be you." He took a seat next to me. "The president of Pleshiwar has canceled Abhwesar's diplomatic status, by the way—and he started singing like a bird. Even as we speak, his colleagues over there are being rounded up." He clapped me on the arm. "And you even found the Eye."

"Will you answer some questions for me?" I asked.

Colin winked at Venus and stood up. "Come on, I'll walk you home."

As we walked, I said, "So, Doc and his buddies really worked for Blackledge."

He nodded. "Yes. They were never really in the military, nor were they from Biloxi. That was all a part of the cover Blackledge came up with after their mission, when it was obvious they were in danger and had to be retired. The Pleshiwarian underground had been trying to overthrow the theocracy for years—but obviously, no country was interested in helping them. The Western powers at that time were too busy fighting communism, and the Pleshiwarians didn't want Communist interference inside their country. Once the uranium was found, of course, the Western powers couldn't allow the Communists to get control of the country—nor could they allow the theocracy of Kali to continue in power." He shrugged. "Several of the Western countries—I don't know which, so don't ask—hired us to bring down the theocracy. Stealing Kali's Eye was deemed the easiest way to do it."

"And the theft really brought down the theocracy?"

He nodded again. "The underground used their religion against them. It worked, the theocracy fell, and democracy found its way to

Pleshiwar. The priests, of course, never took kindly to being out of power—and they recently hired the Wolf to track down the thieves and find the Eye."

I took a deep breath. "So, when you first came here all those years ago, you had a lot of work in New Orleans, didn't you? Looking for the Napoleon death mask, keeping tabs on my uncles, and of course, Doc."

"It's almost like our paths were meant to cross, isn't it?" He smiled at me. "Seriously, Scotty, it's like fate brought the three of us together. Don't you think?"

"I don't know, Colin." I wasn't just saying it. It would be so easy just to fall back into his arms, let him back into our lives. "I mean, we need to talk to Frank."

"Of course," he said, and we fell silent as we walked. "I can't stay here permanently, anyway," he said as we turned at the corner at Barracks. "My work takes me all over the globe. I mean, I can get back here whenever I can…"

"Colin—" I stopped walking. "I can't speak for Frank, but I can speak for myself." I took a deep breath. "Neither one of us ever stopped loving you. That's obvious. Even though we were hurt when we thought—" I inhaled sharply. "Well, you know what we thought. But we never stopped caring about you, or missing you. But what you're asking…" I shook my head. "I don't know if I can live like that—knowing your life is always at risk, that you could be killed and we'd never know." I wiped at my eyes angrily. Stupid tears, anyway. "That was really the worst part of the last three years—wondering if you were dead somewhere, and not knowing."

"Hey." He put his arms around me. I resisted at first, but finally let him hold me. "I wish I could give it up, but I can't. I love what I do."

"I know." I pulled away from him. "And you wouldn't be happy if you gave it up. And if you weren't Superspy Colin, you wouldn't be Colin." I smiled a little ruefully. "You would have never stayed in the first place if it weren't for my uncles and the Russian mob, right?"

"Well, Doc was here." He kissed my cheek. "You have to know that leaving you and Frank was the hardest thing I've ever had to do," he added. "I do love you both." He hesitated. "All the stuff I told you—about what happened to my family, why I left the Mossad—that was all true." His eyes shone with tears. "Scotty, I never thought I'd be able to love another human being again as long as I lived. I thought that part of me died with my family. You and Frank—you made me feel alive—*human*—again." He wiped at his eyes. "I love you both."

"I know you do." I laughed a little. "You let Frank beat you up yesterday, didn't you? You could have killed him with your bare hands if you'd wanted to, right?"

"I don't kill unless I have to—self-defense, or to protect someone else." He started walking again. I fell into step beside him. "So, where do we go from here?" he finally asked when we reached my gate.

"One last question." I held up my hand. "You killed Levi, didn't you?"

He didn't answer.

"He was working for the Pleshiwarians," I went on. "They had no reason to kill him—he was working for them. You did it, didn't you?"

"Don't hate me," he whispered. "He was going to kill you. He'd been hiding on the roof. I saw him climb down—and he had his bag of torture tools with him. He was going to torture you and kill you. I tried to stop him, but it was kill or be killed. I didn't have a choice."

"And how did he end up on my balcony?"

"I lugged his body back up to the roof. I hid his bag of tools in the shed in the courtyard." He gave me a wry smile. "I was going to get rid of the body later. They'll never admit it, but I think the Ninja Lesbians rolled him off." He couldn't look me in the eyes. "Just to fuck with me."

"Nice friends," I replied.

"They really liked you." He still wouldn't meet my eyes. "They thought you and Frank were great—especially during Operation Rescue Mom and Dad."

"Oddly enough, I liked them." I shook my head.

"So, what do we do now?"

This was the moment I'd been dreading.

I had to say good-bye.

"I will love you as long as I live," I said, my voice quivering a little. I stopped and took a deep breath to steady myself to say the words I didn't want to say. "But I can't do this. I just can't. Your work is who you are, Colin. You wouldn't be Colin otherwise. I can't ask you to give up your work, it's not fair to you. But I can't—Frank and I can't—live on, wondering if this is the time you aren't going to come home."

"Maybe," Frank said from behind me, "we can." He put his arm around me. "What is it you always say, Scotty? *Life doesn't give you anything you can't handle, it's how you handle it that matters.*" He put his other arm around Colin. "We love him. He's in our blood, whether we like it or not."

Colin's eyes got wet.

"And life is about grabbing brass rings, right?" Frank went on. "Well, I'd rather have this brass ring for whatever time we can steal with him then never see him again. If he gets killed, well, we'll deal with that when the time comes. But when that time does come, I'd rather have memories to cherish than wish we hadn't made him leave."

My own eyes were getting wet. "Do you mean that?"

Frank kissed the top of my head, and kissed Colin on the cheek. "I mean it."

"In that case," I gave them both a sly look, "we've got some lost time to make up for."

The gate slammed shut behind us as we ran for the stairs.

EPILOGUE

The entire auditorium was dark. The crowd was restless and murmuring amongst themselves.

Suddenly a spotlight shone on a curtain. Over the loudspeaker announced, "Our next contest is one fall, twenty-minute time limit! Introducing first—at six feet four, two hundred and thirty pounds, FRANK SAVAGE!"

The entire crowd started booing, and Mom whispered to me, "What is wrong with these people? Why are they booing Frank?"

Before I could answer, he leaped through the curtain and our little group started cheering. Of course, we were drowned out by all the boos, but we were all jumping up and down and clapping and screaming.

He looked incredible. His head was completely shaved down, as were his torso and legs. He was more tan than I'd ever seen him, and he wore it well. His every muscle rippled as he struck poses, which made the crowd boo him even louder. He was crammed into a pair of skimpy black tights with two silver lightning bolts coming from either side, meeting over his crotch to form an arrow pointing down. It made his bulge look enormous. His oiled skin glistened in the light. He was wearing black kneepads, black elbow pads, and black leather boots that stopped just below his knees. Every muscle was crisply defined. He ignored the boos at first as he started walking down the ramp toward the ring, where his opponent—a lean young man with long hair and wearing all white—was waiting for him. He started flipping off the crowd and acting like he was going to punch certain people who leaned over the rail to get in his face.

"Jesus," Colin whispered from my other side, "he looks amazing. I want him to fuck me right here and now."

"That's later," I whispered back, watching as Frank climbed up on the side of the ring and vaulted over the top rope.

I was so proud I was ready to explode.

It had been four weeks since I'd found the Eye. Abhwesar had been extradited back to Pleshiwar to be tried, and the Eye had been returned to Kali. Frank and I hadn't wanted to keep the fifty grand Blackledge had paid us, so we wrote a check to the NO/AIDS Task Force so the money would do some good for some people. And for two glorious weeks, the three of us had a blast—until the training school reopened and Frank had to go back.

And now he was grabbing that brass ring, experiencing the dream he'd had since he was a little boy.

The referee was patting him down, and Frank was yelling at his opponent. He was doing a great job—the audience absolutely *hated* him.

The bell rang, and Frank started beating on the kid—whose name I couldn't remember. Kid Kharisma, or something like that. He was good—he and Frank worked really well together. Frank had told me that the Kid—despite only being twenty-two—was an old pro and had been working the wrestling circuits since he was seventeen. Kid Kharisma was a lot shorter and smaller than Frank, but he had a great body, too—it just looked like nothing next to Frank's.

Of course, I was just a wee bit prejudiced.

As the match went on, it became more and more apparent that the Kid was just a punching bag for Frank. What was really funny was the way Mom and Dad were getting into it. They were yelling and hollering, screaming at Frank to kill the Kid.

They are so cool.

And like Colin, I was getting more than a little turned on.

At one point, as Frank hoisted the Kid into a torture rack over his shoulders, Colin whispered, "Damn! You think he'll do that to me?"

I smothered a laugh. "Maybe if you ask nicely."

"I'll beg!"

After fifteen minutes of nonstop abuse (the Kid really was a pro) Frank finally pinned him to jeers and catcalls from the audience. They were throwing empty cups and things at him as he climbed the ropes, flexing his arms and swearing back at them. I had to stop Mom from going after a woman in the row behind us when she called him a "cheating dirty son of a bitch."

"It's part of the game, Mom," I whispered as I forced her back into her seat. "They're supposed to hate him."

"I guess." She scowled and looked back over her shoulder. "But that bitch better hope she doesn't see me in the parking lot!"

Frank thought that was the funniest thing he'd ever heard afterward, when we all went out for a celebratory dinner. "Oh, Mom, I wish I could have seen that," he said, wiping at his eyes.

"I'd have snatched her bald-headed." Mom winked at Frank and hoisted her wineglass. "To Frank."

We all clinked glasses, and I whispered to him, "I'm so proud of you."

"Thanks, I love you," he whispered back, and added, "Was Colin serious when he said he wanted me to put him in a torture rack?"

I nodded and tried not to laugh. "I think the three of us are going to have a lot of fun when we get back to the suite."

And we did.

They finally fell asleep, our sweat-soaked bodies entwined, around about two in the morning.

But I couldn't sleep, because I knew what the morning was going to bring.

Colin had another job and had to catch a flight to Paris in the morning. He was supposed to have already left, but he told Angela flat-out he wasn't going to miss Frank's ring debut. We knew nothing, of course, about the job or where he was going, or how long he was going to be gone. Angela had promised to keep us posted, to let us know he was okay—or if he wasn't.

It was going to be hard. But the people who loved cops, soldiers, and firemen had gotten through it all for centuries, and found a way to live with it. Frank and I also had each other—and my family. I knew my heart would sink every time the phone rang when he was out on a job. I knew my sleep would never be as deep as it would be when he was home with us and safe.

Life never gives you anything you can't handle—it's how you handle it that matters.

Life had given me this incredible life, so who was I to complain about it?

I had two wonderful men I loved, and who loved me back. I had a great family. I lived in an awesome apartment in the most fun and crazy city in North America. I had lived through one of the worst natural disasters in the history of this country.

If New Orleans could survive that with her head held high, I knew I could survive anything.

The alarm went off at six, and Colin got up and into the shower.

Frank's hand crept into mine underneath the covers, and squeezed it hard.

Tears welled up, but I bit my lip and forced them back down.

"We can't cry," Frank whispered. "Not until he's gone, okay? He can't be worried about us or he won't be able to do his job."

I nodded. And if he wasn't focused, he could make a mistake—and be killed.

So we made small talk—light idle chatter while Colin got dressed. We joked about Frank's future with the WWE, and how maybe we all three could go through the training—we would make a hot three man tag-team, and become household names…and the room phone rang. Colin picked it up, said "Thanks," and hung it up. "My cab's waiting," he said, hoisting his bag over his shoulder.

He hugged us both at the door, and I couldn't help it. I whispered, "Be safe, please."

Colin didn't say anything, he just nodded and broke free of us and gave us that grin we loved so much. "See you soon," he said, his voice breaking for just a moment.

And the door shut behind him.

I took a deep breath and my eyes filled with tears. Frank and I hugged each other, and we put our heads down on each other's shoulders and cried.

Finally, I wiped at my eyes. "Okay, enough sniveling!"

"Right," Frank said, wiping at his own face.

"We'll see him again, and sooner than we think." I hopped back into the bed. "Come on back to bed, Hot Daddy."

Frank lay down beside me, and we put our arms around each other.

He would come back to us.

I knew it.

About the Author

Greg Herren is a New Orleans–based author and editor. Former editor of *Lambda Book Report*, he is also a co-founder of the Saints and Sinners Literary Festival, which takes place in New Orleans every May. He is the author of ten novels, including the Lambda Literary Award–winning *Murder in the Rue Chartres*, called by the *New Orleans Times-Picayune* "the most honest depiction of life in post-Katrina New Orleans published thus far." He co-edited *Love, Bourbon Street: Reflections on New Orleans*, which also won the Lambda Literary Award. He has published over fifty short stories in markets as varied as *Ellery Queen's Mystery Magazine* to the critically acclaimed anthology *New Orleans Noir* to various Web sites, literary magazines, and anthologies. His erotica anthology *FRATSEX* is the all-time best-selling title for Insightoutbooks. Under his pseudonym Todd Gregory, he published the bestselling erotic novel *Every Frat Boy Wants It* and the erotic anthologies *His Underwear* and *Rough Trade* (released by Bold Strokes Books in 2009).

A longtime resident of New Orleans, Greg was a fitness columnist and book reviewer for *Window Media* for over four years, publishing in the LGBT newspapers *IMPACT News*, *Southern Voice*, and *Houston Voice*. He served a term on the Board of Directors for the National Stonewall Democrats, and served on the founding committee of the Louisiana Stonewall Democrats. He is currently employed as a public health researcher for the NO/AIDS Task Force.

Books Available From Bold Strokes Books

Wind and Bones by Kristin Marra. Jill O'Hara, award-winning journalist, just wants to settle her deceased father's affairs and leave Prairie View, Montana, far, far behind—but an old girlfriend, a sexy sheriff, and a dangerous secret keep her down on the ranch. (978-1-60282-150-7)

Nightshade by Shea Godfrey. The story of a princess, betrothed as a political pawn, who falls for her intended husband's soldier sister, is a modern-day fairy tale to capture the heart. (978-1-60282-151-4)

Vieux Carré Voodoo by Greg Herren. Popular New Orleans detective Scotty Bradley just can't stay out of trouble—especially when an old flame turns up asking for help. (978-1-60282-152-1)

The Pleasure Set by Lisa Girolami. Laney DeGraff, a successful president of a family-owned bank on Rodeo Drive, finds her comfortable life taking a turn toward danger when Theresa Aguilar, a sleek, sexy lawyer, invites her to join an exclusive, secret group of powerful, alluring women. (978-1-60282-144-6)

A Perfect Match by Erin Dutton. The exciting world of pro golf forms the backdrop for a fast-paced, sexy romance. (978-1-60282-145-3)

Truths by Rebecca S. Buck. Two women separated by two hundred years are connected by fate and love. (978-1-60282-146-0)

Father Knows Best by Lynda Sandoval. High school juniors and best friends Lila Moreno, Meryl Morganstern, and Caressa Thibodoux plan to make the most of the summer before senior year. What they discover that amazing summer about girl power, growing up, and trusting friends and family more than prepares them to tackle that all-important senior year! (978-1-60282-147-7)

In Pursuit of Justice by Radclyffe. In the dynamic double sequel to *Shield of Justice* and *A Matter of Trust*, Det. Sgt. Rebecca Frye joins forces with enigmatic computer consultant J.T. Sloan to crack an Internet child pornography ring. (978-1-60282-147-4)

The Midnight Hunt by L.L. Raand. Medic Drake McKennan takes a chance and loses, and her life will never be the same—because when she wakes up after surviving a life-threatening illness, she is no longer human. (978-1-60282-140-8)

Long Shot by D. Jackson Leigh. Love isn't safe, which is exactly why equine veterinarian Tory Greyson wants no part of it—until Leah Montgomery and a horse that won't give up convince her otherwise. (978-1-60282-141-5)

In Medias Res by Yolanda Wallace. Sydney has forgotten her entire life, and the one woman who holds the key to her memory, and her heart, doesn't want to be found. (978-1-60282-142-2)

Awakening to Sunlight by Lindsey Stone. Neither Judith or Lizzy is looking for companionship, and certainly not love—but when their lives become entangled, they discover both. (978-1-60282-143-9)

Fever by VK Powell. Hired gun Zakaria Chambers is hired to provide a simple escort service to philanthropist Sara Ambrosini, but nothing is as simple as it seems, especially love. (978-1-60282-135-4)

High Risk by JLee Meyer. Can actress Kate Hoffman really risk all she's worked for to take a chance on love? Or is it already too late? (978-1-60282-136-1)

Missing Lynx by Kim Baldwin and Xenia Alexiou. On the trail of a notorious serial killer, Elite Operative Lynx's growing attraction to a mysterious mercenary could be her path to love—or to death. (978-1-60282-137-8)

Spanking New by Clifford Henderson. A poignant, hilarious, unforgettable look at life, love, gender, and the essence of what makes us who we are. (978-1-60282-138-5)

Magic of the Heart by C.J. Harte. CEO Susan Hettinger and wild, impulsive rock star M.J. Carson couldn't be more different if they tried—but opposites attract in ways neither woman can resist. (978-1-60282-131-6)

Ambereye by Gill McKnight. Jolie Garoul is falling in love with her assistant. The big problem is, Jolie is a werewolf. (978-1-60282-132-3)

Collision Course by C.P. Rowlands. Tragedy leaves Brie O'Malley and Jordan Carter fearful and alone. Can they find the courage to take a second chance on love? (978-1-60282-133-0)

Mephisto Aria by Justine Saracen. Opera singer Katherina Marov's destiny may be to repeat the mistakes of her father when she becomes involved in a dangerous love affair. (978-1-60282-134-7)

Battle Scars by Meghan O'Brien. Returning Iraq war veteran Ray McKenna struggles with the battle scars that can only be healed by love. (978-1-60282-129-3)

Chaps by Jove Belle. Eden Metcalf wants nothing more than to flee from her troubled past and travel the open road—until she runs into rancher Brandi Cornwell. (978-1-60282-127-9)

Lightbearer by John Caruso. Lucifer dares to question the premise of creation itself and reveals that sin may be all that stands between us and living hell. (978-1-60282-130-9)

Rough Trade edited by Todd Gregory. Top male erotica writers pen their own hot, sexy versions of the term "rough trade," producing some of the hottest, nastiest, and most dangerous fiction ever published. (978-1-60282-092-0)

Late in the Season by Felice Picano. Set on Fire Island, this is the story of an unlikely pair of friends—a gay composer in his late thirties and an eighteen-year-old schoolgirl. (978-1-60282-082-1)

The Lure by Felice Picano. When Noel Cummings is recruited by the police to go undercover to find a killer, his life will never be the same. (978-1-60282-076-0)

Death of a Dying Man by J.M. Redmann. Mickey Knight, Private Eye and partner of Dr. Cordelia James, doesn't need a drop-dead gorgeous assistant—not until nature steps in. (978-1-60282-075-3)

Calling the Dead by Ali Vali. Six months after Hurricane Katrina, NOLA Detective Sept Savoie is a cop who thinks making a relationship work is harder than catching a serial killer—but her current case may prove her wrong. (978-1-60282-037-1)

The Limits of Justice by John Morgan Wilson. Benjamin Justice and reporter Alexandra Templeton search for a killer in a mysterious compound in the remote California desert. (978-1-60282-060-9)

Justice at Risk by John Morgan Wilson. Benjamin Justice's blind date leads to a rare opportunity for legitimate work, but a reckless risk changes his life forever. (978-1-60282-059-3)

Revision of Justice by John Morgan Wilson. Murder shifts into high gear, propelling Benjamin Justice into a raging fire that consumes the Hollywood Hills, burning steadily toward the famous Hollywood Sign—and the identity of a cold-blooded killer. (978-1-60282-058-6)

Simple Justice by John Morgan Wilson. When a pretty-boy cokehead is murdered, former LA reporter Benjamin Justice and his reluctant new partner, Alexandra Templeton, must unveil the real killer. (978-1-60282-057-9)